# BREAK
# THE
# SILENCE

# BOOKS BY D.K. HOOD

*Don't Tell a Soul*
*Bring Me Flowers*
*Follow Me Home*
*The Crying Season*
*Where Angels Fear*
*Whisper in the Night*

# D.K. HOOD

# BREAK THE SILENCE

bookouture

Published by Bookouture in 2019

An imprint of StoryFire Ltd.
Carmelite House
50 Victoria Embankment
London EC4Y 0DZ

www.bookouture.com

ISBN: 978-1-78681-900-0
eBook ISBN: 978-1-78681-899-7

*To Zack Smith—follow your dreams.*
*You never know where they'll lead you.*

# PROLOGUE

## Saturday

Music played so loud it vibrated in Chrissie Lowe's teeth. Students crammed into every spare space talking so loud they sounded like a flock of angry geese. Giddy and uncoordinated, she pushed her way between two huge football players to reach the stairs. The dream date with Seth Lyons—star college quarterback—had faded like a rose in winter. The fruit punch he'd insisted she drink to "loosen up" had the effect of making the room go all misty around the edges. Surrounded by people she didn't know didn't help the wave of rising panic and uncertainty of being the only girl at the party. The niggly feeling something wasn't quite right hit her the moment Seth had refused to give her a ride back to her dorm. His insistence she stay worried her, as did the strange, overly interested looks from his friends. Her legs had become Jell-O and she sagged against the wall. "I don't feel so good. I want to go home."

"And I figured you were all grown up." Seth grabbed her by the shoulders and turned her around. "Go upstairs. You can rest up in my room."

Glad of a chance to get away from the thumping music keeping time to the throb in her temples, she glanced at the wavering stairs. "Up there?"

"Yeah, go right to the end of the hallway." Seth's hand settled on the small of her back and he gave her an encouraging push toward the steps.

A group of juniors she recognized as members of the football team leaned against the walls, drinking beer and watching with interest as she staggered up the stairs. When they grinned at her and made hooting noises like a bunch of deranged owls, her cheeks grew hot with embarrassment. Chrissie smacked away the hands trying to snag her and turned to Seth. "Are these your friends?"

"Uh-huh. Don't worry about those animals." He snorted and high-fived his friends. "It will be just you 'n' me."

A wave of nausea hit her as his overpowering aftershave mingled with the smells of beer and barbecue. She just wanted to lie down and hoped the room would stop spinning. Using the wall for support, she eased her way through the packed hallway and opened the door. It was the usual-sized room but with two double beds, not like the singles in her dorm. "You've double beds?"

"Yeah, us guys need a bit more space than you do." Seth grinned at her. "Sit down. I'll get you a couple of pills." He headed for the open bathroom door.

Warning lights flashed in her brain and the long talk her parents had given her about not drinking or taking drugs filled her swimming thoughts. When she shook her head, her stomach rolled. "I don't need any pills. I just need to lie down for a spell."

"Head all fuzzy?" Seth came out of the bathroom. "Feel like you're gonna spew?" He handed her two pills then a glass of water. "These will make you feel better. You gotta trust me, Chrissie."

She peered at the pills. "Are they like Tums?"

"I guess." Seth sat down, making the bed dip. "Come on, Chrissie. We can't enjoy ourselves with you all messed up like this."

She peered at the pills. "I don't take drugs."

"Do you think I would've asked you to come here if you did?" Seth touched her cheek. "I like you because you're so sweet and innocent."

When he looked deep into her eyes, her stomach gave a little flip. She so wanted to please him but being drunk and alone with him in his bedroom was a big mistake. Swallowing hard, she wet her lips. "I think I should go."

"You don't trust me, do you?" Seth dashed a hand through his hair in an impatient gesture. "You know there are ten girls I know who would've jumped at the chance to be invited up to my room but I chose you—I can't believe you're turning out to be basic." He stood and glared at her. "If you don't trust me, forget it. I'll give you a ride back to your dorm—but don't expect to hear from me again any time soon."

Unable to take his condemnation a moment longer, Chrissie allowed her gaze to linger on his handsome face for just a moment then took the pills.

"See, that wasn't so bad, was it?" Seth gave her a brilliant smile, and sat down again. "Let me help you with your jacket." He tossed it onto a chair then puffed up the pillows and eased her down on the bed. "Lie back and relax. The pills will make you feel so good like you're floating on a cloud." He stood and stared down at her. "Close your eyes. Let me turn down the lights."

Head throbbing, she complied. The door opened and a blast of noise from the party filled the room for long moment before the door closed again, reducing the loud music to a tolerable buzz. *Has he left me alone?* Heaviness filled her limbs and she tried unsuccessfully to lift her arms. A strange numbing sensation had crept over her and she couldn't move. It was as if the bed had turned into quicksand. Frightened, she tried to call for help but only a moan escaped her lips.

Whispered voices deep and masculine surrounded her but she couldn't make out what they were saying. A dizzy, out-of-body feeling swamped her and it was an effort to keep her eyes open. She tried to focus on the faces grinning at her and then darkness closed in around her.

\*

Chrissie opened her eyes, disoriented and confused, and took in the damp lawn outside her dorm. The freshly cut grass prickled her cheek and the world seemed to be upside down. Stifling a moan, she rolled onto her back and stared into the stars, trying to make sense of what had happened. With effort, she sat up, pulled out her phone, and stared at the screen for some moments, not sure what to do. After sending a text, she stood on trembling legs, stumbled at the curb and her phone slipped from her hand. As it fell down a drain, she stared after it in dismay for a long moment before making her way slowly to the front door.

Luckily, the glass door to the dorm lobby remained open on Saturday nights and her room was on the ground floor. She found her key, safe in the zippered pocket of her jacket, and staggered into the building. Empty, well-lit passageways greeted her as she made her way to her room. She passed the noticeboard and, among the coupons for free pizza, she spotted a newspaper article about the Black Rock Falls College football team. Familiar faces grinned out at her from a team photograph. Leaning against the wall for support, she grabbed the pen hanging by a string, circled four of the faces, and then added a sad-faced emoji and her initials.

Outside, the roar of a powerful engine caught her attention and she looked through the glass door as a car, cloaked in darkness, crawled by her building and then stopped. Panic froze her to the spot. She couldn't breathe. The click as the car door shut sounded loud in the stillness, and moments later, a shadow crossed the lawn, coming fast. Chrissie fumbled for her key. Once, twice she tried with trembling fingers to slide it into the lock. Her heart pounded in her chest as the front door whined opened. She dared not scream. *No one must ever know.* As the key slid into the lock, footsteps came down the hallway. She gasped in terror. *I have to get away.*

# CHAPTER ONE

## Monday

Black Rock Falls in August was spectacular. An entire artist's palette of colors painted the landscape, and from Sheriff Jenna Alton's front porch, she could see for miles across the vast grasslands to the mountain ranges. Under a clear, brilliant blue sky, the black mountain peaks stood out like a wall of protection around the town, with the pines of Stanton Forest marching up to meet them in a mix of luxurious greens. Wildflowers spilled over the lush grass surrounding her ranch, and from where she sat, she could see the horses frolicking in the corral. Jenna put her boots up on the railing, leaned back in her chair—coffee cup in hand—and sighed. "It's good to be home." She smiled at Dave Kane, her deputy and close friend. "I kind of missed this place but I sure needed a vacation."

"Me too." Kane yawned. "I wouldn't have minded a couple more weeks' rest." He rubbed the head of his bloodhound, Duke. "But Rowley was worried Duke had started to stress, so next time we'll take him with us."

"That sounds like a really good plan. Think about it—two or three weeks of baking in the sun on a beautiful beach, blue skies, white sand... ah, bliss." She smiled at him. "It was nice to relax for a change, without the constant caseload."

"Maybe we'll be able to catch another week a bit later, but I guess with the county fair and rodeo in town this week, things are gonna start getting crazy." Kane leaned back and dark lashes closed over his eyes. "We might as well make the most of the lull."

Jenna hoped Deputy Jake Rowley would head out to work early as usual and open the office of the Black Rock Falls Sheriff's Department. As far as she was aware, all was quiet in town and she really didn't feel like rushing.

She'd arrived in Black Rock Falls some years prior after giving evidence against an underworld kingpin and landing in witness protection. After spending a year recovering from PTSD, she'd put her name forward in the elections and won the position of sheriff. She'd finally left undercover DEA Agent Avril Parker behind and slipped into her new life with enthusiasm. Dave Kane, an intimidating, six-foot-five sniper, had arrived a couple of years later, and she'd discovered he was an off-the-grid DC's Special Forces Investigation Command agent with incredible profiling skills. He'd just lost his wife in a car bombing and gained a metal plate in his head. They had the same secrets: new identities and faces, not to mention security clearances that went right up to the office of POTUS. During their time together, they'd formed a special bond as close friends. When they had the chance to grab a couple of weeks' vacation, it seemed natural to spend it together.

The outer perimeter alarm sounded then cut out and Jenna jumped to her feet. With one hand on her weapon, she slid into the cover of the house. "It's a white van."

"It's Wolfe." Kane frowned. "Why didn't he call first?"

After spending a week of luxury vacationing in Santa Cruz with Kane, the last person Jenna expected to find on her doorstep was the medical examiner, Shane Wolfe. The Texan ex-marine, who resembled a blond Viking marauder, had been Kane's controller during his time in DC's Special Forces Investigation Command. When Wolfe had suddenly arrived in town with his three daughters, bulging with expertise in forensic science and technology, Jenna had snapped him up as a deputy, and now he carried the office of medical examiner for Black Rock Falls and the neighboring counties.

Wolfe carried a device in his vehicle to allow access to Jenna's ranch security, but it was unusual for him to arrive unannounced. As the van pulled to a halt, Jenna walked back onto the porch to greet him and glanced at Kane. "He doesn't look happy."

"I'm glad you're home." Wolfe climbed out of the van and ran up the steps. "We need to talk."

Jenna waved him inside and led the way to the kitchen, poured him a cup of coffee, and they all sat at the table. "What brings you all the way out here at the crack of dawn?"

"I called both of you earlier but your cellphones gave me the same message: 'I'm not available, call 911.'" Wolfe gave them an exasperated stare. "I knew you'd flown in last night and Rowley told me you'd been by for Duke. Did you forget to turn on your cells?"

Jenna's face grew hot. Yeah, she'd turned her cellphone to vibrate and it was sitting on the bench with her keys. "Seems so, I'm sorry to have worried you. Is something wrong with the girls?"

"No, they're fine." Agitation rolled off Wolfe but he took a deep breath and smiled at Jenna. "Emily is home to finish her degree in Black Rock Falls, so she'll be working with us again." Emily was Wolfe's eldest daughter and as smart as a whip.

"That's wonderful. So, what's up?"

"A call came in on the 911 line yesterday morning from the college about a suicide. Livi Johnson found her roommate Chrissie Lowe, eighteen years old, dead in the shower around seven. Rowley was the first responder and called me." Wolfe sipped his coffee then lifted his chin and looked at her. "I'm not so sure this is a suicide. I've reason to believe Chrissie Lowe was raped before her death but I'll confirm after the post."

Horrified, Jenna swallowed the bile creeping up the back of her throat. "Rowley didn't mention he had an open case."

"He doesn't know the facts as yet." Wolfe leaned back in his chair. "I only did a quick visual examination, we processed the scene, and I removed the body. I've sealed the room as I can't rule out homicide. I notified her parents and requested permission to perform an autopsy."

"What did you find?" Kane shifted in his chair, making the joints creak alarmingly. "Was it homicide?"

"I've yet to make that determination. I haven't performed the post yet. I knew you'd be back today so I waited." Wolfe narrowed his gaze. "As Webber has classes today, would you be able to attend the autopsy this morning?"

Colt Webber, a badge-carrying deputy, worked as Wolfe's assistant and was studying forensic science at college. He sometimes acted as Jenna's representative at autopsies and backup when necessary.

"Sure." She frowned. "You smell a rat, don't you?"

"Definitely." Wolfe waved his cup. "From my initial cursory examination, the method used to cut the veins was unusual. In most suicide attempts the cut is made across the wrist but the incisions in this case run from wrist to forearm. Although, we have established the pocketknife belonged to the victim."

"So, if anyone found her, she'd likely bleed to death before they could help her. It's a no-return move." Kane frowned. "How would she know to do that? It's not general knowledge."

"With all the information available on the internet, I can't be sure." Wolfe sipped his beverage. "Although, she does have a brother in the military—a Navy Seal." He pushed a hand through his hair in an agitated manner. "She could've heard about the technique from him."

"I doubt a brother would discuss killing techniques with his sister." Jenna stood, collected the cups, and placed them in the dishwasher. "Was there anything else?"

"Bruises." Wolfe pushed to his feet. "This morning they are more apparent, and I can't say for sure she wasn't held down in the shower and sliced open to make it look like suicide." He met her gaze. "I'll know more after the post. Can you be at the morgue by eleven?"

Mind whirling, Jenna nodded slowly. "Yeah, sure, we'll be there." She walked Wolfe to the door. "We'll head into the office and see if Rowley has followed up on the case."

"I'm sure he'll have more information." Wolfe smiled at her and headed for his van. "You've trained him well."

Jenna rubbed her temples and looked up into Kane's concerned face. "See, we're home for one night and mysterious things start happening in town." She shuddered. "I'm starting to believe we attract crime."

# CHAPTER TWO

Main Street was awash with brightly colored bunting for the county fair and rodeo. The usually slow-moving town had turned into rush hour with a flurry of people from different committees dashing along the sidewalk to secure a good position for their stalls. Men clutching opposite ends of folded tables carried them from the town hall and set them up. Moments later, a group of women dashed in to erect a sign claiming the spot. Others covered the benches and surrounds with tablecloths and signs. With the fair set to run from Tuesday through Sunday, the influx of tourists alone would keep them busy, but Kane's stomach rumbled at the thought of all the homemade cakes and cookies he could purchase. He slowed his black, unmarked truck— affectionately known as "the beast"—to follow a horse trailer.

"I can hear your stomach from here." Jenna turned in her seat to look at him. "You've only just eaten breakfast. Are you hungry already?"

Nonplussed, Kane smiled at her. "I'm always hungry. I burn up a lot of calories just driving to work."

"Oh, that must be a pain." She chuckled. "You know, I've never heard anyone complain about burning too many calories."

Kane flicked her a glance. "Next time I see someone over two hundred and fifty pounds and six-five, I'll ask them, but I'd guess if they worked out every morning like we do, maybe they'd have the same problem as me." He bit back a grin. "Jealous?" He pulled into a parking space reserved for the sheriff's department.

"More than you know." Jenna sighed, gathered her things, and frowned. "I'm not looking forward to facing an autopsy on the first day back."

Kane met her worried gaze. "Let's hope it's not a homicide, but if it was rape, we'll still be hunting down the animal who raped her."

"Yeah." Jenna slid from the seat. "The beginning of another perfect week." She shook her head and headed for the office door.

Kane stopped at the counter to give the receptionist, Magnolia Brewster—Maggie—a gift from Santa Cruz. "Thanks for holding down the fort and keeping Duke out of trouble during the day." He allowed Duke to slide behind the counter, tail wagging.

"Thank you so much. That hound is always good company and no trouble at all, but I figure he missed you. Rowley was glad to leave him with me, said Duke bossed his dog around somethin' wicked." Maggie shook her head. "I've never seen the like here. He sat in his basket and snored most days."

Kane wondered why Rowley hadn't mentioned the problem. "Duke's mighty territorial; he refused to let Rowley's dog into my cottage last winter."

"Oh, I know. I cared for Spike when Rowley was livin' out at the sheriff's ranch." She looked at the package as if savoring it then turned it over in her hands and beamed at him. "I'll just have to make sure you take a vacation every year if you come back with gifts. Did you have a good time?"

Kane chuckled. "Oh… yeah."

"Hmm, you're not planning on giving out any details, right?" Rowley came up beside him and grinned.

"Nope." Kane smiled at them. "I've gotta go, Jenna's waiting for us." Not wanting to hang around for more questions, he waved Rowley toward Jenna's office and following him took a seat.

"So, what's been happening, Jake? Wolfe dropped by this morning and mentioned a suicide?" Jenna opened her daybook then stared at Rowley. "Have you filed a report for me?"

"Yes, ma'am, it's in your files." Rowley scanned his iPad. "Apart from the suicide, it was the usual: traffic violations, another fight at the Triple Z Bar—seems the local college boys have got it into their heads to go there to drink. Then they clash with the cowboys drifting into town for the rodeo."

"If they're over twenty-one, there's not a lot we can do." Jenna sighed. "I guess the owner could ban them but I figure he likes the passing trade." She scanned her computer. "Now, about this apparent suicide."

Kane turned in his seat to look at Rowley. "What did you make of the scene?"

"Chrissie Lowe was clothed and there wasn't a whole lot of blood. The shower was running. She looked pale, and because of the hot water running over her, Wolfe said it would be difficult to establish the time of death." Rowley cleared his throat. "She had deep cuts up both arms and I found a pocketknife beside her."

"Did you speak to the person who discovered the body?" Jenna leaned forward on her desk. "It was her roommate, wasn't it?"

"Yeah, Livi Johnson." Rowley rubbed a hand down his face. "She was hysterical, sobbing and shaking all over. It was difficult to get anything out of her. I figured I'd go back today and speak to her again." He sighed. "One of the other girls informed me Livi started screaming at around seven Sunday morning. She'd gone into the bathroom after waiting some time without any answer from Chrissie."

Kane frowned. "Did anyone contaminate the scene?"

"Nope." Rowley looked at him. "I was wearing gloves when I turned off the shower and checked for signs of life. Then I called Wolfe. We processed the scene, took photographs, collected prints.

I locked the dorm door and took the key. I collected the next of kin details from Rose Bishop, the dorm director, and Wolfe took over from there. He and Webber took the body to the morgue. He went to speak to the parents and obtained permission for an autopsy." He frowned. "I feel real sorry for her family. They found out earlier in the week their son is MIA. Wolfe mentioned her father is terminal and her mom doesn't look too well either."

Sadness fell over Kane as he exchanged a glance with Jenna. They both understood the pain of losing family. "Okay. Did you secure the victim's cellphone and media device?"

"Wolfe took her laptop but we couldn't find her cellphone." Rowley frowned. "I figure from the third degree you're giving me, this is more than a suicide."

"From Wolfe's initial examination, he believes Chrissie was raped." Jenna pushed the hair from her eyes. "We're going to view the autopsy this morning. We'll need to get a timeline of what she was doing in the hours before she died. Where did she go? Who did she speak to, and who was the last person to see her alive?" She stared at them across the desk. "Kane, I want you and Rowley to do some grunt work. Go and speak to her friends at the dorm and see what they have to say. I'll call the college and get a list of her classes on Friday. I'll need to organize some help from Blackwater so we're free to investigate. With the rodeo in town, we can't leave the office unattended. Once we've attended the autopsy, we can work back from there."

Kane pushed to his feet. "Roger that." He smiled at her. "I'll be back before eleven for the autopsy."

As they headed for the college, Rowley glanced at Kane. "So, how was the vacation? Now Maggie's not listening in, you can tell me."

D.K. Hood

Kane snorted with laughter. "You mean how was it going on vacation with Jenna?" He grinned at him. "It was great."

"Uh-huh." Rowley smiled at him. "Great is good."

"We're just good friends, Jake. Don't read anything into it." Kane looked at him. "We enjoy each other's company is all."

"Okay." Rowley held up both hands in mock surrender. "Good friends, I get it."

When they arrived at the freshmen dorm, they found flowers and a sign with the words "RIP Chrissie." Kane frowned and moved through the girls on the lawn holding a vigil outside the front door. Inside, a woman in her thirties held up a hand like a sentry.

"What do you want, deputies?" The woman frowned. "Haven't these girls gone through enough without you questioning them at a time like this?"

Kane stared at her in disbelief. "We need to interview them while events are still clear in their minds. Now, if you'll step aside, we need to speak to Livi Johnson."

"I'll take you to her—poor thing, she hasn't stopped shaking all day." The woman gave him a contemptuous look. "The ME sealed the room and she's not been able to collect her things. She can't go to class in her PJs. How much longer before we're allowed inside?"

"I'll find out, ma'am, but it won't be for a while." Kane followed her into a large room with wide windows overlooking a neat garden. Floral-patterned sofas surrounded a fireplace big enough to roast a pig. "I'll probably be able to collect some things for her, but as it's a potential crime scene, we can't risk anyone going in and contaminating evidence."

"Contaminating evidence?" The woman had a hooked nose and red hair sticking up in all directions. She resembled a rooster the way she fluffed up and stared at him with beady, black eyes. "Chrissie was in the shower with slashed wrists. It's pretty plain to me what happened: she committed suicide. I've seen it before and it's becoming an epidemic. The moment one thing goes wrong in their lives, they end it."

Surprised by her callous attitude, Kane lowered his voice. "I'm aware the suicide rate among young people has increased, but that doesn't mean we become complacent. In any unnatural death, the ME will make a determination according to the evidence he finds. Right now, he's reason to believe there're a few mitigating circumstances surrounding Chrissie's death."

"Really, how so?"

"I can't say." Kane frowned and took out his notebook. "May I have your name and what position you hold here?"

"Rose Bishop." She gave him a long stare. "I'm the student hall director."

Kane took down the details. "When is the curfew?"

"Curfew? Do you mean when do I lock the lobby door? Eleven thirty every night but Saturdays. It's left open or I'm up and down all night to open it." She turned and headed for the door. "I'll go get Livi." She hustled away down the hallway.

"She was here yesterday morning." Rowley stared after Bishop and frowned. "She spent her time waving her arms around." He turned to Kane. "I tried to interview her but she refused to speak to me. She said the welfare of her girls took priority over anything I had to say to her."

Kane rubbed his chin, wondering if Rose Bishop had anything to hide. "Hmm, well I'm sure she'll make time to speak with us today."

When Livi arrived wearing oversized sweatpants, pale and with eyes red from crying, Kane waved her to a seat. He stared down at Bishop, who'd returned with her. "Thanks, we can take it from here."

"I'm not sure I should leave Livi alone with you." Bishop lifted her chin and glared at him.

Kane sat beside the girl on the sofa and Rowley leaned against the wall, arms folded over his chest. "We'd prefer to interview her alone." Kane looked at Livi. "If that's okay with you? Trust me, I understand what it's like to find a body, and if you're not up to talking to me today, that's okay."

"I'm fine. Mrs. Bishop, I can do this." Livi waited for Bishop to leave the room and looked up at Kane with big, sad brown eyes. "I told the medical examiner everything I know. I woke up, heard the shower running in the bathroom. I waited for about half an hour and then called out. When she didn't answer, I opened the door." She dragged in a ragged breath. "I'm sorry, I don't know what happened to her. I was asleep."

Kane opened his notebook and took out his pen. "You're doing just fine but I need to ask you a few questions about the time before she died."

"Sure." Livi pulled up her knees and hugged them. "Ask away."

"When did you last see Chrissie?"

"Around nine Saturday night; she was heading out to a party." Livi frowned. "She'd met a guy on the football team."

Kane made notes then looked up at her. "Did she mention his name or where the party was being held?"

"Yeah, it was Seth Lyons, the quarterback." Livi gave a little sob of distress. "I told her not to go anywhere near the football team—they've a house off campus and the parties are wild. They do a ton of hazing and it's not safe for a freshman girl to go there alone."

Kane's mind was working at a million miles an hour. "Yet she still went alone?"

"Yeah." Livi frowned. "A few days before she met Seth, she got some bad news from home about her brother going missing. He's a Navy Seal. She told me the waiting was driving her crazy and she needed a distraction."

Kane nodded. "Does she own a vehicle?"

"Nope." She shook her head. "She got a ride but it wasn't Seth who came by. He drives a red Mustang and I saw her getting into a sedan way down the road like it was all secret or something."

"Did you notice the make or color?" Kane lifted his gaze from his notes.

"I think it was silver, could have been light blue. I don't know the make. They all look the same to me." Livi looked at him. "We've made friends with tons of guys and any one of them could've given her a ride."

"Did she date any of them before meeting Seth?"

"Yeah, a few from high school, not many, and the only other guy she knows is Phil Stein, he was at high school with us." Livi wiped her nose with a tissue. "Some of the freshmen can be pests, so we've been hanging with a few of the juniors. It was a surprise when one of the seniors asked her out."

Kane frowned. From the get-go it was becoming obvious more than one person was involved. "Had she been seeing Seth for long?"

"No, she hadn't been seeing him at all. He came up to her in the cafeteria on Friday, waited until she was alone then moved in." Agitated, Livi picked at her fingernails. "He had her up against the wall, sweet-talking her like she was special. She told me he said, 'You're so my type, come to a party with me on Saturday night. Wear something short to show off those fine legs. Don't tell anyone—we don't want anyone showing up to spoil our fun.'" She rolled her eyes. "Of course, Chrissie almost fainted with shock and came back to the table all starry-eyed and madly in love." She choked back a sob. "She told me in confidence, straight away. In fact, she wouldn't stop talking about him. She even drooled over his picture on Facebook and now look what's happened to her."

After making notes, Kane observed her. She seemed to be angry and upset, which was a normal response. After the shock of finding the body of her friend, he was reluctant to push her any further, but he needed more answers and she seemed to be pulling herself together. "Did she speak to anyone else before she left for the party?"

"Yeah, we talked to the other girls over dinner as usual, and she sent a text to break a date with Phil—Phillip Stein, he's a sophomore." Livi frowned. "I figure he was disappointed; he was all over her before Seth moved in. After dinner, we went to our room and just chatted while she had a shower and dressed for her date. I walked out with her when she left and she didn't speak to anyone else at all." Her face crumpled. "I should have gone with her. I asked her but she didn't want me to come."

Kane made a note of the name then looked at her. The girl was becoming distressed again, and he wanted to wind up the interview as soon as possible. "No other phone calls? Texts, social media?"

"No, I don't think so." Livi wiped her eyes with her fingers. "Is there anything else?"

"Yeah, if you don't mind?" Kane glanced down at his notes. "Do you remember what she was wearing when she left the dorm?"

"Yeah, white crop top and pink skirt, silver sandals." Livi gave him a blank stare as if thinking. "Her shoes were missing." She blinked a few times then spoke almost like an automaton. "She was wearing her clothes in the shower but her new shoes were missing and her skirt was torn up one side. Her lip was cut too and she had a bruise on one cheek." She drew a shuddering breath as if all the puzzle pieces had fit snugly into place. "Did Seth hurt her?"

Kane cleared his throat. "I'm not sure. Could you identify her shoes?"

"Yeah, I think so." Tears streamed down the girl's face as she gave a description of silver sandals with rhinestones. "I t-told her not to go."

"Thanks." Kane waited a beat for the girl to settle down. "Could you give me a description of her cellphone—make, cover, or whatever you remember?"

"It had a silver cover." Livi wiped her eyes. "She'd stuck a yellow smiley emoji on the cover. She used them all the time; it was like her logo." She let out a wail.

"Look… ah…" Kane stood. He'd never been any good with tears. "That's all I need for now. If you show me your room, I'll go inside and collect some of your things."

"No, I can't go back in there." Livi shook her head. "My things are all on the right by the window. Chrissie had the cupboard and dresser on the left." She gave him a long, sad stare. "You know, I came here because Black Rock Falls is one of the few campuses which have separate bathrooms in their dorms. Most have communal bathrooms. Now I wish I'd gone somewhere else, and then I wouldn't have found her like that."

Kane nodded. "I'll go get your things." He signaled to Rowley to follow him and headed out the room.

In the hallway, he went straight to Rose Bishop. "Where can we find Seth Lyons?"

"The quarterback?" Bishop's eyes opened wide. "Just a moment." She walked to a noticeboard and scanned a list. "Yes, I thought so— Lyons and a few other members of the football team left early Sunday morning to complete a special coaching session; they'll be back later tonight around nine."

"Okay, thanks." Kane made a note and turned to Rowley. "Show me the crime scene." He pulled latex gloves and booties from his pocket as he walked. "Did you go through hazing in your time here?"

"Nope." Rowley shrugged. "I didn't live on campus, so they left me alone." He glanced at him. "You?"

"I was full grown at sixteen." Kane flicked him a glance. "I was lucky, I guess. I've not met a man yet who's able to intimidate me."

"How did I know you'd say that?" Rowley stopped at a door covered with crime scene tape and pulled out his cellphone. "I took some pictures of the scene. I don't recall seeing any shoes near or in the shower." He handed the cellphone to Kane.

Kane scanned the photographs, zooming in on the position of the body, the pocketknife and an open makeup bag on the vanity. They'd found no note, no fingerprints on the knife. The incisions on her arms showed no hesitation. He glanced around and shook his head. *What happened to you, Chrissie?*

# CHAPTER THREE

Trepidation sat on Jenna's shoulders like a heavy weight as she followed Kane and Wolfe into the morgue. When she'd viewed the crime scene photographs from the case file, an overwhelming feeling of grief had hit her. She'd gazed at the bedraggled image of Chrissie Lowe, a young woman with all her life ahead of her. Had a monster raped her, perhaps murdered her, or left her so damaged she'd taken her own life?

Jenna bolstered her courage, determined to find out what had happened to Chrissie and bring the person to justice. Inside, the too familiar stink of the morgue seemed to crawl toward her in a cloud of cold. She grabbed a face mask from the box on the counter, pulled it on, then collected a pair of gloves. Nothing extinguished the smell of death no matter how cold or how much antiseptic Wolfe used. It seemed to cling to her clothes and hair as if an entity. She eyed the jar of mentholated salve Kane was applying under his nose and took it from him. "Thanks."

"You're welcome." Kane added his face mask and took a position on Wolfe's right.

Jenna joined him and stared down at the body covered in a white sheet. She looked at Wolfe. Dressed in green scrubs, with mask and gloves, he barely resembled the tough Texan deputy she'd first met. "Do you have a time of death?"

"When was she last seen alive?" Wolfe pulled back the sheet, folded it, and laid it under the gurney.

"Her roommate said she left at nine and was seen getting into a silver or light blue sedan shortly after." Kane's eyes narrowed. "She was discovered at seven Sunday morning."

"Okay." Wolfe pulled down his microphone and started to dictate his findings, giving the date and persons present, and the name and relevant details of the deceased. "Time of death is currently open and can be gauged between nine on Saturday night and seven Sunday morning. The findings will change due to the following circumstances. Further investigation into finding the last person to see her alive at the party would lessen the TOD. The temperature of the hot shower increased rigor, but from the condition of the epidermis, I would determine the immersion in hot water lasted approximately four to five hours post-mortem."

Jenna moved closer and winced at the array of bruises on the young woman. "Have you taken swabs?"

"Yes, I found no foreign DNA evidence." Wolfe raised his head from examining the bruising. "Her clothes were wet and gave up no viable DNA whatsoever." He frowned. "The bruising on both upper arms is consistent with pressure from large hands. I believe someone held her down for an extended period to do this much damage. There are no defensive wounds and her nails aren't broken. Not to fight back is very unusual." He pointed to Chrissie's thighs. "The bruising is consistent with rape. You can clearly see fingernail gouges in her flesh." He sighed. "The handprint on the face is from a slap, looking at the impact area; I would say this injury caused the split in her lip." He indicated to the X-rays on the lightbox. "She has no broken bones and no signs of head trauma. I've taken blood samples and have started a toxicology screen. I'll be checking the stomach contents at the conclusion but she is showing a high blood-alcohol level. Enough to impair her reasoning and cognitive skills."

Jenna wanted to look away, run out of the room, go straight to the college, line up every damn man on campus and scream at them until she discovered the culprit. Instead, she drew a deep breath and called on the logical part of her brain. She needed answers, and although Chrissie had passed, the young woman had the answers to all their questions. She waited expectantly for Wolfe to finish. "What conclusions do you have for me?"

"I can confirm she was raped over a period of some hours. This is not one man; it's many men." Wolfe's gaze met Jenna's.

An overwhelming rage balled up inside Jenna. She stared down at Chrissie's angelic features and understood how terrified she'd been during her ordeal. Helpless and drunk, she'd had no chance to defend herself. Jenna dragged her gaze away from Chrissie's face and looked at Wolfe. "If she recognized any of them, or threatened to go to the cops, they could've staged her suicide."

"Exactly, and this being the case, I'll leave the cause of death verdict open until I've examined the injuries microscopically and gained more information. It will take a few days, I'm afraid." Wolfe peered at her over the top of his mask. "I'll roll her over."

With Kane's help, Wolfe turned over the body and examined every inch of Chrissie's deathly white skin, cataloging every scrape and each bruise, then turned it back. Jenna hated watching autopsies but it was part of the job, and when it involved a young woman, it just about broke her heart. No matter how caring or respectful Wolfe was, it came down to the awful truth that Chrissie had gone out to meet the boy of her dreams and a group of men had raped her. Had she been murdered or decided to kill herself rather than live with the memory?

Jenna concentrated on the evidence and allowed the various scenarios to settle in her mind. No matter how she personally felt about this victim, she needed to be objective and find out the absolute truth. She would need to speak to the roommate and ask her some personal questions about her friend. Kane had neglected to ask Livi how long she and Chrissie had been friends.

"Jenna." Wolfe was stitching up the body. "You okay?"

Jenna frowned at him. "I'm just fine."

"I'll send you a full report once I've analyzed the stomach contents, but from the smell, I'd say it was juice laced with vodka and likely Bourbon—a potent mix. From the amount, I'd say she vomited at some time before she died."

"Poor girl." Jenna pushed a lock of hair from Chrissie's face. "We'll find out who did this to you, I promise."

"We'll find them." Wolfe finished, covered the body, and then wheeled it into the storage locker. As the metallic door slammed shut, he turned and looked at her. "I ran a full toxicology screen on her blood but I also ran specific tests here for Rohypnol and GHB, the date-rape drugs. I'll go and see if they're ready as the full tox screen will take up to three weeks to come back from the lab." He pulled off his gloves and strode from the room.

Jenna moved to Kane's side. "I need to speak to Livi and get some personal details. I also want to find out a bit more about Phillip Stein and see if we can get a list of the boys Chrissie knew, although I'm leaning toward the football team for the rape."

"The girl's in bad shape; maybe we should leave it until tomorrow." Kane shrugged. "But you're the boss."

"We'll give her some space. It's unlikely she'll forget what happened during her lifetime." Jenna removed her gloves and mask then tossed them into the trash. "It's so much harder watching an autopsy of a young woman. The brutality she endured makes me so angry."

"I've seen the hardest of cops faint in an autopsy or, worse, spew—as if the smell isn't bad enough." They walked through the doors and out into the hallway.

Jenna sighed. "Wolfe does help by making it all very technical. I found a few things interesting from his examination: prior to the rape she wasn't sexually active, and her attackers used protection, which means it wasn't a spontaneous attack. The few leaves of freshly cut grass caught in the rolled-up material of her top are apparently from the lawn outside her dorm, which means someone delivered her to the residence hall and dumped her on the grass."

"As no one witnessed her return, we don't have a valid timeline." Kane pushed his hands into the front pockets of his jeans and sighed.

Jenna leaned against the cold white wall and folded her arms across her chest. "Yeah, we do."

"How so?" Kane mimicked her pose.

"We know someone gave her a ride just after nine and Livi found her at seven. If she'd been immersed in water for four to five hours, that would have her entering the shower at between two and three Sunday morning." Jenna looked at him. "If we find out the distance from the residence hall to Lyons' house, we'll have a time of arrival at the party."

"If she arrived at the party." Kane raised one eyebrow. "The car was obviously owned by someone she knew or she wouldn't have gotten inside."

Jenna straightened. "We know Seth Lyons drives a red Mustang." She gave him a long look. "So why wouldn't he give her a ride in his vehicle?"

"Maybe because it sticks out like a sore thumb, and if he'd planned to rape her, why advertise his presence?" Kane frowned. "Livi mentioned she overheard him telling her to keep their date a secret."

Jenna's ears pricked up. "And why didn't you haul his ass in for questioning?"

"Oh, I'd have been all over him like a rash." Kane eased away from the wall, dropping his hands to his waist. "He's away with the rest of the team. He left Sunday morning and the bus gets in around nine. I heard the guys drink on the way back to campus, so to avoid an under the influence defense, we should wait to speak to him until first thing in the morning."

Before she could reply, a swish of doors opened, heralding the arrival of Wolfe. She stared at him expectantly. "Did you find anything?"

"Sure did. I have a positive for gamma-hydroxybutyric acid or GHB." Wolfe held up a sheet of paper. "From the concentration in her blood, I'd say she took it around eleven. It was a high dose—one pill would have knocked her out with the amount of alcohol she consumed—but I figure this was at least double."

Jenna pushed the hair from her eyes and frowned. "I've no reports about anyone supplying GHB in my town." She looked up at Wolfe. "The last case involving a date-rape drug was injected and they can't possibly be from the same dealer."

"Nope, the last case involved ketamine and was an injectable anesthetic." Wolfe frowned. "GHB is a street drug, so if it's not supplied here, someone is bringing it in. Like it or not, this drug is available all over." He looked at Jenna. "This answers a ton of questions. The drug is fast-acting and remains active for several hours. Chrissie would've had difficulty speaking and certainly wouldn't have been capable of fighting back."

Jenna chewed on her bottom lip, thinking back on other cases involving similar drugs. "I figured date-rape drugs made a person forget what had happened, so that rules out suicide, doesn't it?"

"Think about it." Wolfe's gray gaze became compassionate. "This poor girl likely wouldn't have remembered the details while she was semi-conscious. I figure someone slapped her face, split her lip, and then threatened her. She'd have been aware of what had happened to her. She'd have been in a considerable amount of pain."

She stared at Kane. Having a profiler on the team gave her insights into the criminal mind. "Give me something, Kane. What kind of man does this to a defenseless young woman?"

"I don't think this attack was random. I figure we could be looking at serial rapists. We haven't had this happen before—the suicide angle, I mean—so I don't know if they planned on killing her. I agree with Wolfe. Threatening her would be their only option to keep her quiet." Kane rubbed his chin, making a rasping sound. "These guys have a system. They single out potential victims, find their weak spot, and then use that as leverage to threaten them into silence."

Horrified, Jenna swallowed hard. "Are you sure they've done this before?"

"It's likely. They're well organized." Kane shrugged. "They all used protection, made sure the car giving her a ride was nondescript. If it's a group, like a gang or a football team, they'll all lie for each other. You can be sure whoever is involved will have an iron-clad alibi."

"That may not be enough." Wolfe stood feet apart with his hands on his hips. "The bruises on her are significant and show defined handprints. I'm sure one of them shows the outline of a ring. I'll be looking closely at the images to see if we can use them for identification. We do have the technology to take latent fingerprints from skin, but as she was submerged in water for some time, it will be impossible."

Anger simmered just under the surface and Jenna would use it to push to find who'd abused Chrissie. "Thanks, that's all very interesting. I'll need your report as soon as possible." She sighed. "I guess I'll have to break the sad news to the parents about the rape before the media gets hold of the story."

"They're coming in this afternoon. They'll want to make arrangements and won't be happy I'll have to delay my findings." Wolfe gave her a long, considering stare. "They'll have questions and I figure

I'm the best person to answer them. I'll call when they leave so you can organize a press release if you feel it's necessary."

"Thanks, I'd appreciate that. I don't envy you the task; there's nothing worse than adding more misery to grieving parents." She turned to Kane. "We'll head back to the office. If we can't interview Seth Lyons or his friends, I want background checks on him and every member of the football team. We'll check out Phillip Stein as well. I want to discover everything about them. By the time I've finished with them, we'll know how many times a day they go to the bathroom."

# CHAPTER FOUR

## Monday evening

He'd always been logical and considered each aspect of a situation. Watching the causes and effects of people's actions had become a way of life. He peered out from the cover of bushes to the dark driveway, taking in the array of buildings on the college campus. Streetlights lined the walkways in pools of yellow in an effort to make it safe for students to move from one place to another—but was it safe? *He* lurked in the shadows and could pluck an unsuspecting person at random and dispose of them in seconds. In truth, if he decided to kill them all, no one would be safe from him.

The leaves on the maple trees fascinated him. Each a replica of thousands of others, only differing in size or color. The pine he leaned his back against was the same. The bark and needles had the same design as the others. Insects too, ants, butterflies—each species in nature resembled each other as if cloned. Apart from man, most species shared a similar if not identical genetic code. It seemed only when man became involved and bred to his own preference did a species make a dramatic change. Yet nothing on earth acted like man, and having a higher intelligence came with a price. He often wondered if God created each man with a unique DNA code, to prevent people from getting away with murder.

He relaxed, used to waiting. He'd never understood impatience. Things happened in their own sweet time, and he welcomed the chance to ponder the meaning of life—or death. As the cool evening air rustled the leaves, he focused on two giggling girls in shorts and bare midriffs running along one of the footpaths with ponytails bobbing. Many things happened on campus at night. The swimming pool, gym, and library remained open until very late. Students used rooms for discussions and club meetings. It seemed the place rarely slept.

In the distance, he heard the shifting of gears and the whine of brakes as a bus rounded the end of the driveway, leaving a cloud of toxic fumes caught in the streetlight as it labored toward them. The group of players aboard all received special treatment from Coach, being the few he liked to parade before the scouts.

As they stepped from the bus he made his way along the shadowed walkway toward the college, mixing with the students returning to their dorms. By the conversations, some members of the team planned to use the gym and pool. He smiled into the dim light and pulled his baseball cap down to cover his eyes. Patience was a virtue he had in spades, and his was just about to pay out in silver dollars. His next strike would be tonight.

# CHAPTER FIVE

Alex Jacobs stared at his reflection in the mirror above the sink. He raised both arms to admire his bulging biceps and grinned. A six-two man with a brilliant white smile looked back at him, tanned with neat blond hair. He'd created his body over a few years of hard work in the gym. His efforts had paid out and he took pride in his physique. His place on the football team as left tackle was secure, as was his friendship with the quarterback Seth Lyons.

He strolled into the gym, glad to see the place empty and quiet. At this time of night, he usually had the place to himself so a slight movement in the shadows surprised him. The figure hadn't moved and just leaned against the wall, watching him. Alex gave him a wave but had gotten no response by the time he reached the weight training bench. He'd planned to do a few reps on the weights and didn't need a spotter. It was just a regular workout. The guy's rudeness unsettled him. He didn't like people staring at him as if he'd become their night's entertainment, but maybe the guy was too shy to approach him. Being his size and a celebrity on campus, it happened.

After loading the weights onto the bar, his attention drifted to the person in the shadows, but he'd vanished. Had he imagined him? A niggle of unease slid down his spine. As a senior in Black Rock Falls, and with the town's reputation of being serial killer central, he'd be stupid to continue without checking if the guy was hiding somewhere.

He picked up the barbell he used for arm curls as a weapon and walked with purpose toward the glass doors leading to the hallway.

He peered outside and looked both ways. It was quiet with only the distant hooting of an owl flying overhead. Most of the students would be in their dorms by now, or maybe a few had gone to the library to prepare for the morning's classes. One of his teammates, Pete Devon, would likely be doing laps in the pool, not lurking in the shadows.

As he strolled back to the weight training bench, he couldn't shake the feeling he wasn't alone. "You're losing your mind, man."

His voice sounded loud in the empty room but he shrugged and then took his position on the bench. He took a deep breath and then closed both hands around the bar. Engrossed, he lifted the weight with ease, completed five reps, then rested the bar back on the rack. When a man wearing a baseball cap pulled down over his eyes slid into his periphery, his heart skipped a beat. Where had he come from and how the hell had he snuck up on him without a sound? Alex sat up so fast his head spun. He reached for his towel and wiped down his face. He let out a relieved gasp. "Oh, it's you. Are you waiting to do weight training?"

"Nah." His friend leaned against the wall. "I wanted to talk in private about the party last Saturday night."

Alex allowed the smile to creep over his face. "She was pretty hot, huh?"

"Quiet too." Shadows covered the man's face. "I like them quiet."

"Me too." Not wanting to elaborate, Alex dropped back on the bench. He preferred to be alone in the gym. "I'm cooling down. I'd better finish my workout."

"You'll burn muscle using light weights on fast reps. If you change to heavier weights and do slower reps, you'll build harder muscle." His friend peered down at him and smiled. "I'll spot you if you want me to add some more?"

Not wanting to appear weak, Alex nodded. "Sure, thanks."

He waited while his friend added substantially more weights to the bar and noticed his thin leather gloves. He grinned. "I guess you've gotta take care of those hands, man." He gripped the bar.

"Yeah. I wouldn't be much use without them, would I?"

"Nope." Alex looked up at him. "Why are you really here?"

"Do you figure we should get that girl again?" The man rested his hands on the bar. "She was very cooperative."

Alex strained through the first rep, glad when his friend lifted the bar back onto the rack. The weight was punishing and much more than he preferred. "She was wasted, man." He grinned. "I can't wait to see the shots we took, and the vid will be a classic." He heaved the bar off the rack, dropped it to his chest, then heaved it up again, grunting through the pain.

He repeated the movement three more times and his muscles stung with the effort. "This will be the last rep. I'm all in."

"Sure." His friend's mouth twitched into a smile. "The last rep it is."

Alex grunted, pushing up with all his strength, but no help came to lift the bar onto the rack. Panic curled in his belly and sweat ran down his face. Muscles bulging with effort, he sucked in a deep breath and heaved but couldn't lift the heavy weight the last few inches. Elbows locked and arms shaking with the burn, he stared at him. "Hey, give me a hand here."

"There's a small problem with seeing Chrissie again. She was found dead yesterday morning."

The heavy weight vanished, and panting with the effort, Alex stared into the man's cold eyes. His friend suspended the weight over him as if it weighed nothing and held it like he was taunting him—but why? "What! Shit, what happened to her? We all enjoyed every minute and she never complained, not once."

"Neither will you."

As if in slow motion, Alex watched in horror as the bar slipped from the man's fingertips. He had no time to react. A loud crack filled his head and then a clanging sound as one side of the weight bar slid to the floor. Hot burning pain shot through his neck and up into his brain. He couldn't breathe and his arms refused to move. Blood gurgled up his throat, spilling over his tongue in a metallic rush. He heard whistling and the outer door open then close before his sight folded in at the edges.

# CHAPTER SIX

The 911 chime of her cellphone dragged Jenna out of her dream. She pawed at the bedside table, snatched up her phone, and accepted the call. "911, what is your emergency?"

*"There's been an accident at the college gym. There's a body. I didn't know who to call."*

Jenna turned on her bedside lamp then grabbed her pen and notebook. She noted the time: it was a little after one. "This is Sheriff Alton. Who am I speaking to, and can you give me some details, please?"

*"This is John Beck. I'm the janitor. I was locking the gym when I found him. I figure he's been dead for a while."* Beck took a shuddering breath. *"Done dropped a barbell on his neck."*

"Okay, stay where you are and don't touch anything. We'll be there soon."

With Kane at the wheel, Jenna sat back in her seat sipping a freshly brewed coffee and snapping fully awake. "So, did you uncover any dirty little secrets?" She sighed. "I only found their driving records; nothing in juvie and no crimes since they turned eighteen."

"I gained access to their college records. Phillip Stein is an elite athlete, mainly snowboarding and winter sports." Kane flicked her a glance. "He's every mother's dream: clean-cut, has a high IQ, and is pursuing a career in IT."

Jenna frowned. "He's a contradiction to the usual nerd stereotype; he excels in sports as well?"

"Yeah, but I guess dating a snowboarder doesn't come close to dating a quarterback." Kane snorted. "I've never been able to understand the dynamics of dating in college."

"What about Seth Lyons?"

"He's a mixed bag." Kane turned onto Stanton Road and accelerated toward the college. "Troublemaker, makes a game out of the rules. After some roughhousing last semester, the dean removed most of the football team from the resident halls. They rent a big old house out on Pine." He sighed. "All the complaints against them are much the same: drinking, loud music, fighting… but no reports of abusing women."

Jenna stared at the dark forest as they flashed by. It was dark and dangerous by night with only small pools of light from the streetlights guiding their way. They turned into the college's sweeping driveway, through the wrought-iron gates, and stopped beside Wolfe's white van. Jenna grabbed the thermos and cups and headed for the gym. "I hope this is just an accident."

"It would sure make life easier." Kane strode along beside her. "I take it they don't have CCTV inside the gym?"

"I'm not sure but there's a camera over there." Jenna pointed to one just above the entrance to the amenities block. "I hope it's working."

"I'll ask the janitor." Kane gave Wolfe a wave. "Although, if that's him with Wolfe, he doesn't look so well."

Jenna walked up to a man in his forties, dressed in coveralls and looking sheet-white. "Mr. Beck?"

"That's me." Beck leaned heavily against the wall.

Jenna pulled out her notebook. "Do you recognize the victim?"

"Sure do, Alex Jacobs, the best left tackle the Black Rock Falls football team has had in years." Beck scrubbed a trembling hand down his face as if trying to erase the memory. "To see him like that, dear Lord, made me sick to my stomach."

"Deputy Kane has a few questions for you." Jenna turned to Wolfe. "What have we got?"

"Likely an accident, it's hard to tell. He's not been dead long, maybe one to two hours."

She followed Wolfe into the gym and stared at the broken body. It would take a long time to forget the young man's bulging eyes and open, bloody mouth fixed in a scream of terror. "If we can get the footage from the CCTV outside, we'll be able to find out what time he arrived and if anyone else was here."

"It's unusual for a weightlifter to risk lifting so much weight without a spotter." Wolfe frowned. "Plus, the position of his hands concerns me. I've seen this type of accident before and it's unusual for the hands to be below the waist. You see, when the victim is struggling to take the weight, he traps at least one hand under the bar on impact." He held his arms up as if demonstrating.

Jenna nodded. "Maybe his spotter dropped the barbell then panicked when he saw he'd killed him?"

"Maybe. I'll check it for prints." Wolfe shrugged. "Is that coffee?"

"Yeah, I figured you'd need some." Jenna placed the thermos on a nearby table. "I'll go see what Kane has gotten from the janitor."

She made her way outside the gym and ran straight into the dean of the college. David Bent was an imposing, tall, thin man in his sixties with black hair graying at the temples. He wore a robe over his pajamas. "Mr. Bent, I'm sorry but you'll have to remain here. The ME is on scene."

"What happened?" Bent stared over her shoulder then returned his gaze to her. "Is Jacobs dead?"

Jenna rested a hand on his arm. "I'm afraid so. It appears he dropped the weight bar and it struck him across the neck. Does he normally have a spotter?"

"I'm not aware of every student's habits on campus, Sheriff." Bent gave her a look of disdain. "I'm sure his friends will be able to answer all your questions. Lyons and a group of seniors on the team live out on Pine. Their house is set back from the first corner, you can't miss it." He cleared his throat. "Coach took a few of the football team out for a training clinic. They left early Sunday morning and returned around nine last night."

"Yes, I'm aware of the trip." Jenna made a few notes. "Is it unusual for the team to go away on a Sunday?"

"No, and they had the opportunity to spend both days with professional players." Bent gave an exasperated sigh. "Those that needed to go to church or whatever did so before they caught the bus." He stared back at the hallway leading to the gym. "Two deaths in the same number of days will ruin our reputation."

"I'm sure the parents of the students won't be worrying too much about the college's reputation." Jenna couldn't comprehend his apathy. "They'll want to know what happened." She narrowed her gaze. "I'll need Jacobs' next of kin details so I can make arrangements to inform his parents."

"I'll have to open my office." Bent's brow furrowed. "Come with me and I'll get you the information."

Jenna shook her head. "I see you have your cellphone with you." She pulled a card from her pocket and handed it to him. "It will be easier if you send me the information in a text. I can't leave the scene until the ME has removed the body." She gave him a long, appraising look. "If you'd call your security team to keep the students away from this area, I'll follow up with you in the morning."

"I've already notified them and they're heading this way as we speak." Bent hunched his shoulders. "Are you sure I'm not needed here?"

Jenna shook her head. "I don't need you but I'm sure the students gathering out on the lawn require an explanation. As you mentioned, two deaths in as many days will be unsettling."

"Yes, yes, they'll disperse once I tell them there's been an unfortunate accident." Bent looked exhausted. "I'll find you that information." He wandered off as if in a daze.

Jenna hustled toward the janitor's office and met Kane on the way out. "Do you have anything?"

"Yes and no. First, the janitor doesn't usually lock up the gym or the pool. One of the security guards on duty called in sick and he volunteered to lock up. The CCTV screens are in the security guard's office." He frowned. "The other guard is out on patrol somewhere on the grounds."

"Apparently, he's on his way." Jenna looked up at him. "So, what else did the janitor say?"

"By all accounts, Jacobs was a close friend of Seth Lyons. They went everywhere together. Lyons might have been the last person to see him alive… and maybe Chrissie. There's something else." Kane pulled out his cellphone. "He let me into the security guard's office and I took a look at the CCTV files. I've emailed you and Wolfe a copy of the footage." He pulled up the file and handed the phone to Jenna. "There's Jacobs arriving at 9:15 p.m. Just after, there's a malfunction and the camera goes down until 12:30 a.m. The janitor goes in at 12:55 a.m. and that's him running out to vomit in the garden. That must've been when he called you."

Jenna frowned. "Did you ask him if the CCTV goes offline often?"

"I did." Kane raised one dark eyebrow. "He said I'd have to check with the security guards but as far as he knows it hasn't failed before tonight." He rewound the video. "See that flash? I figure someone disabled the camera with a laser pointer."

"Oh, wonderful." Jenna rubbed her temples. "Why does everything have to be so darn complicated in this town?"

# CHAPTER SEVEN

Alex Jacobs' parents were out of Louan an hour's drive north of Black Rock Falls. Jenna called the Louan Sheriff Department and asked a very reluctant and grumpy man to notify Jacobs' next of kin. She disconnected and waited for Kane to help Wolfe load the weighty body into the back of the van. For now, the gym would remain closed. Crime scene tape covered the door and Wolfe had pocketed the key. She turned to Wolfe. "What next?"

"I have my suspicions." Wolfe removed his gloves and mask then rolled them into a ball. "I'll put him on ice and come back tomorrow with Webber. I doubt we'll find anything incriminating; the students wipe down the benches after each use. I only found one set of fingerprints on the bar. So many people use the gym, it would be impossible to implicate anyone even if I did return a verdict of homicide." He sighed. "The best course of action is to wait until his parents come by to identify the body. I'll obtain permission for a post then I'll make a decision."

"Sure, thanks." Jenna walked back to Kane and they headed for his truck. She had two deaths and two reasons to speak to the members of the football team. "We'll go wake up Seth Lyons. I know where he lives."

"You don't figure Lyons is going to step up and admit to raping Chrissie, do you?" Kane gave her an incredulous look. "He'll just sit back and wait, hoping it all blows over. How are you planning to play this?"

Jenna pulled open the door and climbed inside. She waited for Kane to slide behind the wheel. "Straight down the line. I'd want him to believe we're looking elsewhere."

"Sure." Kane headed toward Stanton Road. "I'll follow your lead."

They drove for some time in silence and then she waved a hand as the headlights picked out a road sign. "That's Pine. The frat house is on the first bend." She pointed. "That must be the entrance."

They turned in and took a winding, tree-lined driveway, drove past a no-entry sign blocking another small road and then they came to a parking lot. A pathway led through the trees to the house. Jenna peered into the darkness. "Why not have parking closer to the house?"

"The no-entry sign on the other road likely leads to the house." Kane frowned. "They don't like visitors." He pointed through a gap in the trees. "The lights are on. Don't they ever sleep?"

"Where exactly did you go to college?" Jenna giggled. "Oh yeah, I know the drill. If you tell me, you'll have to shoot me." She gave him a long stare. "I figure you went to OCS."

"Yeah, Officer Candidate School was part of my training like hundreds of others. I've several degrees in different fields, not that they're worth anything now with my new name and all." His expression was shadowed in the dark car interior. "I completed a variety of complex training, Jenna, at Quantico just like you. It's not like civilian college; we didn't have the time or energy to stay up all night." He waved a hand toward the frat house. "These kids figure education is a game; for me, getting it right was the difference between life and death."

Sobered by her own dark memories, she could only imagine what Kane had endured during his deployment. "Ah, yeah, I know what you mean." She turned her attention to the front door. From what they could see through the trees, it stood wide open and light spilled out onto the porch. "Either they don't seem to be too worried about security or something's wrong. I figure we play it safe and forget the path. If we keep to the tree line, we won't be spotted from the house."

"Roger that." Kane killed the lights and coasted into the bushes beside the driveway.

Jenna slipped silently from the seat and closed the door. Seeing the cobwebs hanging down from the trees, she shuddered. "Ah… you mind taking the lead?"

"Nope." Kane looked at her and grinned. "Worried about ghosts?"

"Nope, spiders." She moved behind Kane's big frame as they ran in the shadows. Underfoot twigs cracked and she stumbled over the remnants of a garden border. "Dammit." She untangled her foot from a mess of dead vines and hurried after him. Kane had reached the bottom of the steps to the long, wide porch and then vanished into the shadows. Jenna hightailed it across the driveway and went to his side. They stood listening for some moments. Soft music drifted out the open door but apart from the strains of a country singer, the place was deadly quiet. "I hope they're not all dead in there."

"Well, I guess a mass murderer would be a change from the usual deranged psychopaths we attract around here." Kane's smile showed white in the darkness. "Sorry, I couldn't resist, but I don't smell death—booze and sweat maybe, but not murder."

Amazed by Kane's ability to sum up a situation in seconds, she moved closer. "What if someone poisoned them or is holding them at gunpoint?" She lifted her chin. "I figure we proceed with caution."

"I always do." Kane eased his way up the steps and pressed his back to the wall beside the front door.

Jenna followed and, weapon drawn, waited for him to turkey-peek around the front door. "What do you see?"

"Bodies everywhere. The front door leads straight into a family room." Kane turned back to look at her. "I can't see or smell blood, so maybe they've all passed out."

A noise from inside prickled the hairs on the back of Jenna's neck. "What was that?"

"There's something moving in there." Kane took a step forward and the boards under his feet gave a loud moan. A strangled cry came from inside. "Stay back."

The next moment a large calico cat shot out the door, carrying part of a slice of pizza, and took off into the darkness, tail fluffed out like a raccoon. Jenna jumped back then stared at Kane. "What the—?"

"If animals are raiding the place, something's up." Kane holstered his weapon, pulled on latex gloves, and then moved to the doorway.

"I'm going in." Jenna peered around the door and raised her voice. "Sheriff's department."

When nobody moved, Jenna holstered her weapon and followed, pulling on gloves as she walked. She went to the first young man spread out on a sofa beside another with his head hanging over the arm. She touched his face. The warm skin under her fingers and the rapid eye movement under his lids told her he was in REM sleep. She checked the other man and found him to be fine. "They're asleep."

"So are these over here. We have six guys. Do you know how many live here?"

Jenna shook her head. "No, but they're all seniors."

"Well, Jacobs was one of them and there could be more asleep upstairs. I figure two to a room, they'd fit ten or more people in here. There has to be six bedrooms in a house this size." Kane wrinkled his nose and bent over. "And look what we have here." He held up a glass bong and a substantial bag of weed. "I bet you know what this is?"

Jenna took the bag from Kane, peered inside, and examined the weed. "It looks and smells like Ghost Train Haze or maybe Train Wreck." She glanced up at him. "It's been some time since I've seen any weed, and new strains are coming out every day. Whatever, it's a federal offense to bring it into Montana. We'll bag the evidence."

She looked around at the sleeping bodies. "Wake them up one at a time, get their names and prints. I doubt any of them have a medical marijuana permit but you can ask—but I figure this bag is way over the limit."

As Kane went to work rousing the sleepy young men, Jenna took in the surroundings. The place was a mess. Beer and liquor bottles littered the coffee tables and the floor around the sofas. Empty wrappers from a variety of junk food, half-eaten hamburgers, and cartons of Chinese takeout littered every spare space. She moved slowly through the ground floor, passing a number of rooms set up for studying, with desks and laptops left unattended. A staircase led into darkness, but at the end of the hallway, she found the kitchen. Four coffee machines sat on a counter amid piles of dirty dishes, some with mold growing on rancid food. She heard footsteps and spun around as an athletic young man strolled into the room. Clean-cut and wearing a muscle shirt and shorts, the guy had blond hair and piercing, emerald-green eyes.

"It's the maid's day off." He gave Jenna a crooked smile. "What brings you here in the middle of the night, Sheriff? Somebody die?" He leaned against the counter with one hand a little too close to a kitchen knife.

Jenna eased to the other side of the table then faced him, one hand resting on the handle of her weapon. "And you are?"

The young man looked abashed, almost insulted, and she caught a gleam of cruelty in his eyes.

"Seth Lyons." He waved a hand to encompass the house. "My dad pays for all this so me and my boys can be alone, and here you are walking right in as if you own the place."

Jenna lifted her chin. He was smaller than she expected for a football player, maybe five-ten with an athletic build. "The front door was open and we called out. When none of your friends moved, we entered the premises to offer assistance."

"I see." Lyons crossed his arms over his chest. "That doesn't answer my question, Sheriff. Why are you here?"

"We found Alex Jacobs dead in the gym approximately an hour ago. I believe he lives here." Jenna watched Lyons' reaction and it was as if she'd punched him. "Is he a friend of yours?"

"Dead? How?" Lyons scrubbed his hands over his face. "Heart attack?"

Jenna frowned. "Did he have a heart problem?"

"Not that I'm aware of, but he pushes himself hard and his old man died of a heart attack recently." Lyons pulled out a chair at the table, pushed away the plates to make a space, and dropped into the seat.

"When did you last see him?" Jenna went to the sink, took a clean glass from a shelf, filled it with water, and handed it to him.

"When we got back from training camp." Lyons leaned back in his seat and sipped the water. "We all came back here but he decided to stay on campus and lift some weights."

Jenna was making a mental calculation. Six men asleep in the family room, Alex, and Seth. "How many of you live here?"

"Eight." Seth gave her a long look. "Sometimes more on the weekends when members of the team drop by."

Not wanting to disclose any information about the cause of death, Jenna cleared her throat and moved on. "When was the last time you saw Chrissie Lowe?"

"Chrissie?" Lyons' demeanor changed in a split second from relaxed to wary. He paused for some moments as if thinking but Jenna could see a man searching for a plausible story to tell her. It came soon after. "In the cafeteria on Friday. I asked her to party with us on Saturday night but she was a no-show. Why do you want to know about her?"

*Oh, you're good.* Jenna leaned on the table and stared at him. "Really? A no-show, huh? Which one of you drives a silver or light blue sedan?"

"Most of the boys drive trucks and my ride is a Mustang." He shrugged and stared out into the passageway. "I don't know anyone who drives a sedan except maybe my old man." He turned his attention back to her. "You've ignored my question and expect me to answer yours. Why do you want to know about Chrissie?"

Jenna ignored him. "So, if I ask all the guys living here, they'll tell me Chrissie Lowe has never been here, is that right?"

"I'm not sure many of them would have met her. Alex did, and Pete." Lyons grinned. "You want it in writing, Sheriff?"

"Yeah, I do." Jenna pulled out her statement book and handed it to him. "Write it down and sign it. I'll ask Pete to do the same and I'll be on my way."

"You still haven't told me why." Lyons stared at her. "Has she made a complaint against me?"

"No, she hasn't said a word." Jenna straightened but her eyes never left his arrogant face. "Because she was found dead on Sunday morning, right after your date. I gather you missed the news tonight?"

"Yeah, we were on the bus." He gave her a direct, cold stare. "Shame, she was a nice girl." He set about writing the statement.

With his uncaring attitude toward the death of a young girl he'd thought worthy of asking on a date, Jenna needed to push harder. He and his roommates had gone to the top of her suspects list for Chrissie's rape. "How many people came to the party?"

"Not many—ten, fifteen maybe. They drift in and out all night." Lyons signed the document and handed it to her. "It's invitation-only."

"How many of them were women?" Jenna noticed the way he hunched his shoulders and one hand partly obscured his mouth. *He's hiding something.*

"I don't recall." Lyons' eyes flashed in annoyance. "I noticed a couple of girlfriends. The guys take them up to their rooms, so the majority were guys. It's not like we don't invite girls but we have a bad rep and they often refuse to come here."

"How so?"

"Aw, come on, Sheriff." Lyons barked a laugh. "We study and train hard all week, then on the weekends we party. That's why we're off campus. It was move out here or leave, so we came out here."

Jenna nodded then pulled out the trump card. "I see. Would you be willing to give a DNA sample?"

"No way." Lyons scowled at her. "That comes close to the same as microchipping a dog. I don't want my private information in the FBI database."

"Okay." Jenna waved a hand toward the hallway. "My partner is talking to your friends. Why don't we join them?" She wet her lips. "Do you mind if I grab a glass of water?"

"Knock yourself out." Lyons placed his empty glass on the table then stood and headed out the door.

Jenna waited a beat, then without a second thought, she pulled an evidence bag from her pocket and placed the glass inside. After filling out the label, she pushed it into her pocket, removed her gloves, and made her way to the front of the house. *Not so clever after all, are you, Mr. Lyons?*

# CHAPTER EIGHT

Kane had the men in the family room spread out away from each other. He'd established the bag of weed and the bong belonged to a young man living in the house. The guy in question suffered from epilepsy and was legally engaged in the medical marijuana program. He carried a card as proof. The others denied smoking the illegal substance and to prove their innocence had agreed to submit to drug testing, which he conducted on the spot. To his surprise they'd all come up negative. They informed him all members of the football team had agreed to random drug testing after one of them had been caught with drugs and suspended last semester.

He hadn't informed them about Alex Jacobs' death and had only just finished entering their information into the files when another young man strolled into the room. Kane took in his pale face and strained expression then noticed Jenna coming behind him down the hallway.

"Did he tell you? Alex is dead." The man scanned the room. "And that freshman girl I invited to the party on Saturday night, the no-show, she's dead too." He stared at the others. "The sheriff wanted my DNA but I refused. I'm a suspect because I asked her out on a damn date and you guys know I was with you all Saturday night. I didn't leave the house until we all caught the bus on Sunday morning."

A barrage of questions followed and Jenna hustled into the middle of the room.

"We're not accusing anyone of a crime but we'd like to know if any of you saw Chrissie Lowe on Saturday night. She's the girl Seth asked to the party." Jenna pulled out her cellphone, brought up a picture of Chrissie, and showed it to each man. "Did you see Chrissie at any time on Saturday night or early Sunday morning?"

"I was in the cafeteria with Seth when he asked her out on a date." One of the men glanced at Lyons. "I'm Pete Devon. She was a no-show, just like he said."

"So, she's never been in the house?" Jenna frowned.

"Not that I recall." Pete shrugged.

"Can I have that in writing?" Jenna handed him the notebook and pen she was carrying. "Seth has already given me a statement."

"Sure." Devon took the statement book and, resting it on the arm of a chair, started writing.

Kane considered the body language of each man as he peered at the image. All of them to a man glanced at Chrissie's photo, denied knowing her, and then looked straight at Seth Lyons. They all had the same confused expression and one of them shook his head slowly. Kane could tell by their reactions they all recognized her and he figured at least two of them had been involved in the rape. Lyons' speech when he'd walked into the room had given them all just enough information to keep their mouths shut.

After waiting for Jenna to finish, he cleared his throat. "Mind if we check out upstairs?"

"Why?" Lyons folded his arms across his chest. "We haven't broken any laws."

Kane took a step closer to him. "I'd like to close this case up tonight. It's late. We just want to establish that you're the only members of the household." He let out a long, seemingly exhausted sigh. "I don't want permission to search, just look."

"Sure, but I'm coming with you." Lyons led the way to the stairs.

Kane headed after him; he'd caught Jenna's confused gaze and given her a nod. As Lyons opened every door, Kane noticed a common theme running through the house: each room was dirty and littered with laundry until he came to the room at the end of the hall. When the door opened, the smell of bleach hit him in a wall of fumes. The bed had crisp, clean sheets and was made up in almost military-style precision; not one speck of dust covered the floor. "Who sleeps here?"

"I do, and Alex." Lyons' brow wrinkled into a frown. "I like things clean."

*Or he's covering up trace evidence after raping Chrissie.* Kane gave the room a cursory once-over then nodded. "So I see."

"The house isn't a mess all the time. The cleaner comes tomorrow. They come once a week but the guys live like pigs." Lyons followed behind him. "What happened to Alex? The sheriff refused to tell me, and his mom will have questions."

Kane stopped walking and turned to look down at him. "We're not sure; accident most likely. We'll know more after the autopsy. When did you last see him?"

"I already told the sheriff. We got off the bus and he headed to the gym." Lyons shrugged. "He goes there late; he likes the quiet."

Kane took in the man's unusual demeanor. His best friend had died and he didn't seem to care. "Didn't you wonder why he hadn't come home?"

"Alex?" Lyons gave him an incredulous look. "Nah, I figured he'd taken a ride down to the Triple Z, maybe had too many beers and decided to sleep in his truck." He gave him a slow smile. "Or found a woman to spend the night with; he's a big star on campus."

*Then why the need to drug and rape young women?* Kane bit back a retort and nodded. "Okay, thanks."

He made his way downstairs and heard Jenna telling the others she was sad for their loss. He followed her out the front door and they hurried through the shadows to his truck using his Maglite to find their way. The house was set back on the lot, offering Lyons and his friends a place far enough from the road to muffle any loud music—or the screams of the women he raped. Safely inside the truck, he headed down the driveway, turned onto Pine, and then headed for home. He glanced at Jenna. "I figure Lyons and his buddies raped Chrissie."

"How so?" Jenna turned in her seat to look at him. "We don't have any proof and they all said she was a no-show at the party."

Kane gritted his teeth, wondering how many times they'd lured girls to their house. "The place is a mess but Lyons' bedroom, which he shared with Alex Jacobs, was spotless and they'd used bleach to wash things down. Clean sheets, the works. It was one of the best clean-up jobs I've seen for a long time. They're all very aware of DNA and leaving trace evidence." He sighed. "Did you like his little speech when he came into the room to give his friends a heads-up?"

"Yeah, it was a bit hard to miss." Jenna rubbed her temples and sighed. "Now he knows Chrissie is dead, they'll all cover for each other, and by now, he's likely coaching them not to say anything."

Kane thought for a moment. "We need to get more information about what happened to Chrissie."

"I'll see if I can get it out to the media. We'll need her parents' blessing, but if we can get other rape victims to come forward, we could make a case. We'll guarantee to protect their identities. I figure the DA will go along with the idea, and I could insist they hear the case in a closed court. I'll speak with him later." Jenna yawned. "Right now, I need to sleep. I'm having trouble staying awake."

"I'm tired too." Kane accelerated along Stanton Road, his head-lights picking out an owl flying into the forest and the reflections of many sets of eyes peeking out of the dark trees. "I have a bad feeling about Lyons—something about him is waving a red flag at me."

"I figure I saw the evil in him earlier in the kitchen." Jenna leaned back in her seat and looked at him. "It upset him that his best friend had died, but when I asked him about Chrissie it was like I'd flipped a switch. His personality changed and his eyes disturbed me; it was anger or as if he was just on the edge of losing it. Like a cat just before it pounces."

Kane rubbed his chin. "Hmm, and he directed it toward you, huh?"

"Yeah, he didn't like me being there, period."

"Interesting. He likes to take his anger out on women." Kane stared at the dark, winding road ahead. "Rape is never sexual, it's violence. If Lyons planned to rape Chrissie all along, he could've encouraged his friends to participate."

"I find it hard to believe all of them are violent rapists." Jenna frowned. "You're the expert on behavior, so just how did he encourage them to rape an unconscious girl?"

"It would've started off slowly." Kane glanced at her. "He'd have used peer pressure, insisting they complete a ritual hazing before allowing them to live in the house. If one or two of them had concerns, the fact she was unconscious and couldn't see them would've made a difference. To them it wouldn't have appeared so violent. Once they'd agreed and Lyons had implicated them, he'd have gained their silence and an alibi."

"How does he know the girls won't go to the cops or tell someone?" Jenna didn't sound convinced. "I sure would."

Kane turned into their driveway. "I figure this isn't his first time. Men like this gain control by threatening to hurt someone the victim knows, or they go after their reputation by making sure everyone in school knows they're easy." He pulled up outside the ranch house. "Or maybe they have pictures."

"If they did this to Chrissie," Jenna turned to face him, "I'll take them all down."

Kane smiled at her in the darkness. "That's my girl."

# CHAPTER NINE

## Tuesday

As he had little to occupy his day, he decided it was time for more observation. He slid his vehicle into a space at the back of the student parking lot and turned off the engine. He could remain in his vehicle all day if he chose to. No one policed entry into the designated parking areas—such was the security around campus. It was a terrorist's dream. The weaknesses in the school's defense amused him. The wired CCTV system was sporadic and didn't cover all entrances. Anyone could easily disable it by cutting the power source or simply aiming a laser pointer at the lens of a camera to disable it for a couple of hours. Laser pointers were the easiest option as the beam travels long distances and the user could remain hidden.

Using his drone, he'd followed six security guards as they patrolled the complex. Another three worked in a small office surrounded by screens, viewing the CCTV footage or issuing ID cards to the students. It hadn't taken too much time to discover they worked eight-hour shifts, so at any time, only two men strolled around and none of them worried too much about security. In fact, for most of the time they were either smoking, eating, or chatting to each other about sports. He wondered if he arrived carrying an AK-47 and strolled through the hallways killing at random, would they stand and fight or turn tail and run? He decided on the latter.

He set up his iPad and made himself comfortable then maneuvered his tiny drone to rise up into the air and scan the area. The minute panoramic camera and sensitive speaker gave superior clarity of picture and sound. As small as a hummingbird, it wouldn't attract attention and landed perfectly on the windowsill outside the football players' locker room. He listened with interest at the conversations; not one mentioned the suicide. It seemed the death of Jacobs—and the player the coach would pick to take his place on the team—consumed them. As the team members left the locker area to shower before heading to class, he zoomed in and listened to a hushed conversation between Dylan Court and Pete Devon.

*"Seth's found another girl. He wants to meet her later tonight at the pool. She gets there around eight thirty."* Court wasn't looking at Devon; his eyes were constantly scanning the locker room. *"You'll be doing laps as usual and he'll go to watch. You told us no one else goes there that late at night, so no one will see him talking to her. When she's finished, he can follow her out and use his charm to get her to come to the house on Saturday night."*

*"I figure we should cool it for a couple of weeks."* Devon rubbed the sweat from the end of his nose with the back of his hand and then shook his head. *"Jesus, you're talking about Brook? Hell, man—I know her."*

*"Yeah, she's a loner and a perfect choice."* Court snorted with amusement. *"Her mother lives alone."* He poked Devon in the chest. *"Come on now, don't tell me she doesn't deserve it. You've seen her teasing the guys."*

*"Nah, touch her and she'll squeal like a stuck pig."* Devon glared at him. *"Her father works for the DA's office."* He shook his head. *"I'm not going there, man."*

*"Dammit."* Court punched his locker door. *"Seth won't like it. We'll find someone else. What about that new girl, Emily Wolfe? Seth has her on his list."*

*"She's hot."* Devon smiled. *"I like blondes but she'll take time, she's a loner."*

*"Hmmm."* Court stared into space. *"I guess we could ride out to Aunt Betty's tonight after dinner and see who is hanging in town?"*

*"No can do."* Devon stripped off and wrapped a towel around his waist. *"Coach said if I don't do laps every night to build muscle over the injury from last season, I'm on the bench. I'll be done by nine thirty though, I'll join you then."* He headed for the shower.

The drone returned with swift efficiency and he stowed it away then leaned back in his seat, contemplating the information. He remembered the coach's wrath—vividly. One small infringement of his rules and a player could be outed. The fat, balding, loud-mouthed man was no role model for his players. He'd be the first one in his sights if he ever decided to return with that AK-47. He smiled into the sunshine at the visual image of the coach riddled with bullets and then his thoughts returned to the conversation in the locker room. Such loyal friends, but if they wanted to survive, they'd need to keep their mouths shut.

# CHAPTER TEN

Ears ringing from an overindulgence of coffee and eyes heavy with lack of sleep, Jenna scanned the files, making sure every detail was up to date. After obtaining the approval of Chrissie's parents and running her idea by the DA, the callout for other victims of rape went out over the media. The Victims of Crime hotline workers would be handling the delicate issue but no one had come forward yet. Jenna had checked out any dropouts from the college as well. She'd followed up four from the previous year and been shut down each time. All had insisted they'd moved college for logical reasons and didn't want to be involved in her line of questioning. So she had nothing to tie Lyons to any blackmail conspiracy or rape. Chrissie's roommate would be her only chance of getting some information or even gossip about what really happened on campus.

She'd called the college, and rather than pull Livi out of class, she'd decided to wait and speak to her at eleven, when she had a break. If Kane went with her, he could hunt down Phillip Stein and find out his story.

When a shadow crossed the door, she glanced up. "Ah, Rowley, what have you found for me?" She waved him into a seat.

"Not much." Rowley sat and glanced down at his iPad. "Lyons is the son of John Wakelin Lyons, old money with shares in just about everything, from housing to goldmines." He frowned. "Lyons is what I'd call the usual bad boy and spent most of his first year suspended, but then everything changed when he became quarterback. He's an integral part of the team and lives a charmed life on campus. It seems he can do no wrong, and if he's caught skirting the rules, it goes by unchallenged. Although, he was asked to move his friends off campus after a number of fights broke out in one of the dorms."

Jenna tapped the pen between her fingers on the desk. "Hmm, so I figure his father pays off any potential problems?"

"Seems so." Rowley cleared his throat. "There is a division in the team to some extent: Lyons has the team members from wealthy families in the house off campus, and I figure they're under his protection."

"How so?" Jenna placed the pen on the table.

"Well, although they've been implicated in incidents over the last couple of years, nothing is on their records, and nothing has been reported to us at all." Rowley gave her a troubled stare. "And I've checked them all out. Trust me. No one is that squeaky-clean."

"I gather all the guys in the house with Lyons are important team members as well?" Jenna shook her head. "Winning is everything, so I guess the dean lets things slide rather than lose a darn football game."

"Yeah, it's important for them to win." Rowley leaned back in his seat. "The chance to impress a scout and turn professional is the dream. It looks good for the school too." He glanced down at his notes. "I hunted down everything I could find on Chrissie as well. Normal kid who won a full scholarship to college, well liked, quiet, studious girl. She's never had as much as a detention. Her family lives in town, including a grandpa and one cousin—but decided to live on campus." He lifted his gaze. "That's all I have, ma'am. Do you want me to go out on patrol now? We have an influx of visitors. Main Street looks like a lineup at Aunt Betty's on discount Fridays."

With the rodeo in town, it would only be a matter of time before all hell broke loose. The last thing she needed during rodeo week was a desk full of unsolved cases. Jenna glanced at the clock. "Ah, sure, but wait until Deputy Walters arrives. He's due in soon and I want someone here. I'll be heading out with Kane around eleven to interview Livi Johnson, and then we're going straight to Alex Jacobs' autopsy."

"Yes, ma'am." Rowley stood. "I heard from Wolfe. Jacobs' parents will be arriving this afternoon to view the body." He cleared his throat. "I'll go and update the files with this info before I leave." He headed for the door.

Jenna made a few notes in her daybook then looked up when Kane poked his head around the door. She could always count on Kane to arrive bearing food and couldn't help smiling as he slipped inside the door carrying freshly brewed coffee and takeout bags from Aunt Betty's Café. She took the coffee from him. "Don't tell me you've decided since we have to work through lunch attending an autopsy, it would be good to eat at ten?"

"Something like that." Kane dropped into a chair and opened one of the paper bags. "Cherry pies, still warm from the oven. I've died and gone to heaven." He sniffed the pie and hummed in pleasure. His eyes met hers. "And I found a silver sedan."

Astonished, Jenna stared at him. "You sure it's the one that Livi saw Chrissie getting into?"

"Not one hundred percent but maybe ninety-nine percent." Kane bit into the pie, moaned, chewed, and swallowed. "I chased down silver and light blue sedans in the local area and luckily there are fewer than a hundred or so in town. I narrowed the search to the area surrounding the college, and guess what?"

Impatient, Jenna stared at him. "Go on."

"The janitor owns a silver sedan, and when I called him, he told me he'd wanted to drive the car to church on Sunday but found vomit in the floor in the back." Kane took another bite and seemed to take forever to swallow. "He lives on campus and leaves his car in the parking lot. His spare set of keys are on a nail in his office and he rarely locks the door. He put it down to a student prank." He gave Jenna a long look. "Wolfe said Chrissie vomited sometime before she died. Whoever gave her a ride to the party probably took the janitor's car and used the same car to take her back to the dorms."

Food forgotten, Jenna reached for her phone. "We need to get Wolfe onto it straight away. I gather the janitor cleaned up the vomit?"

"It's with Wolfe already." Kane smiled at her. "He pulled up the carpet and is doing tests as we speak. One thing, though: the entire car was wiped down for prints but Webber found hairs on the back seat—they're the same color as Chrissie's. He found other hairs as well and a few other stains. They were tearing the car apart when I left."

Jenna leaned back in her seat and took a long breath. "Great job. If Chrissie was in the back seat, that tells me more than one guy was in the car with her."

"Maybe two carried her to the vehicle if she was still groggy." Kane sipped his coffee. "Dumped her in the back seat—just a minute, she had a split lip. It was still bloody after being in the shower for hours; she would've bled over the back seat if she was lying down, and from the pool of vomit, she'd have been on her left side."

Excited by the revelation, Jenna leaned forward, all hint of tiredness gone. "They'd have turned off the interior light so nobody would recognize them and could've missed the blood on the back seat in the dark." She reached for a paper bag and took out a pie. "One thing's for sure, if they've left any trace evidence, Wolfe and Webber will find it."

"Another thing." Kane's gaze had wandered to the last cherry pie and remained there. "I made a few inquiries about Jacobs. I wanted to make sure he hadn't been in any fights lately or had any enemies." He lifted his attention back to her. "He was in a fight with a guy by the name of Owen Jones. I asked the janitor if there was any scuttlebutt about Jacobs, and he said Jacobs and a few other members of the team—Lyons' crew, we'll call them—told the coach he'd attempted to sell them drugs. A fight broke out between Jones, Lyons, and Jacobs, and the coach benched Jones then later the dean suspended him from college for the entire semester." He shrugged. "Although they carried out a search and found nothing. I figure Lyons' crew set him up to get one of their own on the team."

"So, is he back now?"

"Yeah, started back for the fall semester." Kane leaned back in his chair and sighed. "If Wolfe suspects homicide in the Jacobs case, we'll need to take a look at Owen Jones."

"Yeah, if he's as innocent as you say, he sure has a motive." Jenna sipped her coffee. "I really don't have time to watch football but Rowley explained how important being on a winning team is to these guys. The chance a scout might see them could mean a million-dollar career."

"Yeah, and to have that snatched away on a lie…" Kane shook his head. "That would make me angry but not mad enough to murder someone."

"So, we have Stein, but who else would want to kill someone for raping Chrissie?" Jenna shrugged. "Chrissie could've mentioned to anyone that she was going to the party and they'd assume the team was involved."

"We'll need to take a close look at her family and their movements around the time of Jacobs' death as well." Kane made a note. "I'll see what I can find out."

"Great." Jenna noticed Kane's attention had drifted back to the pie. "Ah, do you want to eat that pie while it's fresh? I'm having trouble finishing mine."

Kane gave her a smile to light up a room. "I thought you'd never ask."

# CHAPTER ELEVEN

Kane followed Jenna into the college cafeteria and pointed out Livi. Jenna had decided to speak to the girl alone, hoping she'd be more forthcoming speaking to a female officer. He headed for a group of students and asked if anyone knew Phillip Stein. They pointed out an athletic young man sitting alone in the corner wearing a T-shirt, jeans, and a baseball cap worn backward. Kane went over and introduced himself. "Mind if I sit down and have a word with you?"

"Is this about Chrissie?" Stein lifted his chin almost defiantly. "I wasn't with her on Saturday night. You need to be speaking to Seth Lyons."

Kane pulled out a chair and sat down. "I've already spoken to him. Tell me about your relationship with Chrissie. How long have you known her?"

"I knew her in high school and then ran into her again the day she started here; she'd gotten turned around and I took her to class." Stein stared into space as if remembering the moment. "She was a beautiful soul, gentle, and soft-spoken. I'll miss her."

Kane noticed the sorrow in his eyes. "You cared for her?"

"Yeah, it was heading that way, but we never really went on dates—as in out on a date. It was lunch here in the cafeteria and coffee at Aunt Betty's when we met up in town." Stein shrugged. "She was kind of innocent—know what I mean? I wanted to take things slow."

"So it was a shock to you when she told you she was going to a party with Lyons." Kane watched his reaction. "Did it make you angry?"

"Angry?" Stein's eyes narrowed. "Hurt maybe, disillusioned yeah, but not angry. I told her to have a good time and I'd call her on Sunday. She told me I was good old reliable Phil." He snorted. "I figured if she had one night with that animal, she'd decide I was the better choice."

Kane frowned. "He insists she didn't show."

"Then who raped her?" Stein's voice was low and deadly. "It must have been bad. She killed herself, didn't she? That's what Livi is telling everyone."

"Her cause of death is undetermined at this time." Kane studied his face. Anger shimmered under his surface of calm.

"Is that right? So you figure maybe someone followed her home and killed her to keep her quiet? I wouldn't be surprised. We all know what goes on at Lyons' house." Stein grimaced. "Chrissie isn't the first girl to come back from there messed up."

Intrigued by this information, Kane leaned forward. "Do you have any names or is it just a rumor?"

"We hear things but you'll never get any proof. It's common knowledge Lyons' daddy pays off any problems. I wouldn't be surprised if he makes them sign some kind of document to keep his boy safe from jail." Stein met his gaze. "So no, I don't have any names."

"Okay." Kane leaned back in his seat. "Can I ask where you were on Saturday night?"

"Sure, in my room studying." Stein gave him a determined look. "I didn't go out, check with my roommate or ask the others. I was there all night."

"And last night around nine?"

"I'd heard about Chrissie on the news and called her parents. I spoke to her dad. He asked me where she'd been and if I knew anything. I told him about her date with Lyons. Her dad was a mess—it was the worse call I've ever made." Stein shrugged. "After, I went for a walk around campus to clear my head."

Kane pushed to his feet. "Okay, thanks for your time." *I need to find out if Mr. Lowe is capable of murder.*

Jenna found Livi with a group of friends, and after introducing herself, she took her to a quiet corner of the cafeteria. She sat opposite, and seeing the girl was picking at her fingernails, she squeezed her arm. "I know this has been a terrible time for you, Livi, but to understand why Chrissie killed herself and to find the men who raped her, I really need your help."

"I told Deputy Kane everything I know." Livi lifted a distraught face and peered at Jenna through red-rimmed eyes. "She was my best friend so I knew her better than most."

Jenna took out her notebook and pen. "Did Chrissie have many boyfriends?"

"No, she was pretty quiet. She dated a boy in high school for a month or so and then his family moved back east." Livi frowned. "I guess you could count Phil but he wasn't really a boyfriend, he was more of a friend. They had lunch together sometimes and he'd study with her in the library; he's one year ahead of her and real smart, so I guess she kinda used him, to help her."

Jenna unfolded her notebook on the table. "Did she ever consider dating him?"

"Yeah, she wanted to go to the dance at the showgrounds next Saturday night. I'm going but she didn't have a date." Livi lowered her gaze to her fingers again. "She figured if she went out with Phil, she could convince him to take her to the dance." She made a waving gesture with her hands. "Then she blew him off for Seth without a second thought."

Jenna made a few notes. "Was Phil angry?"

"Nope, he made a study date with her for Monday." Livi shrugged. "Maybe he just liked her company. One thing's for sure, he's not afraid of Seth Lyons."

Jenna leaned forward. The conversation just got interesting. "How so?"

"Oh, they had a disagreement in the cafeteria. Seth walked in with his friends and told Phil he was sitting at his table. When Phil refused to move, Seth pushed him. Well, Phil is real strong. He just stood up and glared at him. Next minute, Seth threw a punch and Phil ducked and then laid him out cold." She brightened. "Then he sat back down, looked at Seth's friends, and told them to take out the garbage because it was starting to smell. Everyone started laughing. Seth was like a mad bull and threatened to get even."

A cold chill blew across Jenna's neck. Had Seth chosen Chrissie to get back at Phil? She frowned. "Could Seth have known Phil was seeing Chrissie?"

"I don't see why not." Livi stared out the window but it was obvious she wasn't seeing the lush green grass and flowerbeds. "Yeah, I recall Seth being in here when Phil was having lunch with her, and they were together in the library at least four times a week."

Jenna slid her pen back into her pocket and folded her notebook. "You've been very helpful. I hope I haven't taken up too much of your time."

"I'm fine, my next class isn't until two." Livi stood. "I'll be getting back to my friends now." She hurried away.

*

"How did you go?" Kane touched her back then dropped into the seat beside her.

Jenna smiled at him. "Oh, she was a wealth of information. I'll tell you on the way to the morgue." She frowned. "There's something else." They stood and headed out the building to the truck. "I figure we have an ace up our sleeve already."

"How so?" Kane started the engine and headed the truck down the campus driveway.

Jenna smiled at him. "Webber. He's a student here, remember? We'll get him to go undercover and find the dirt on our Mr. Lyons."

"They'll know he's a deputy, and what about his age?" Kane frowned.

"No one here will remember he's a deputy and he hasn't mentioned it to anyone. He was only in uniform for a couple of months before he started working with Wolfe, and he'd pass for early twenties, easy." She smiled at him. "If they do remember, he can say I fired him last year and he joined the ME's department. Think about it, Kane. Webber ticks all the boxes. He was at college last year, uses the gym and the track. He'll pass without notice."

"Maybe." Kane shrugged.

Jenna sighed. "Now all we have to figure out is how he can get close to Lyons."

"He tries out for the team. They'll be looking for a replacement for Jacobs." Kane turned at the end of the driveway onto Stanton Road. "I know he played football in high school and he's fit. Worst case, he'll be on the bench but will train with the guys. If he fits in, they might even ask him to move into their house."

Jenna snorted. "That's not a safe place to be if they discover he's on the job." She took her gaze away from the crowds as they drove into town and glanced at him. "I've been in deep; it's deadly." She sighed. "Maybe you should talk to him? It's more like an order coming from me."

"Sure. He'll be at the autopsy." Kane slowed as they passed the hot dog vendors on Main.

Jenna poked him in the arm. "Stop looking at the food. You just ate and we have an autopsy to attend."

"Sure, sure." Kane grinned at her. "I'm good. Emily always leaves cookies in Wolfe's office."

# CHAPTER TWELVE

Colt Webber had transferred to Black Rock Falls from Boston and spent a short time as deputy before taking Wolfe's offer to become his assistant in the ME's office. It was a complete change of career, but going back to college at twenty-nine to complete his studies in forensic science had been a breeze. He'd the added bonus—and salary—of remaining a deputy, being around if Sheriff Alton needed an extra hand. Neither he nor Wolfe had a problem in their dual roles; in fact, they all worked together like a well-oiled unit. He enjoyed working with Wolfe; the man's font of expertise and easy Texan manner made each day an adventure. The course was becoming a breeze, and in one year's time, he'd graduate.

In the morgue, he'd prepared the instrument tray and specimen receptacles, and had the corpse on the autopsy table, when he heard footsteps and voices in the hallway. It was a surprise when Kane beckoned him outside and they strolled into Wolfe's office.

"We have a situation." Kane leaned one hip on the edge of Wolfe's desk.

Webber frowned, hoping he hadn't been the cause, but Kane appeared animated rather than condescending. "What can I do to help?"

"Have you ever been undercover?" Kane folded his arms across his chest.

Webber shook his head. "Nope."

"We need someone to get up close and personal with the college football team." Kane's serious expression unnerved him. "They don't have an age limit, and you're fit. How long since you played?"

Astounded by the request, Webber's mind seemed to run in circles. "Ah, I played touch last weekend. I work out with Rowley every day. I'm fit." He smiled. "You want me to try out for the team? How so?"

"Yeah, that's the general idea. Of course, we'll supply a tracker and anything else you need to get the information we require. It would be best if you avoid us and add any info you find to the case files. I'll make sure to check them daily." Kane narrowed his gaze. "We suspect Seth Lyons and his crew are raping girls off campus, and could be the reason behind Chrissie Lowe's death."

"I gathered that from the case file but you've no proof." Webber stared at him. "If Chrissie hadn't been under the shower, maybe we'd have found some trace evidence." He let the battered image of Chrissie Lowe slip into his mind. "To get close, I'd need to get into their house, and they're not going to risk divulging anything to a stranger." He snorted. "I won't get near Lyons. I'll be on the bench. I don't figure Coach would consider an old man like me for the team."

"Did you know the coach is ex-military?" Kane's smile spread over his face. "I've asked Wolfe to speak to him. You'll be playing before you know it." He gave him a direct stare. "The thing is, Colt, are you ready to step up and get the proof we need to stop these animals?" He stared him in the eyes. "It's a request, not an order. You could be dealing with a killer."

Webber considered the implications and dangers. He'd be running with the pack and would have to lower his own moral standards if what Kane said was true. "Yeah, I can take care of myself, but I'd need a damn good cover story. As sure as the sun rises in the morning someone will remember me being a deputy, and there's no way they'll discuss anything in front of me if they believe I'm still in law enforcement."

"We've already worked on a cover story but we'll keep it simple and as close to the truth as possible." Kane straightened. "You arrived in town, moved in with your aunt; we'll use Wolfe's housekeeper if necessary as a cover. The scholarship is no secret, so go with that angle. You worked as a deputy for a time and then argued with me, so Jenna fired you. You figure I'm an arrogant asshole and you took the offer of a job with the ME."

Webber grinned at him. "How did you know?"

"Arrogant, huh?" Kane laughed and headed for the door. "Touché."

# CHAPTER THIRTEEN

Attending two autopsies of young people in the same number of days disturbed Jenna. Sure, she held it together using her professional façade to cover her inner feelings, but deep down she held a yawning sorrow and some measure of responsibility for deaths that occurred in Black Rock Falls. She'd sworn an oath to do her best to keep the townsfolk safe and uphold the law, and yet two young people had died in unusual circumstances. If Wolfe ruled the cause of death for Jacobs accidental, and Chrissie's a suicide, she'd still find it difficult to accept. With the football team containing her main persons of interest for Chrissie's rape, Jacobs' death seemed a little too convenient.

She pulled on a face mask, took a deep breath, then followed Wolfe through the doors into the clinical cold of the morgue. She'd never quite met an ME like Wolfe before; although a very imposing man in stature, he had a wonderfully calming presence. His soft voice and respectful manner during an autopsy made surviving the horrible experience a whole lot easier. She nodded to Kane and Webber, chatting over Jacobs' corpse. She wished she could switch off completely like Kane. His training as a sniper gave him the ability to drop into a zone of peacefulness. She'd witnessed him do this a number of times; it was as if the man she knew had left the building—she'd seen the same in a murdering psychopath as well but there was a difference. Kane had compassion in spades and had an inbuilt need to protect everyone even if it meant risking his own life.

Wanting to keep the mood light, Jenna moved to Wolfe's side as he checked the instrument tray and adjusted the lights and microphone into position. "How do you feel about Emily moving back to Black Rock Falls to complete her degree?" Wolfe's daughter Emily had secured a place at the local college for the fall semester.

"Since the college expansion, she'll be able to complete her Bachelor of Forensic Science here and she's also considering a criminal justice degree, which will set her up if she wants a career in CSI or as a medical examiner." Wolfe peered at her over his mask and his eyes crinkled at the corners. "Then she has hands on here with me as well, which is an advantage. I have to admit that girl is a sponge for knowledge; she excels in everything she does and she loves studying in the new building." He laughed. "And I kinda like having her living at home again." He pulled on his gloves with a snap. "Anna and Julie are over the moon to have their sister back."

Jenna nodded in agreement. "I enjoy her company too." She sighed. "When we get these cases sorted, you should bring the family over for a barbecue."

"You won't be able to drag them away from the horses." Wolfe glanced over at Kane. "You know they'll bug you for a ride."

"I enjoy their company." Kane pulled on a face mask. "Do you think Anna is old enough for a pony? It's her birthday soon."

"Dang, not you as well." Wolfe snorted. "They've both been at me for months to buy them one. I ask them, 'Where can we keep a pony? When do I have time to care for one or take them for rides?' Then I'm the bad guy for a week."

"We've got the space." Jenna looked at him. "One little pony isn't too much more to care for, and I know Atohi has one for sale." She smiled behind the mask, remembering the beautiful paint pony their Native American friend had raised on the res.

"Is it okay if I buy it for her birthday?" Kane looked at Wolfe. "I'll take full responsibility for everything. It won't be any extra work or expense for you, but it will make it safer for her when she comes by to ride the horses."

"Hmm." Wolfe's gaze moved from one to the other. "She's been pestering you as well, hasn't she?"

"Nope." Kane shrugged. "She hasn't said a word. We just figured it would be easier than riding with me when she comes by. I can't risk her on my stallion alone."

"I'll think on it." Wolfe waved a hand toward the body. "Let's start." He pulled the sheet from Jacobs' body and switched on the microphone. "We have the body of Alex Jacobs, twenty-two years old, Caucasian, weight two hundred pounds, height six-one. The body appears to be in excellent physical shape. Apart from the trauma to the neck, there are no signs of external damage apart from a small bruise to the left hip. I would estimate the bruise to be approximately six days old."

Jenna watched as the autopsy progressed; the heart, lungs, and other organs all presented as normal, and the blood tests conducted by Wolfe earlier had not given a result for alcohol. As Wolfe progressed to dissecting the neck region, she moved forward as he explained.

"As you can see from the X-ray alone, the damage to the atlas and axis… ah, the upper part of the cervical spine, is severe. Blunt force trauma crushed the larynx and hyoid bone. I'd say paralysis would've been instantaneous; the spinal cord damage alone would have killed him instantly." Wolfe looked up at them. "Herein lies the problem." He removed his gloves and went to his computer. "Here are some images of similar fatalities during weight training using a similar bench." He scrolled down the page. "And here are the images taken at the scene." He glanced at the others. "As I mentioned before, all of the other victims have their hands under the bar. All of them tried to prevent the bar from crushing them. Why does Jacobs have his hands hanging down both sides of him?"

"I examined the equipment." Kane pointed at the screen. "As you can see from the images, the rack wasn't damaged and the equipment is solid. He couldn't have missed the rack and dropped it, and the bar couldn't have rolled off the rack. If the bar had slipped, his hands would be gripping the bar and he'd have tried to maneuver the weight away from him."

"This is why I believe someone else was involved." Wolfe narrowed his gaze. "I've lifted weights, and unless he tried to commit suicide by throwing them in the air in the hope of dropping them on his neck, I doubt he'd have gotten his hands out the way in the split second it takes for that amount of weight to drop." He looked at Jenna. "I'd like to know how much weight he usually presses. According to the bench press standards, a male novice at 200 pounds should be able to press around 140; an advanced around 300 pounds. Including the weight of the bar, he was lifting in excess of 300 pounds. In my opinion, going on his physical shape, he may have been able to lift it a few times with a spotter. The only logical conclusion is his arms were down because someone had taken the weight and he thought they had placed the weight on the rack. If they dropped the weight on him, he wouldn't have had time to react."

Jenna allowed the information to sink in then looked at him. "So you're saying we have a homicide?"

"Nope, I'm saying someone else could've been involved." Wolfe gave her a long look. "What if it was an unfortunate accident? The spotter was lifting the bar the last inch and it slipped out his hand. Maybe he'd gotten scared and hightailed it out the gym." He sighed. "Until we discover the truth I'm leaving the cause of death open."

He pulled on a fresh pair of gloves. "I'll finish up here and release the body to the mortician."

Jenna removed her mask and gloves. "Thanks, we'll look into it some more."

"Before you go." Wolfe turned back to her. "The vomit in the car matches the stomach contents of Chrissie Lowe, and the hair is the same color. I found a set of her prints under the edge of the car seat and matched the blood in the car to her type; the DNA test is running now. I don't have any doubt that Chrissie was in the janitor's vehicle." He waved a hand toward the counter. "I found other hairs, at least five different people. I've obtained samples from the janitor and his wife and discounted them. I've taken samples from Jacobs and we have Lyons' fingerprints from the glass but right now, I've no other samples to use as a comparison. There was no other trace evidence or prints apart from the janitor's, and they were fresh." He frowned. "It's going to be difficult proving who raped her without evidence. I'll take some prints from Jacobs' hands and see if they match the marks on her arms. I found a groove on his pinky finger, which makes me believe he wore a ring. If we can link the ring to the mark on Chrissie's arm, it will put him at the scene of the rape. If we can implicate him in the rape, the rest might fall like a house of cards."

Jenna exchanged a glance with Webber. "As Colt's willing to infiltrate their house, we'll get the creeps. Sooner or later one of them will break the code of silence."

# CHAPTER FOURTEEN

Kane stood for a few seconds to inhale the fresh breeze and rid his nose of the smell of death. As Jenna walked to his side, he turned to her. "We'll need to keep a close eye on Webber if he manages to get close to Lyons." He led the way to his truck. "I don't trust that guy."

"Me neither." Jenna glanced up at him. "Oh, and Rowley hunted down Owen Jones. I figure we go see him and find out his angle on the fight with Jacobs, but first, I need a moment to get my head straight after the autopsy."

Kane opened the door of his truck. "Sure. Wanna take a break at Aunt Betty's?"

"That sounds like a plan." Jenna smiled. "A strong coffee will help to remove the horrible morgue taste in my mouth."

Kane grinned at her. "Hush, don't say that too loud—people will figure you've been snacking on tissue samples."

"Ewww." Jenna pulled a face. "Now I've lost my appetite." She climbed into the passenger seat.

Kane slid behind the wheel. "Nah, Aunt Betty's pecan pie would tempt a saint."

He headed slowly through town. A carnival atmosphere filled Main Street, and visitors' horse trailers arriving for the rodeo made up the majority of traffic. The Jumpy Castle was in the park, and with school out for the day, kids ran in all directions, eating great clouds of cotton candy, or ketchup-dripping hot dogs. "The clowns are absent this year."

"I'm not surprised—the last time they showed, the parents kept their kids away." Jenna sighed. "Not that I blame them. I've hated clowns all my life, and ever since we had some involved in a pedophile ring, I hate them even more."

Kane pulled up outside Aunt Betty's Café, glad to find a parking space, and climbed out. Inside, the noise was way above his comfort level, which was unusual. He cast his eye over the patrons and a few of the locals gave him a nod. The ruckus was coming from a group of cowboys, and he stopped to glare at them. When Jenna turned to stare at them as well, the men elbowed each other and kept their heads down, and the café quietened to its normal hum of polite conversation. They went to the far end of the counter to avoid the line, and Susie Hartwig dashed over to take their order.

Kane followed Jenna to their reserved table and sat down. "It sure is nice to have this table and fast service for the department."

"Yeah, we'd never find time to eat otherwise." Jenna smiled as Susie filled two cups with coffee then left the pot and fixings. "Thanks, Susie."

"Your order will be right out." Susie frowned at Jenna. "You feeling okay, Sheriff? You look a might pale today."

"We've come from an autopsy." Jenna lifted her cup. "It wasn't pleasant."

"Oh, I see." Susie looked mortified. "I'll be back before you know it." She hurried away.

Kane sat back in his seat, running the case through his mind. "We need to find Jacobs' pinky ring." He glanced at Jenna over the rim of his cup. "If it's bulky, like the impression Wolfe found on Chrissie's arm, it places him at the scene of the rape and gives Phillip Stein a motive."

"How would he know Jacobs was involved?" Jenna gave him an inquisitive stare.

"Jacobs and Lyons were like this." Kane crossed his fingers and held them up. "They're roommates and Stein knows Chrissie went on a date with Lyons the night of the rape. It's also likely Lyons was in the vehicle that gave her a ride to the party. From what we know about Chrissie, it's unlikely she'd have gotten a ride from a stranger, which tells me the rapists planned to use the janitor's car."

"Hmm." Jenna stared into the distance. "Do you figure Stein would kill on a hunch?"

Kane shrugged. "He knew Chrissie; for all we know he could've followed her to the house." He sipped his coffee. "He might be able to provide the missing link we need to prove Chrissie was there. If he hung around until she left, he'd have a pretty good idea what happened to her."

"Yeah, but murder?" Jenna shook her head. "If he was a friend and saw her dumped on the lawn outside her dorm, he'd help her… maybe call the paramedics, not leave her alone."

Kane placed his cup on the table. "Maybe she didn't want his help—she'd been drugged and raped. I figure the last thing a woman would need would be a man around."

"Maybe, but then she had her roommate." Jenna frowned. "We still don't know for sure if she killed herself. Someone could've taken her into her room and staged the suicide. The idea she killed herself doesn't fit her outgoing profile. Women are speaking out now, and the support network is there. If we consider Lyons' father might have offered her compensation to keep her mouth shut, it makes less sense. It had to be something or someone else."

Kane rubbed his chin. "Like I've said before, the men who pack-rape a woman and get away with it usually have some way of intimidating her to keep her silence."

"I guess so. But whether or not she committed suicide isn't the issue right now, it's who killed Jacobs." She sighed. "It ties in; two deaths happening so close together is more than a coincidence. When you looked around Lyons and Jacobs' room, did you notice a ring?"

Kane shook his head. "I wasn't looking for one, but even if he wore it regularly, it would make sense for him to remove it to lift weights. I'd say it's in his locker at the gym." He sighed. "We'd need a warrant to search it."

"Not if we asked the parents if we could collect his things. I'll call Wolfe and find out if they've arrived to view the body yet." Jenna pulled out her cellphone and made the call. "Has Jacobs' family arrived yet?"

*"Yeah, they're waiting in my office to view the body."* Wolfe cleared his throat. *"What do you need?"*

"Permission to go through his locker at the gym." Jenna exchange a glance with Kane. "We're chasing down his pinky ring. If it matches the mark on Chrissie Lowe's arm, it will place him at the scene during the rape."

*"Sure, I'll ask them to sign a statement to the fact, and I guess you'll want to include his bedroom?"*

"Yeah, and we'll need you there as well, but I figure Lyons is too smart to leave any evidence." Jenna glanced up as Susie delivered their meals and paused until she walked away. "Do you have time this afternoon?"

*"I'll make time."* Wolfe's voice lowered. *"If this is a group of predators, we need to take them down and soon."*

"We sure do." Jenna frowned. "Let me know when you have the doc signed. We're heading over to the college to interview Owen Jones."

*"Oh, I'll get it signed."* Wolfe disconnected.

# CHAPTER FIFTEEN

There was something special about sitting in Aunt Betty's Café watching the world go by. The tourists invading Black Rock Falls amused him, and now with a string of psychopathic killer novels on the market, the place was humming. It was as if people flocked here on the off chance they'd be involved in a brutal murder. He shook his head. It didn't work that way; most killers had a darn good reason to snuff out the life of a stranger. He'd always been an observer of life, from the strangest of insects to the biggest predator of all: man. He liked being a dominant male. A predator.

People needed to face facts. Nothing law enforcement could do would stop a psychopath hell-bent on killing. They'd walk over hot coals to reach their target, and no amount of sweet-talking would make them stop. When the urge came along, the control vanished like water vapor. He wouldn't consider himself a psychopath because he only killed people who deserved it.

He took another bite of his burger and chewed slowly. His attention moved to the sheriff. A woman of average height in her thirties, attractive with raven-black hair that hung like wet silk to her shoulders. The bare arms protruding from her regulation shirt showed a muscular definition from working out regularly, which made him believe she preferred to handle situations herself rather than rely on her deputies. His attention slid down to her small hands with neat nails. She wore only one ring, no wedding band, and he wondered why she'd remained single in a town dominated by men.

Although, he'd never seen her without the big deputy at her side, and the way they leaned toward each other, they acted like friends.

He wished they'd sat closer to him, so he could listen in on their animated conversation. He craved information, but after watching the news and listening to the scuttlebutt around campus, he'd discovered little about the investigation into Jacobs' death. He'd done his job well and people wouldn't be wary if the sheriff believed his death had been an accident. Suspicious people caused problems by noticing things they normally missed.

The day was dragging, each hour moving so slow it was as if the hands on the clock had stopped then suddenly decided to move again fifteen minutes later. He stared at his empty coffee cup and sighed. After planning his next move to the second, he had little to do but wait until dark.

The waitress left the sheriff's table and headed his way to refill his cup. She gave him a bright smile and he felt his mouth curling up to return it. "Why thank you, ma'am."

"Is everything okay?" Her smile lingered.

"Yeah, thanks." He waited for her to sashay away and finished his meal, leaving a generous tip.

As he left, he cast another glance at the sheriff. Some part of him felt sorry for her. If, by chance, she discovered someone had murdered Jacobs, she'd never pin it on anyone no matter how hard she tried. He smiled to himself. *No evidence, no witnesses, no case.*

# CHAPTER SIXTEEN

The young woman at the counter of the college office tossed back her long blonde hair and looked up at Kane with an interested expression, and then looked over at Jenna. She smiled at her.

"We're looking for Owen Jones. He's a junior."

"Oh, everyone knows Owen; he was on the football team and he's back this semester. We have a new system here. We issue students with a swipe card and they scan them as they enter each lecture hall or the library. It's so we know who is inside each building should there be an emergency of some kind." She pointed down the hallway. "If you go down to security, they'll look him up on the computer and find his location, and then they'll escort you to him."

"Okay." Jenna turned and headed down the hallway.

"Weird security system." Kane fell into step beside her. "The students log in and out of lectures or whatever but there's no security to stop anyone wandering in."

"It's not a prison, and it's normal for students to have free access to common areas." Jenna chuckled. "I guess you'd have them all frisked before they passed through the gate?"

"I'd have airport-type security scanners on every darn gate at all schools if I had my way." Kane narrowed his gaze. "Carry weapons all you want but don't take them into schools."

"I'm sure that's every parent's dream, but do you know how long it would take to scan every student in a school?" Jenna slowed her pace as they reached the security office. "It will never happen."

*

After discovering Jones was in the library, they followed a security guard through the building.

"I'll do the talking." Jenna looked up at Kane and smiled. "We don't want him running for the hills, and he will if you lean on him."

"I was going to take the sports angle to ease him into spilling his guts." Kane frowned. "Leaning on him would work too."

"Like I said." Jenna narrowed her eyes at him. "I'll do the talking."

The security guard asked them to wait in the hallway and he went inside the library to collect Jones. The hallway led out to a landscaped garden with benches set under trees. A couple of students sat on the lawn chatting. When Jones came out with the security guard, Jenna took in the muscular young man, tall and strong with chiseled features. She pulled out her notebook and looked up at him then introduced herself and Kane. "We understand you had a fight with Alex Jacobs and a few of his friends; can you tell us what happened?"

"The fight was ages ago, why drag it up now?" Jones gave her a disinterested stare. "I did my time and I'm back now. Why? Is someone causing trouble again?"

Jenna shook her head. "No, but the ME has left his cause of death open on Jacobs, and we're speaking to anyone who may have had a reason to cause him harm."

"He don't hurt that easy." Jones snorted. "I busted a finger punching him, and he didn't go down." He gave her a direct stare. "Do I care he died? No, I don't. He and Seth Lyons are both liars like the rest of those animals. Lyons' daddy buys him out of trouble, and trust me, he's gotten in more trouble than any man I know."

"Maybe you should explain what happened to cause the fight?" Jenna led the way outside to a secluded bench. She sat down and he dropped reluctantly onto the seat beside her.

"Lyons and Jacobs wanted me off the team." Jones shrugged as if reluctant to talk about it.

"Why?" Kane dropped onto the grass and raised one eyebrow. "They must have had a reason."

"I can't go into it. Let's just say I didn't want to move out of the student halls and into their house." Jones pushed both hands through his unruly hair. "So they went to Coach and told him I tried to sell them drugs. The dean organized a search and they found a pipe in my room. I wanted them to test me but that didn't happen." He stared into the distance and anger flashed in his eyes. "They set me up, and Coach told me I had a choice: sit on the bench for the season or he'd call the cops and have me charged, which would mean the end of my scholarship." He looked at Jenna. "I took the penalty but went postal on Seth; Alex was never far away, and after he got involved, things got nasty. I was suspended for the rest of the semester." He gave her a wry smile. "I'm still on the bench."

Jenna scanned his expression and the flash of annoyance. "So, you went on the coaching trip on Sunday. What did you do on Monday night after you got off the bus?"

"I didn't go on the bus but I like to run and usually try and fit a session in each afternoon." Jones rubbed the back of his neck. "I worked in the library all day and needed to loosen up, so I ran some and then I went back to my room and slept."

"What time was that?" Kane's voice was conversational.

"Darned if I know." Jones shrugged. "Around ten maybe."

Jenna made a few notes. "Did you see anyone during this walk, or stop and talk to anyone?"

"There were people, yeah, but I don't remember anyone specific." Jones looked into the distance then shook his head. "Nah, I didn't talk to anyone. I was listening to some tunes." He pulled a phone out of his pocket with earbuds attached. "Why? You think I killed Alex?" He chuckled. "How?"

"Maybe you spotted for him in the gym and dropped the bar on his neck." Kane had dropped into his dangerous mode. "You had a motive to kill him. He had the coach bench you and that led to your suspension. If you take him out, a spot on the team becomes available."

"I didn't kill him. He's not worth my time." Jones grimaced and looked away with a disgusted expression. "And I play wide receiver, Alex played left tackle. You really think after what happened, I'd put my body on the line to protect Seth Lyons in a game?" He shook his head. "I hope the SOB gets what's coming to him."

Jenna leaned forward, noting the agitation in the young man. "Because he planted the pipe, or is there something else you're not telling us?"

"You know, Sheriff, there are just some things a guy doesn't discuss in the presence of women." Jones stared at his hands. "Let's leave it at that?"

A number of things ran through Jenna's mind but she stood and exchanged a knowing look with Kane. "I'll wait inside." She headed for the door then leaned against the wall and watched as Kane asked questions.

Moments later, she noticed Seth Lyons heading her way and moved toward him in an effort to stop him seeing Kane talking to Jones. She searched her mind for a few questions she could ask him, anything to delay his movement along the hallway. "Ah, Mr. Lyons. Just the person I wanted to speak to."

"Yeah?" Lyons gave her an insolent look. "What now?"

Jenna took her time taking out her notebook and flipping through the pages. "When did you last call Chrissie Lowe? I assume you called her to arrange a ride to the party. We know she climbed into a gray sedan."

"I didn't call and I don't have her number." Lyons huffed out a sigh. "I spoke to her in the cafeteria. I guess she made her own arrangements for a ride." He moved into her personal space. "It's all over, some guy raped her. Look at me, Sheriff. Do you honestly think I need to rape girls?"

Unfazed by his bravado, Jenna leaned in slightly and lowered her voice. "You've a bad reputation with women on campus, but no one has made any complaints against you. I'm starting to believe you have someone on the faculty protecting you."

"I don't need protection." Lyons clamped his hand around her arm and glared down at her. "But maybe you do. My dad is a very powerful man with friends in high places. Everyone has secrets, Sheriff, and if you keep harassing me, I'll find out yours, and come next election you won't get any votes."

Straightening, Jenna met his smug expression. His grip on her arm painfully ground the bones together. He was enjoying intimidating her, and with no one in the hallway to witness his behavior, it would be her word against his. She slid her Glock from the holster and pressed it against the zipper of his jeans. "Didn't your daddy ever tell you not to threaten a woman with a gun? Take your hand off me, turn around, and walk away before I arrest you for assault."

"Okay, okay. Jesus. I'm sorry." Lyons dropped his hand and backed away, hands held up in surrender.

Jenna holstered her weapon. "I'll be watching you, Lyons."

"Yes, ma'am." Lyons hurried toward the library.

Jenna turned to see Kane walking toward her. She stared at him. "Well?"

"What was going on with Lyons?" Kane turned to stare after him.

"I wanted to stop him from seeing you with Jones and asked him a few questions he didn't like. He grabbed my arm and tried to threaten me—"

"He did what?" Kane gaped at her with an expression of disbelief. "What did he say?"

Jenna shrugged. "It was nothing and I handled it. What did Jones say?"

"His girlfriend, a freshman, left mid-semester after she was dragged into a car and raped." Kane's expression looked like the sky before a thunderstorm. "Jones tried to make her report it but she refused to say who'd raped her. Not long after, Lyons made a comment about Jones's girlfriend, saying she was 'tasty.' When Jones confronted his girlfriend about it, she packed up and left college."

Jenna swallowed hard. She'd just experienced the evil side of Lyons. "Did he give you the girl's name?"

"Nope." Kane pushed his hands into his pockets. "He said she'd been hurt enough and he'd deny he told me." He looked at her. "It would be reaching to get Lyons charged with rape after so long. If he's been doing this for some time, we might be able to get a group of women to come forward, but one on one without a shred of evidence will be hearsay at best."

"Uh-huh." Jenna chewed on her bottom lip. "Nothing Jones said convinced me he isn't responsible for Jacobs' death."

"There is one thing." Kane's brow furrowed, making his eyebrows join in the center. "If Jones and Jacobs were enemies, it isn't likely Jacobs would allow him to spot him. I don't figure Jacobs would put himself in such a vulnerable position."

"Hmm, that's a point." Jenna's cellphone chimed and she glanced at the screen. "It's Wolfe."

*"I have permission for you to search Alex Jacobs' locker, but I figure unless Seth Lyons agrees, you'll need a search warrant for his bedroom.*

*It's Lyons' room too, and his father owns the house. Another thing: Kane mentioned it was bleached and clean as a pin. I figure we'd be wasting our time doing a sweep this late in the game; these guys are way too smart to leave any evidence."*

Jenna sighed. "Roger that. Send a copy of the doc to my phone; we'll go see the security guy again and get access."

*"It's on the way."*

Jenna disconnected and waited for the message to arrive. She glanced at the file and turned in the direction of the security guard's office. "Let's go check his locker at the gym."

After showing the security guard the paperwork, they collected a forensics kit from Kane's truck then followed him to the gym. The guard took them into the locker room and used a pair of bolt cutters to break the padlock. Jenna noted the whiteboard with names and numbers listed. "Are those the names of people and corresponding lockers?"

"Yeah, they all have a combination lock, so they don't need to carry keys. They pick a locker then add their name to the list." The security guard stood to one side.

A whiff of body odor crawled up Jenna's nose as she opened the door and peered inside. "So the lockers are used by anyone?"

"Yeah, but only male students. The women's locker room is next door."

Jenna nodded, pulled on a pair of gloves, and used her Maglite to look inside. There on the top shelf was a large gold pinky ring sitting beside a watch. "Get a photo of the ring, Kane, then we'll bag it along with the watch."

She labeled the evidence bags and collected the items, and then they bagged his clothes, including a baseball cap and a jacket with the football team's logo on the back. "That's it." She turned to the guard. "Thank you for your help."

"No worries, ma'am." The guard strolled away.

"From the stink coming from his jacket, Jacobs wasn't much into personal hygiene." Kane wrinkled his nose. "If he was involved in Chrissie's rape, I wonder if Wolfe will be able to pull any trace evidence from his things."

"We'll drop by on the way back to the office." Jenna glanced at the bagged items. "We need to find evidence against at least one of the guys in Lyons' house."

# CHAPTER SEVENTEEN

It had been a long day, and after entering all the day's information into the files, Jenna glanced at the clock. It was a little after seven, and a spell in the hot tub, dinner, and an early night were calling her name. She'd come up against a brick wall with her investigations and would think on them overnight and start fresh in the morning. She closed down her computer, collected her things, and then headed out her office to the reception area. The place was quiet and Maggie had left for the day, leaving Rowley on the counter. She strolled down to Kane's desk and waited for him to stop typing. "Let's call it a day, I'm beat. It's my turn to cover the 911 line tonight so I'm planning on getting an early night."

"Sure, give me five." Kane smiled at her and went back to his computer.

Jenna walked to the counter. "No one has been in for a couple of hours, we've no outstanding warrants or misdemeanors to worry about, I'm going home."

"It's been pretty quiet in town today." Rowley picked up a bunch of keys, slid on his hat, and moved around the counter. "I figure things will pick up as the rodeo starts tomorrow."

Jenna sighed. "It would be nice if one festival and rodeo went off without a hitch. Those cowboys seem to get pleasure out of knocking each other senseless or causing trouble with the locals."

"It's a small price to pay for the revenue it brings the town." Kane walked up behind her, pulling on his jacket. "Duke, where are you?" He peered around the counter and grinned at his dog. "Time to wake up and go home to sleep some more." He rubbed the dog's head then looked at Jenna. "Ready?"

Jenna nodded. "Yeah." She turned to Rowley. "See you in the morning."

Having Rowley lock up and open the office worked to her advantage; as he arrived at the office at the crack of dawn each morning, it meant she didn't have to dash into work. By the time she arrived at around eight thirty, he'd dealt with most of the walk-in complaints and had the coffee machines bubbling. Of course, she made sure he was paid for his overtime. To her, finding a dedicated deputy like Rowley had been a dream come true.

She followed Kane outside and dumped her things in his truck. The smell of popcorn and hot dogs drifted on the breeze, and people moved along Main Street, chatting loudly. She sighed with relief. The festival, for once, was going on without incident. Her heart sank at the sound of a dirt bike coming fast, and she turned to see who was stupid enough to speed past the sheriff's office. The bike came right at her and screeched to a halt, turning sideways with the effort to stop. She recognized the rider as Atohi Blackhawk. He often helped with cases.

"What's the hurry?"

"A mess of joggers are getting into one hell of a ruckus on the path that goes to the top of the rapids. There's a crowd of college kids watching." Blackhawk pulled off his helmet and frowned. "I figure someone is gonna get killed." He pushed long black hair from his eyes. "I would've tried to break it up but they're tough guys and no way was I getting involved."

"Okay, lead the way." Jenna jumped into the truck. "Joggers?"

"I'm guessing they're from the college; there's a switchback path that follows the river to the top of the rapids then comes down through the forest and ends up back at the parking lot. All the college kids use it to reach the rapids. They jog and hang out there." Kane backed out of the parking space and followed Blackhawk through the traffic. "Do you remember Mayor Petersham made a big deal out of clearing it last year so it was a safe trail for the students to use?"

Jenna nodded. "Yeah, vaguely. His speeches tend to go on so long I tune out after he's finished speaking about our budget for the year." She yawned. "I hope this won't take long; this day's been hard enough already." She glanced at the forest as they sped by; this late in the day the shadows seemed to stretch forever.

"It's going to get longer if we have to walk to the top of the rapids." Kane glanced at her. "Maybe Blackhawk will lend us his new dirt bike?"

"Maybe it will all be over by the time we get there." Jenna shrugged. "How long can a fight last?"

"It depends." Kane pulled up behind Blackhawk and they jumped out the truck.

Jenna buttoned her jacket. "Where did you see them?"

"Way up the top of the trail." Blackhawk handed her a helmet. "Here, put this on." He removed his helmet and handed it to Kane. "Take my ride, I'll wait here."

"Thanks." Kane tossed him his keys. "Duke will be glad of the company."

After pushing on the helmet and fastening the chinstrap, Jenna climbed on behind Kane and they took off at breakneck speed up the trail. She clung on to him as the powerful bike bounced over the uneven ground littered with tree roots. How people ran up here, she'd never know. The cool evening air seeped through her jacket and she wished she had thought to pull on a pair of gloves. The dirt bike's engine sounded louder as they moved deeper into the forest, and although the trail was wide, as the light dimmed the tall pines seemed to close in around them, bringing back horrific memories of atrocities she'd witnessed in this forest since arriving in Black Rock Falls.

"I see them." Kane's voice seemed to catch on the wind, and she would have missed it if she hadn't been stuck so close to his back. "Just ahead." He slowed the bike and then stopped it some ways from a crowd.

Legs still trembling from the vibration, Jenna climbed awkwardly from the seat and glanced up at him. "Let's hope we can defuse the situation and let them go with a warning. I don't like the idea of making an arrest then trying to get them back to town this late in the afternoon."

"It will be slow-going." Kane headed toward the crowd. "Sheriff's department. Break it up, folks."

The wind had picked up and a cloud of spray from the roaring falls washed over Jenna as she headed after Kane. Ten or more young people, all dressed for running, stood in a circle in a small clearing close to the edge of the rapids. She heard the sound of a slap and inwardly groaned; it sure sounded like a fight. Resting one hand on her weapon, she followed Kane through the small gap in the crowd. "Come on now, people, it's getting late. Get on your way and give these folks some air." She pushed between two tall, young men and took in a brawl between four others. She recognized all of them: Owen Jones, who they'd interviewed earlier, and Seth Lyons, Pete Devon, and Dylan Court, who they'd met at Lyons' house. She raised her voice above the noise of the water. "Hey, break it up."

Seeing Kane moving to the left, she moved to the right, circling the fighting men. The roar of the rapids rushing down the mountainside was deafening, and it was likely none of the men could hear her. The fight was anything but fair: Lyons and his friends had Jones cornered, and he'd become a punching bag. Ignoring the wet grass and slimy rocks, Jenna took a dangerous path closer to the edge of the rapids to avoid them. She edged closer so Jones could see her. Using her harshest voice, she yelled at them. "Hey, that's enough! Break it up!"

"You should learn to keep your mouth shut." Lyons aimed a punch at Jones's stomach. "I wouldn't want you to have an unfortunate accident."

*

Owen Jones dropped his hands and, astonished, turned to see the sheriff heading his way. The next moment, Seth Lyons moved in with an uppercut. The impact radiated through his teeth. The follow-through was a hard push to his chest. He staggered back, and as his feet slipped on the mossy wet rocks, he went into an uncontrollable slide toward the rapids. Arms flailing, he grabbed desperately for the soaking branches, but to his horror, they slipped through his fingers like wet spaghetti. The roar of the falls was deafening but he could hear raised voices from above him. Unable to stop his momentum toward the gaping abyss behind him, he cursed as the ground under his feet vanished.

Airborne for a millisecond, he seemed to hang above the churning water and then dropped fast. Air and water buffeted him and fear froze his senses for a split second, but he'd skied on higher slopes than this. The next moment, the instinct to survive broke through and he sucked in a deep breath before hitting the freezing water. The air rushed out of him on impact and the bubbling depths enclosed him. Lungs bursting as white, foaming water surrounded him, and unable to determine which way was up, he forced himself to relax. The moment his body started to rise, he kicked madly, broke the surface, and gasped for air.

Ice-cold, churning water slammed down on him as he kicked hard, but a current strong enough to shred clothes had him in its grip.

He had no chance of swimming wearing shoes and kicked them off. When he broke the surface again, he realized he'd landed where the water pooled before it raced a hundred feet or so to plunge over the rapids. Bobbing in the rushing water like a cork, he tried desperately to grab at rocks but the icy depths had him in their grip and it was like fighting against the strength of an elephant.

Cold seeped into his bones, and with his strength deteriorating, he had to make a choice. Die here or live. There was only one chance of survival: he had to go over the edge and ride the rapids. He'd watched people in kayaks maneuver their vessels over the waterfall. Downstream the water was wild but not deep. Taking a few deep breaths, he surrendered to the current, folded his arms over his chest, and allowed the water to hurtle him to his fate.

# CHAPTER EIGHTEEN

Heart racing, Kane dashed to the edge of the falls, concerned for the young man. He stared into the swirling rock pool below and heaved a sigh of relief. Jones had survived the fall but was flailing his arms in a desperate attempt to swim to a rock. He turned to Lyons. "Did you push him?"

"No, and I have witnesses." Lyons waved to his friends. "Don't try to pin this on me. Owen started it, ask anyone."

Kane hurried downstream, unfastening his belt and intending to dive, but stopped when Jenna ran up behind him and grabbed his arm. "What?"

"It's about six feet deep down there—you dive in, you'll break your neck." Jenna pointed down the trail. "There's another access point on the big sweeping bend. It will take him time to maneuver around the rocks. If we ride down there, we'll be able to catch him before he reaches the next falls."

Kane gave her a nod and they took off running. He had the dirt bike hurtling down the trail at full throttle in seconds. Behind him, Jenna clung on tight, moving with the bends. People heard them coming and pressed into the trees as Kane dropped one boot to the ground to slide the bike around the tight bends. Trees flashed by in a blur of green and the bike bucked dangerously over the uneven ground, but he pushed the speed to the limit. "Come on, come on."

Ahead he could see the sweeping bend. "Hang on."

Kane took the turn so fast and low, his knee brushed the ground. When they reached the bend, he could hear Jenna yelling behind him to stop. They leapt from the bike and he took off, stripping off his weapon and jacket. He kicked off his boots and waded into the deep, swirling water. Behind him, Jenna followed suit, gripped tight to the waistband of his jeans and followed him. The current was fierce, and every step felt as if he had great weights tied to his legs. They stood together with a huge boulder at their backs and stared into the light. He set his feet apart to keep his balance and then looked up at the swirling water tumbling down the mountain. "Can you see him?"

"Has he gone past?" Jenna was already shivering.

Kane turned and searched the lower reaches but could only see white water. "I don't think so."

Anxiety gripped him as he scanned the swirling bubbles trying to catch a glimpse of Jones. Seconds ticked by, each one stretching like a lifetime, and then out of the swirling, misty haze, a head popped up. "There." He pointed as Jones came hurtling toward him at speed. He gritted his teeth and then lunged at him, snagging one flailing arm. It took all his strength, but with Jenna's help, he dragged him onto the boulder.

The young man coughed, spluttered, and then spewed. Kane helped him to sit up. "Where does it hurt?"

"Everywhere." Jones's voice was a husky squeak and his teeth chattered violently. "I'm s-so cold." He looked at Kane. "Thanks for saving me. You too, Sheriff Alton."

"If you're okay, let's get out of this freezing water." Jenna squeezed Kane's arm. "Oh good, help has arrived."

Kane heard someone yelling close by and turned to see a chain of college students making their way through the turbulent water. He grabbed hold of Jones's arm, and with the students' help, they staggered out of the rapids and collapsed on the riverbank. Jones's friends surrounded him, offering him towels and thumping him on the back.

"I've called the warden." A bright-faced young man smiled at Kane. "He's just up the mountain a ways. The paramedics are on their way too. The warden said he'd take Owen down the mountain to meet them."

"Thanks." Kane rolled over to see Jenna shivering beside him. "You should've stayed on the bank."

"You needed my help." Jenna's teeth chattered like castanets. "Did Lyons push him?"

Kane shook his head. "I didn't get a clear view with everyone around them but he stumbled back real fast."

Kane pushed to his feet and went to retrieve their weapons, boots, and his jacket. He pulled on his boots and went back to Jenna. She was shaking so bad, he worried hypothermia might set in. He smiled at her. "You'd better wear my jacket. You're soaked through."

"What about you?" Jenna blinked up at him and peeled off her wet clothes.

"I'm fine. Being tall has its benefits." Although his jeans were wet through, his top was dry. "Here, put it on."

"Lyons and his buddies took off like greased lightning." Jenna shrugged into his jacket and rubbed her arms. "Once we deliver Jones to the warden, there's nothing more to do here."


The warden arrived with hot coffee in a Thermos, and they sat with Jones as he recovered. He wanted to tell his story so they listened to his explanation of what happened. "So, what caused the fight?"

"Nothing, just Lyons mouthing off as usual." Jones dragged a hand through his wet hair.

"Did he push you toward the rapids?" Jenna leaned forward. "It sure looked like it to me. Come into the office in the morning and we'll charge them with assault."

"I'm not sure if he pushed me and there's no way I'm getting involved with an assault charge against Lyons." Jones coughed a few times. "Can we leave this to another time? I nearly drowned and my head hurts."

"Okay." Jenna nodded. "But we're here to help. If he's threatening you, we need to know."

"You sure don't know too much about Lyons, do you? He threatens everyone." Jones handed the warden his cup. "I need to get warm, ma'am, and the warden has offered me a ride down the mountain to meet the paramedics. I can handle it from here if that's okay?"

"Go right ahead." Jenna turned to the warden. "Thanks for your assistance today."

"Just doing my job." The warden mounted his horse, pulled Jones up behind him, and then rode away.

Kane stared at Jenna. "It seems everyone is scared of Lyons." He gave her a long look. "He even got away with threatening you."

"No, he didn't." Jenna lifted her chin and her eyes danced with mischief. "He grabbed my arm and I pulled my weapon and aimed it kind of low. He got the message real fast that I'm not a woman he can intimidate."

The daylight was fading fast and long shadows spread across the clearing. The temperature had dropped considerably and the ride down the mountain would be freezing. "Okay. You ready to go?"

"Yeah." Jenna stood, swamped by his jacket. "I could wear this as a winter coat." She grinned at him.

Kane stored her wet jacket and then climbed onto the dirt bike. When Jenna jumped on behind him and slipped her arms around his waist, he turned his head to speak to her. "I figure we came close to witnessing an attempted murder. If Jones wasn't so fit, his chances of surviving the rapids would've been limited."

"Yeah." Jenna rested her chin on his shoulder. "We need to be keeping a close eye on Lyons. He's shaping up to be our number-one suspect. He's so arrogant, I figure he wouldn't have thought twice about following Chrissie into her room and killing her or murdering his best friend."

# CHAPTER NINETEEN

It was close to nine thirty when Pete Devon walked out of the locker room and made his way to the college's Olympic-size swimming pool. He'd delayed his regular session to avoid Brook, the girl Seth had mentioned as a perfect candidate for the next party. He stood for a moment, inhaling the familiar smell of chlorine, and then his gaze settled on someone gliding along his usual lane. To accommodate students who liked to train, the college had divided half the pool into lanes, and he preferred swimming laps in the middle one. Disgruntled, he stood observing the swimmer's technique. The man cut through the water with a smooth stroke and his turns were fast. As a likely member of the swim team, he took priority over an injured football player.

Pete dove in and counted the laps in his head. Training in the pool had become almost mechanical and he enjoyed the quiet time alone to think. He'd been paranoid since discovering the girl—what was her name? Ah yeah, Chrissie—had died after willingly allowing half the team to have sex with her. Yeah, she'd seemed a little drunk at the time, but hey, she probably needed the courage. Seth had insisted she'd been more than willing, and nothing they'd done had pushed her over the edge. In fact, Seth had made sure she'd gotten a ride home, and she'd been fine when Pete and Alex had driven her back to her dorm. Now the cops were interviewing everyone, as if they figured someone had murdered her.

He pushed his arms out to touch the wall and his fingers met solid flesh. Unable to stop, he collided with someone. He trod water and then chuckled. "Oh shit, I'm sorry. I didn't know you came here, man." He ducked into the next lane.

"There's lots of things you don't know about me." His friend's face broke into a grin. "Ever played Shark?"

The way he looked at him disturbed him. The smile didn't reach his eyes; instead, cold orbs fixed on him, empty of emotion. *What did I do to upset you?* He cleared his throat. "Nope, can't say that I have. It sounds like a kids' swimming game?"

"You could say that, but it's more of a race. How fast do you figure you could swim with a shark chasing you?" His smile didn't fade.

Pete shrugged. "Pretty fast, I guess." He continued treading water.

His friend waved him away in an arrogant gesture. "Go on, I'll give you a head start and then try to catch you. I'll be the shark. Unless you're chicken."

Pete shrugged. "It sounds a bit childish. Okay, so if I play your stupid game, what happens if you catch me?"

"I'll kill you." A sinister chuckle came from deep in his chest. "Okay, in five seconds. One, two…"

# CHAPTER TWENTY

## Wednesday

It was a little after seven when Jenna's cellphone chimed the 911 ringtone. She'd just sat down to eat breakfast in Kane's cottage and hoped the cowboys arriving in town hadn't started to make trouble. She took one bite of her eggs then reluctantly answered the call, putting the phone on speaker to allow Kane to listen. "Sheriff Alton."

*"This is Bob Jamison. I'm a paramedic over at Black Rock Falls General. The cleaner at the college called us out to the pool for a suspected drowning."* He waited a beat. *"There's a deal of blood on the ladder and trauma to the victim's face. We hauled the body out of the water from the other side, left it on the gurney and sealed the area. I figured you'd want to take a look, in case it's suspicious."*

Jenna exchanged a glance with Kane. "Yeah, we'll get the ME out there. Can you wait until he arrives and tell the cleaner we'll need a statement?"

*"Sure, but she's pretty shaken. We have her in the back of the bus. A security guard came to look and he recognizes the body but can't give a positive ID—he doesn't know his name. Says he believes he's on the football team and swims here almost every night, same time."*

"Thanks. Keep him there as well." Jenna disconnected. It was about a half-hour drive from her ranch to the college, but Wolfe could get there in ten minutes. "Rowley's close. I'll send him out to hold down the fort until Wolfe gets there."

"You finish eating." Kane picked up his cellphone, made the calls and then disconnected.

Jenna sneezed and looked at him. "Thanks."

"You okay after the freezing-cold swim?" Kane's gaze moved over her.

Jenna swallowed the mouthful of eggs. The previous evening, they hadn't discussed saving Jones. She'd just wanted to soak in the hot tub then get an early night. "The rapids moved faster than I imagined."

"It was just as well we had the dirt bike or we wouldn't have gotten there in time." Kane frowned. "The bends slowed him down some, but it was closer than I'd have liked."

Jenna reached for her coffee. "Did many of your things get wet?"

"Nothing above the waist." Kane frowned. "You?"

"Yeah, most of my stuff is ruined, but my phone came through okay." She finished her coffee and stood to collect the dishes. "I have a drawer filled with everything I need at the office. It was just as well I didn't lose my keys, my wallet, or my phone." She rinsed the plates and slipped them into the dishwasher. I have new cred packs at the office as well; mine is a little wet but my creds are fine." She sighed. "My notebook is toast but I have a spare. Thank goodness my files are up to date." She glanced at him. "I guess you'll need replacements for everything as well?"

"No, I'm fine. My notebook was wet too." Kane smiled at her. "I've replaced it with a digital pen. I can use it on my cellphone screen and it converts my notes to text via Bluetooth. I've been itching to try it."

"Wolfe?" He always had the best gadgets. "That would save tons of time updating files manually. I'll ask him to get me one too."

"Don't worry him, I'll order you one online."

Jenna smiled at him. "Thanks."

"Jenna." Kane leaned against the counter and looked at her with a concerned expression. "If this is an 'accidental'"—he made quotes around "accidental" with his fingers—"drowning, it means three college kids have died in about the same number of days. Jacobs' death is suspicious, and I figure if this victim is on the football team as well, it has to be connected."

Jenna had come to the same conclusion. She messed with the dishwasher and then turned it on before straightening to look at him. "Yeah, if he is, something's not right." She blew the bangs from her forehead. "I'm ready to leave. We'll head out to the college first. Let's just hope another killer isn't stalking Black Rock Falls."

It was a magical day when summer mellowed into fall, and Jenna decided it was her favorite time of year in Black Rock Falls. Each season had its own glory, but as Kane drove toward town, she opened her window and allowed the wind to tousle her hair. Glancing in the side mirror, she could see Duke's reflection, his long ears flapping and lips vibrating in the airstream as if he was singing. Glad to be alive, she inhaled the crisp morning air, almost tasting the flavors of the season. The smell of pine and then wood smoke intermingled with the last sprinkle of fragrant wildflowers. She inhaled, appreciating the fragrant air filling her lungs. Her mind filled with the horrible experience of watching Jones coming close to drowning and what had happened in the college pool. Did the fight by the rapids have anything to do with it?

The landscape changed dramatically as they left the open grass-lands and moved through town then out onto Stanton Road. The rolling green pastures and grassy hills soon became a forest of tall pines, growing so close together a bear could be a yard away and hidden from view. The dark, rough-barked trunks lined the roadside like a row of sentries, hiding the many secrets within.

"What's on your mind?" Kane glanced at her for a second before returning his attention to the road.

Jenna dragged herself from her thoughts. "If both these deaths are homicides, what's the possibility they are revenge killings for Chrissie? Have you had time to look into her background yet? Is her father capable of murder?"

"The father is terminal and too ill to murder anyone. Her grandpa is in his eighties so we can rule him out. Her brother is the eldest by six years and MIA in the Middle East somewhere. From all accounts, her sister and mother wouldn't be strong enough, but she does have a cousin in town: Steve Lowe." The nerve in Kane's cheek twitched. "He's twenty-one, six feet tall, and works at the feed store in town. Their families live one street apart so I'd guess Chrissie and Steve spent plenty of time together as kids."

"Hmm. So he's a possible. We'll need to speak to him." Jenna chewed on her bottom lip, thinking through the circumstances of each case. "The cases are coming along so fast I can't seem to get a foothold on any of them. We haven't gotten any real proof against the men we feel might be responsible for Chrissie's rape, and if Wolfe rules Jacobs' death as murder, we have two persons of interest in the case, maybe three if we include Steve Lowe. I feel a little out of control right now, as if the cases are sweeping us along on a mystery ride."

"Then we take it one step at a time. I really don't recall any of our cases being easy, and we made it through okay." Kane turned the corner onto the sweeping driveway leading to the college. "Once we find out the drowning victim's name and Wolfe has made a determination, it will make life easier." He smiled at her. "You know darn well, once you lay the cases out on the whiteboard everything will fall into place." He chuckled. "Knowing you as I do, you'll have figured out a list of possible suspects by noon."

They parked beside Wolfe's van and walked to the amenities center. Jenna glanced at Kane. "I'll speak to the paramedics and the cleaner. Find out who opened up this morning and which security guard locked up last night. I'd like to know how come he missed seeing a body floating in the pool."

"Okay, and I'll go check the CCTV footage as well." Kane frowned. "If someone tampered with the cameras again, I figure we have a killer on campus." He headed off with Duke at his heels, tail wagging.

A shiver ran down Jenna's spine and she pushed away the familiar rush of dread that gripped her at a crime scene. The back of the ambulance was open and a middle-aged woman was sitting inside, wrapped in a blanket. Jenna couldn't see Wolfe or Rowley anywhere, so she approached the two paramedics speaking with a security guard. "Which one of you called it in?"

A short man with close-cropped hair and a round face held up a gloved hand. "That would be me, Sheriff. I'm Bob Jamison."

Jenna nodded. "Okay. Is the woman who found the body well enough to make a statement?"

"Yeah, she's a bit shaky but she should be okay." Jamison nodded toward the entrance to the pool. "The ME is inside with the other deputy."

Jenna pulled a pair of surgical gloves from her pocket and pulled them on. "I'll go see the body then come and speak to the cleaner. What's her name?"

"Gladys Birch." Jamison cleared his throat. "I called the dean as well and he's on his way."

"Thanks." Jenna headed for the entrance to the pool. *Maybe he'll be able to ID the body.*

# CHAPTER TWENTY-ONE

Kane stared at the footage on the screen in the security guard's office and shook his head in disbelief. The camera outside the entrance to the amenities center had blinked out in exactly the same manner as the previous night and around the same time. In the hour before that, two students had entered the pool area, one male and one female. This time, the camera activated again at 10:35 p.m. and caught the security guard entering the building at 11:05 p.m. Seconds later he came out, locked the gate, then went on his way.

He straightened and cast his gaze over the security guard. The man was in his sixties with a belly hanging down over his belt. His white-streaked greasy hair hung down each side from an attempted comb-over. It was only a couple of hours max since he'd started work but his clothes looked as if he'd slept in them. Pudgy hands with dirty nails gripped a stained coffee cup. Kane wrinkled his nose, wondering how he kept his job. An odor like the football locker room after a game with added onions hung in the office as thick as fog. "Did you have the system checked out after the last failure?"

"Me? No, the request for maintenance was sent through the normal channels. Who the hell knows if anyone will come out and fix the darn thing." The security guard shrugged. "I didn't go inside the pool either, I just unlocked the gate for the cleaner and left. I had a couple of students waiting on me to unlock the gym."

Kane made a few notes. "Do you keep a log of your shifts?"

"Yeah." He pushed a tattered book in Kane's direction. "It's just for when we do our rounds, and we make a note if anything unusual happens." The guard placed his cup on the desk and leaned back in his chair, making it groan under his weight. He folded his arms across his substantial waist and looked at him. "There's no mention of the malfunction. I guess the guys were out on their rounds."

*How convenient.* Kane glanced over the entries and snapped a few shots of the relevant pages over both days with his cellphone camera. "I'll need to speak to the guard who locked up last night."

"That would be Dirk Voss. He locks up and Tim Brannon handles the library. By eleven most of the students have left." The guard was scanning a file on his computer. "I've found his number. I'll give him a call." He dialed the landline and after a brief explanation handed the receiver to Kane.

Kane took the warm, greasy receiver and, avoiding contact with his skin, gave his name. "What time did you lock the amenities center last night?"

*"Around eleven."* Voss sounded as if he'd just fallen out of bed.

"Did you go inside to make sure no one was using the pool?"

*"Kinda. I went to the doorway and called out, waited some, then called out at the entrances to the locker rooms. It was as quiet as a tomb."* Voss yawned. *"Why? Did I lock someone inside? All the kids have cellphones—one call and someone would go let them out."*

Annoyed by the man's unprofessional behavior, Kane stared at the floor. "I'll need you to come by the sheriff's office this morning to make a statement. Your inability to do your job could've cost a man his life. The cleaner found a body floating in the pool this morning and he's been there all night."

*"You sayin' that's my fault?"*

Kane grimaced. "I'll leave that to the sheriff to decide. If you're a no-show by noon, I'll be dropping by to haul your ass downtown."

He dropped the phone onto the cradle and reached into his pocket for a card. "Email me a copy of that section of tape. You do know how to do that?"

"Yeah." The guard took the card from Kane. "I'll do it now."

Kane nodded. "Thanks, I'll show it to the sheriff." He headed out the door, glad to be breathing fresh air again. "Come on, Duke. Let's go see who's been killed this time."

# CHAPTER TWENTY-TWO

Wolfe's investigation was in full swing as Jenna walked poolside. Markers littered the area around the ladder, and to one side the uncovered, pale-skinned body of a young man lay on a gurney. Wolfe was deep in conversation with Rowley and they both looked up at once as she approached. "What have we got?"

"At first glance, an accident." Wolfe walked her to the body. "He slipped climbing up the ladder and fell, hitting his nose on the top rung, fell into the water, and drowned."

The chlorine in the water hadn't disguised the smell of death: not rancid yet but the awful smell of the first signs of decay. The young man's face was a mess, his nose near flattened and the tip pushed up. His skin was pale and rippled from a long time spent submerged in water, and his eyes stared into nothing, cloudy like a dead fish. She frowned. "So, what makes you think otherwise?"

"Every death is suspicious unless proved otherwise. Do you know what he was doing prior to his death?" Wolfe looked at her expectantly.

Jenna dragged her gaze away from the body. "If he's on the football team, yeah I do. They all went to a coaching clinic or whatever over the weekend. They train every morning, and if he lived in Lyons' house, there's a possibility he could've been involved in Chrissie Lowe's rape. Why?"

"See here on his ankles, both sides have a tiny, half-moon indent?" Wolfe pulled a magnifying glass from his pocket and handed it to her. "I'm not 100 percent sure but I figure they're nail marks. Sure, they could've happened during group sex, I've seen worse injuries; but if not, someone could've grabbed his feet as he was climbing the ladder and pulled him in a downward motion. He'd lose his grip and his face would hit the top rung." He cleared his throat. "I have to consider every angle before I make a decision, Jenna."

"That would take strength." Rowley stared into the pool as if weighing up the facts. "Because some of him would've still been in the pool. It's hard to exert force under water."

Jenna nodded, glad to see Rowley add his conclusions. "That makes sense. So is this another probable homicide?"

"Ah…" Wolfe frowned. "When I've conducted an autopsy, I'll let you know my decision."

"Do you have a TOD?" Jenna pulled out her notebook and found her pen. "I gather he's been in the water all night?"

"Yeah and the water temperature messes with the readings, so I don't have a time of death, but going on the skin deterioration, I'd say at least eight hours." Wolfe pulled a body bag from his kit. "We'll get him loaded into the van." He looked at her. "We need a positive ID. Have you found anyone who might know him? I'll need permission from his next of kin."

Jenna shook her head. "Not yet. Do you mind waiting until the dean gets here? He might recognize him."

"Sure." Wolfe indicated with his chin toward the locker rooms. "While we're waiting, I'll take a look in there as well. I found a towel on the bench, so I gather he left his belongings in a locker. The students are required to carry a photo ID card with them. Emily has just gotten hers."

"I'll go. They leave them open, so the locked one will be his." Rowley headed off in long strides.

"Call me when you locate the locker and don't touch anything," Wolfe called after him.

Jenna looked at him. "No Webber this morning?"

"No." Wolfe shook his head. "I thought it best as he's trying out for the football team." Wolfe had lowered his voice to just above a whisper. "I figure the less time he's seen with us, the better. I've given him backdated paperwork to say he's been doing an internship in my office since starting college, just in case Seth Lyons questions him. Webber seems to believe Lyons is involved in the rape case and will be trying to get closer to him." He narrowed his gaze. "I don't envy him."

Footsteps in the hallway caught Jenna's attention and she turned to see Kane with David Bent, the dean, coming toward them. She stood her ground and waited for them to reach her. She took in Bent's neat appearance: professional in a dark brown suit with leather patches on the elbows, but his expression was one of horror at the sight of the body. She waved her hand toward the corpse. "Do you know this man?"

"Ah, yes. Dear God, what happened?" Bent stared at the corpse and then slowly back to her. His Adam's apple moved up and down as if he couldn't find the words. He visibly gathered himself. "It's Peter Devon, another member of the football team."

*Another coincidence?* Jenna made a note. "Thank you. Ah, the medical examiner will be able to give you the details." She indicated to Wolfe.

"Right now, it looks as if he slipped getting out the pool and struck his head." Wolfe moved to her side. "I'll be able to give you more information once I've completed my examination."

Jenna glanced at him. Wolfe was a master of not offering a cause of death without absolute proof. She led Bent away from the body.

"We'll need to notify his next of kin. Mr. Wolfe will need their permission to conduct an autopsy."

"He's out of Helena and his father is a close friend of mine." Bent pushed a hand through his hair in an agitated manner. "I think it should come from me. I'll make a video call."

"Thank you." Jenna took a card from her pocket and handed it to him. "We'll also need permission to search his belongings, including his vehicle. I know it's difficult to ask for things like this, but I can assure you it's necessary."

"Why?" Bent narrowed his eyes at her. "Is there something you're not telling me, Sheriff?"

Jenna shook her head. "No, you have the same information as I do right now, but when an unusual death occurs, we make sure no stone is left unturned. A scanned copy will be fine. If you can arrange to have the parents send it straight to me, we'll be able to release the body to them without an unnecessary delay."

"I'll see what I can do." Bent turned away and left, muttering under his breath.

Jenna turned to Kane. "Get anything out of the security guards?"

She listened as Kane went over everything he'd discovered. "Another CCTV failure? Well, that's convenient. Take a look at the body—what do you see?"

Jenna waited for Kane to examine the crime scene and chat with Wolfe. Then Kane pulled on a pair of gloves and assisted as Wolfe maneuvered the corpse into a black body bag and zipped it up.

As Wolfe packed up his forensics kit and collected the samples, she turned her attention back to Kane.

"So, Wolfe's not making any hasty conclusions, huh?" Kane moved to her side. "Looking at the damage, someone smashed his head into the side of the pool." He shook his head. "Unless this guy was drunk or taking drugs, why would he slip? He's hanging on to the railing with both hands. If he slipped, he might have grazed his shins on the ladder but I doubt he'd let go. If he slipped and let go, I'd say he'd fall backward into the water, not drop like a stone with enough force to break his nose. The water would have slowed him down some, enough for him to grab the railing."

Jenna indicated to Rowley, who was heading toward them from the locker room.

"I found his locker." Rowley smiled at Kane. "I bet you could open it in a second."

"Probably." Kane glanced at Jenna. "Do you want me to take a look?"

"We'll take a look." Jenna made her way to the locker room. "I've asked for his parents' permission to search his belongings and vehicle. I can't see a reason why they'd refuse."

"Well then, in case they refuse, we'll lock it again." Kane shrugged. "No harm, no foul." He glanced at her. "If we find damning evidence, we'll post a guard or add another lock until we obtain a search warrant. There's always a way."

Jenna snorted. "I'm padlocking the gate to the pool. No one is getting in here until Wolfe makes his decision. Right now, as far as I'm concerned, this is a crime scene."


As Rowley had suggested, Kane had opened the combination lock in a few seconds. She looked at him and raised both eyebrows. "How did you do that?"

"Once Bent told you his name, I looked him up online. Found his date of birth and a few images of him with the football team. I tried his date of birth first, then doubled up his team number and it opened. People are creatures of habit; they use familiar numbers so they don't forget. It's a locker, so he wasn't too worried about security."

Jenna peered inside. She could see a gym bag, clothes hung on pegs, and a pair of worn sneakers with socks balled up inside. She found a set of keys in his pants pocket, and a pair of sunglasses lay on top of his bag. "See if he left his phone inside the bag."

"Interesting." Kane had placed the bag on the bench and was searching every crevice. He held up a cellphone then pulled another from a zipped compartment. "Why would he need a second phone?"

Jenna moved closer. "Can you get into it?"

"Oh, yeah." Kane scanned the calls and frowned. "No calls made but he uploaded image files from the same number, this number. It's a burner. I figured as much. You can buy these at any 7-Eleven." He opened the image gallery and dropped his hand to his side, obscuring the view. His gaze lifted to Jenna. "This only proves he likes rough sex but it's not Chrissie Lowe. The woman looks of age as well."

"Let me see." Jenna narrowed her eyes at him. "I know you believe seeing images like this will bring on my PTSD but I'm over it, Dave. I've dealt with many rape cases in my career and I can't lead an investigation from the sidelines." She held out her gloved hand. "Show me."

She flicked through the shots, sickened by the content, and then lifted her gaze. "Oh, they're smart. I can't make out one face in these shots apart from the girl. We can't even prove Devon was involved. Anyone could've given him this phone. For all we know, this might be a fetish."

"It could also be his girlfriend." Rowley peered at the screen. "They're adults and there's no law against group sex."

Jenna looked at Kane. "It's too much of a coincidence, finding these images when we have a rape case on campus. We'd need the cooperation of the woman involved, but finding her might be a problem. What do you think?"

"If we plan to use this as evidence, we need to pack it up neatly and obtain a search warrant." Kane pointed to the screen. "Look around the room in the images. I figure it belongs to Lyons. I checked his room at the house, and this one has the same drapes and nightstand. We blow these up and we'll get the location." Kane rubbed his chin. "Although, if we find this girl, I doubt she'd admit to any wrongdoing."

Jenna stared at him in disbelief. "Why? If someone raped me, I'd sure want them locked up for a long time, and this is proof."

"Proof she was raped but no evidence to point to the men who raped her. Unless we can find some distinguishing marks on the men involved." Kane shook his head. "It takes a twisted bunch of guys to rape a woman. This isn't sex, it's violence, and I figure they're using these shots as blackmail to keep their victims quiet."

# CHAPTER TWENTY-THREE

A crisp morning breeze brushed Colt Webber's face and tousled his hair as he ran through the tunnel and out to join the football team. The memories of the roar of the crowd, the scents and smells of a stadium packed with people at high school, filled his head. He could still see the cheerleaders clear in his mind. Heck, it seemed like a moment ago.

He had to admit the idea of being undercover both thrilled and unsettled him. He'd heard rumors about Lyons: his arrogance and temper had gotten him into trouble many a time. The fact the man had backup in the form of a number of heavyweights made his threat real and disconcerting. Up to now, his life at college had been enjoyable and he'd taken to his subject with enthusiasm, made new friends, and enjoyed working beside Shane Wolfe in the ME's office. He'd become a sponge soaking up the wealth of information that poured from his mentor. His career change from deputy to ME's assistant might not have eventuated. On arriving in Black Rock Falls, his immediate attraction to Wolfe's eldest daughter Emily had been a mistake. At seventeen, Emily was too young to be seeing a man in his twenties, and Wolfe had made it clear he didn't want his daughter involved with him. Emily, a sensible, smart woman, hadn't taken much convincing and they'd walked away as friends.

To get his foot in the door with Lyons and his buddies, he'd dropped by a training session to speak to the coach. He'd told him that he'd played football in high school and wanted to try out for the team. Coach had made him drop and do thirty pushups. He'd smiled to himself. Since arriving in Black Rock Falls, he'd trained daily with Jake Rowley and was fitter now than he'd ever been in his life. He'd completed his pushups on his knuckles. He'd impressed Coach and noticed Seth Lyons watching him like a hawk. He wondered now if the quarterback's attention was a good thing or a potential threat. *Time will tell.*

He swung his helmet as he walked and joined the other players making their way to the coaching team for morning practice. They went through a fitness training session and then Coach concentrated on plays. After watching from the bench for some time, Coach called him over. He wanted him to try out for the position of wide receiver and had him running and catching balls. One thing he could do well was catch a football.

After countless resets, Colt pulled off his helmet to wipe the sweat from his eyes and Coach strolled over to him with Seth Lyons.

"As Devon hasn't graced us with his presence this morning, without offering a reason, I'm benching him." Coach gave Lyons a look that prevented any arguments. "Lyons, this is Colt Webber."

A pang of regret gripped Colt. Wolfe had called him earlier about the death of Pete Devon. Obviously, the news hadn't spread yet. He took the hand Lyons offered and smiled. "Nice to meet you."

"Where've you been playing?" Lyons gave him a confused look. "And why the hell haven't you tried out before now? I've seen you around, you were here last semester."

Colt shrugged. "I'm out of Boston. Last semester I was way too busy to commit to joining a team."

"Too busy how?" Lyons rested his hands on his hips and lifted his chin as if assessing him.

"Working." Colt met his gaze. "I held down two jobs but since I've gotten a scholarship I have more free time."

"When you two have finished passing the time of day, I want to try a few plays with him and see if he fits." Coach stared at him. "How fast can you learn plays?" He handed him a playbook.

Colt grinned. "Pretty fast."

"Good. We'll go with the first two in the book." Coach walked away and left him with Lyons.

"They're pretty simple." Lyons went through the moves. "Got it?"

Colt nodded. "Yeah."

After spending a great deal of time setting and resetting the plays, Colt had his head firmly back in the game. It had been as easy as riding a bike and he figured age had given him more strength and speed. When Coach called practice to a halt and sent the players to the showers, he figured even without Wolfe's intervention, he would've made the team.

"Webber, and you too, Lyons." Coach waved them over and stared at Webber as if assessing him. "Okay, I'm giving you a shot, but you'll need to learn the plays."

"Alex's playbook is in my room. I'll give it to him. It will save time and it's not like Alex is going to need it any longer." Lyons glanced at him. "We'll need to study this together. I don't like mistakes during a game."

"I want him up to speed by the weekend." Coach walked away without a backward glance.

"Where are you staying?" Lyons narrowed his gaze. "On campus?"

"Nah, I've got a room at my aunt's house in town." Colt fell back on the cover story Kane had created.

"Your aunt's house?" Lyons cringed. "Are you a monk or something?"

Colt chuckled. He needed to convince Lyons he was as sleazy as he was. "Nah, the opposite, but my scholarship doesn't cover accommodation. Not that I take girls home; having any visitors causes her a problem." He winked. "It doesn't slow me down though. I've got a nice ride and Black Rock Falls has old abandoned ranches all over so I don't go hungry."

"I figure we're gonna get along just fine." Lyons slapped him on the back. "We, ah, me and some of the guys live in our own house. It's a big old ranch house out on Pine at the first bend. Living in the dorms was way too restrictive and the dean kept sticking his nose in our business."

Colt indicated with his chin toward the college. "I figure the dean believes he's a prison warden the way he keeps tabs on everyone's movements with those damn swipe cards. There are far too many rules. We're adults not kids."

"I'm liking you more by the minute." Lyons chuckled. "Exactly. And as far as I'm concerned football has the only rules I intend to live by."

"That's me, hard and fast." Colt grinned. "And never drop the ball."

"We're having a wake to send off Alex on Thursday night, why don't you come along?" A serious expression crossed Lyons' face. "You'll have heard about Alex Jacobs' accident? We want to say goodbye in our own way."

As Pete Devon's death would be all over campus by the time they arrived at class, Colt wondered how it would affect Lyons. He plastered a grim expression on his face and nodded. "Sure, I'll be there."

"I'll supply the entertainment and beer." Lyons gave him a long, considering stare and then seemed to make up his mind. "Why don't you drop by tonight? I'll give you the book and we'll go over the plays."

Not believing his luck, Colt nodded. "Sure."

"Around nine would be good." Lyons turned to go. "I'm hitting the showers."

Colt stood for a few seconds watching Lyons strut toward the tunnel. Stage one had gone better than expected but he needed to be living in the house and that would take some doing. *What will I need to do to gain his trust?*

# CHAPTER TWENTY-FOUR

He strolled from the football field, puzzled by the morning's events. He'd seen Webber around the college and hadn't realized he'd played football. He must have used someone's influence to get himself on the football team so fast. *Who is this guy?* He opened his laptop and in seconds had hacked the college's student database. After scanning the files, he found Webber's details. The man was on a scholarship and interned at the ME's office. Webber had already completed his first year's internship at the ME's office and wasn't one of the usual brain-dead jocks. A guy like Webber would ask questions, and from his direct stare and confident walk, he was nobody's fool. Yet if he was a player when it came to girls, a player would be useful.

He allowed ideas to percolate through his mind and then snapped his fingers. Of course, Webber would have access to a variety of drugs. Who better than someone working in the ME's office? Surely, samples of different drugs would be available for testing. In any case, everyone in town was aware Shane Wolfe had been a medic in the military before taking over as ME. As a deputy, he'd often been at the scene of an accident, patching people up before the paramedics arrived. Oh yeah, working alongside him, Webber would have access to drugs.

He figured Webber would make the team. It didn't take a fool to see how enthusiastic Coach had been toward him, and he wasn't nice to anyone. Webber was an unknown quantity and he'd have to tread easy, but over the last couple of days things had worked out just fine. He'd taken out two of the team without breaking a sweat. In truth, when it came to dying, they'd became weak momma's boys.

# CHAPTER TWENTY-FIVE

Rushed off her feet, Jenna sat in on the interview with Dirk Voss, the security guard from the college. She'd given Kane the lead as he'd spoken to the man on the phone earlier.

"Run through your routine for locking up; what do you do from, say, seven." Kane's face was void of expression.

"Let me see, I'm in the office until eight thirty, when we both go on patrol. We split up and do a general walk-through. After, we come back here, have a cup of coffee, something to eat, and then we go out again around eleven to lock up the amenities areas. Then we come back here. We stay here most of the night unless we have a perimeter alert or something similar."

"So, the office was unattended during the camera blackouts at around nine, nine thirty on both nights the fatalities occurred?" Kane lifted his gaze.

"Yeah, seems so, we didn't see anything wrong." Voss frowned.

"Run through what you do before you lock up the gym and pool." The nerve in Kane's cheek twitched. "What precautions do you take to ensure nobody is locked inside?"

"I usually go in, check the pool, walk through the locker rooms and the gym areas, then lock up." Voss frowned. "I'm not irresponsible."

"So, what happened the night Pete Devon died?" Kane leaned back in his chair and gave him a stare that could freeze an ocean. "Seems to me you should've found Devon in the pool, maybe in need of resuscitation. Instead, we have a dead body floating in the water all damn night."

"I wanted to get back to the office to catch a TV show." Voss dropped his gaze. "I'm sorry."

"Go tell that to his parents." Kane looked at Jenna. "Is there anything else, ma'am?"

Jenna stood. "No, get his statement then cut him loose." She used her card to open the door and headed back to her office.

It was a little before five by the time Jenna had gotten all the necessary search warrants and permission from Alex Jacob's parents to search his vehicle and possessions at the house. Their probable cause had been flimsy for Pete Devon's drowning but Jenna had offered the judge two alternatives. The first, as a member of the football team living in Lyons' house, Devon had become a person of interest in the rape of Chrissie Lowe, and secondly his suspicious death had sent up a red flag. As his cellphone records and personal possessions could hold crucial evidence in both cases, the judge had agreed to allow them to search the entire house on the off-chance Wolfe picked up some trace evidence. Warrant in hand, she waited for confirmation that Rowley had the contents of Devon's locker secured in the evidence room, and then she left with Kane for Lyons' house.

"I figure it's going to be difficult, finding the last person to have seen Devon alive. I mean, with the number of students milling around campus at night." Kane maneuvered his truck through town and out onto Stanton Road. "It would've saved the grunt work if we'd asked the dean to put an announcement over the loudspeaker at the college."

Jenna turned in her seat to look at him. "Yeah, it would've saved time, but it could also bog down our investigation with hearsay. We don't have the manpower to interview everyone who was on campus both nights." She watched the darkening forest flash by and tried to keep the cases separate in her mind. "I sure need to get the three cases laid out on the whiteboard. With the number of clues piling up, it will be easy to overlook crucial evidence." She sighed. "It's never this difficult; we usually have random murders and a list of suspects but these cases are all intertwined. It's hard to keep them all straight in my head, as in who was where with whom at what time, because it seems to be the same group of people."

"It certainly revolves around the football team." Kane glanced at her then returned his attention to the road.

"I figure we investigate Chrissie's rape separately for now." Jenna leaned back in her seat. "Finding out where it happened and who raped her is crucial. Let's hope we find something we can use tonight."

"I remember the layout of the room. It was Lyons' bedroom in the image for sure." Kane grimaced. "Problem is, believing the rape is the motive for killing two players may be a mistake."

"How so?"

"It's too easy." Kane frowned. "Chrissie was a freshman; who on campus would care enough to kill for her apart from Stein?"

"No one." Jenna shrugged. "Phillip Stein is our only suspect. I still think we need to look at the cousin."

"Yeah, he's a maybe if it's a revenge killing but we can't overlook Jones and anyone else who might have a beef with the players." Kane turned onto Pine Road.

Jenna frowned. "Or the coach." She chewed on her bottom lip, thinking. "Hmm, we have two pivotal players removed from the team right before the start of the season. It might be payback."

"And successful teams do get a ton load of enemies." Kane turned onto the driveway leading to the house and continued along the forest-lined driveway. "It looks like we'd better include the coach in our inquiries but he isn't liked so we'll have a list a mile long."

Jenna pointed ahead at the small parking lot. "Ah good, Wolfe is here. He's bringing a piece of Chrissie's clothing so Duke can have a sniff around." She turned to look at Duke, who was sitting up in the back seat in his harness. "I'm starting to love that dog."

"That's good, he kinda likes you too." Kane pulled up beside Wolfe's van and slid out. "I'll grab Duke."

Jenna climbed down from the cab and met Wolfe. "I figure we take as many images as possible. If we can locate the rape room, it will at least be a start on the Chrissie Lowe case."

"Sure. I'll be looking for evidence in the Devon case too, so we'll need media devices, anything he would have social interaction with, online gaming for example. We'll need to look at both the football players' deaths from every angle. If I discover it's homicide, who had it in for them?" Wolfe dragged his kit out of the van. "I figure these could be hate crimes, and if they are, who hated the shiny boys on campus enough to kill them?"

Jenna nodded. "That's a good point. We discussed the cases in the truck but as everything is happening so fast, we'll need a meeting to brainstorm these cases and get everyone on the same page. Even if you're not convinced the last two deaths are accidents, the killer is trying to make us believe they are, which brings us back to the question: did Chrissie commit suicide or was she murdered?"

"I'm leaning toward suicide right now and I haven't made a determination on the other cases yet, Jenna; they may be tragic accidents." Wolfe looked perplexed. "Okay, what did you come up with?"

"If we're looking at homicide, we have a direct link to the football team." Jenna looked up as Kane joined them with Duke at his side. "Maybe the killer's motive is to destroy the team. First, Chrissie dies after a brutal rape, and she was supposedly heading for Lyons' house on the night it occurred. It wasn't exactly a secret she was going to the party with Seth Lyons; at least two people knew: Livi and Stein." She narrowed her gaze. "So, someone could've intervened. I think Lyons is a creep but he could be telling the truth and she didn't arrive at the party. If so then someone is trying to shift our focus onto the players. We didn't arrest anyone, so the perp moves it up a notch and takes out two key players. This tells me someone has a beef with the entire team or the coach."

"I like the way you think out of the box but three murders means we have a serial killer loose in town again. I know we've had our fair share of psychopaths of late, but we can't assume every death is a murder." Wolfe rubbed his chin. "If this is the work of a serial killer, we'd see similarities in the cause of death. So far they're miles apart—if they're homicides."

"If they are, I'm seeing cold and calculating." Kane rubbed his chin. "A sociopath tends to be more hot-headed and does things on the spur of the moment without thinking of the consequences, yet in both cases the CCTV cameras were disabled. The killer walked in and walked out and nobody noticed him. To me that says planned, not out of control, heart racing, and sweating." He stared at Wolfe. "I guess you'll know more after Devon's autopsy?"

"Yeah, I'll do the post first thing in the morning. I've already extracted a sample of bone marrow for diatom testing." Wolfe met his gaze. "I'll be able to give you the results later and explain the tests involved in a suspected drowning." He sighed. "I realize the CCTV camera going offline at the same time each night seems suspicious but we can't rule out a malfunction, or someone turned it off for a short period of time—maybe a security guard to cover something else. You'd have to go back over the last six months and see if it's happened before around the same time."

"That's impossible—the drives are overwritten every week." Kane rubbed his chin. "It's an old system; a malfunction is possible."

Jenna lifted both arms into the air and then dropped them at her sides. "Darn it, every time we find evidence, something wipes it out."

"Hello, what's this?" Kane turned a full circle then looked at Jenna. "See the devices hidden in the trees?" He pointed in two directions. "That's a Wi-Fi silent alarm. They've installed an early warning system for unwanted visitors and we've already tripped it." He shook his head. "When we came via the tree line last time, we didn't set it off—no wonder Lyons was surprised to see us."

Jenna frowned. "They know we're here now, so let's get it over with." She turned back to Wolfe. "How do you determine if someone murdered Devon or he just slipped and drowned?"

"Drowning is more difficult to prove than murder, believe it or not." Wolfe headed down the pathway and walked toward the house, his boots sounding on the cement pathway. He turned to them and raised a pale eyebrow. "Although, from my initial examination, if someone murdered Pete Devon, they covered their tracks like a pro."

# CHAPTER TWENTY-SIX

They made their way along the tree-lined pathway to the house then paused at the foot of the steps. Jenna looked at the vehicles parked close by. "The road with the no-entry sign must lead right here. I figure they send their visitors the other way, so they have a warning of any unexpected arrivals. She placed her hands on her hips and looked at Wolfe. During a search for trace evidence, the ME took seniority. "How do you want to play this?"

"One of them might have been the last person to see Pete Devon alive, and if we had a timeframe for his movements it would help. My TOD is an educated guess right now." Wolfe scratched his chin as if considering his next words. "With the Chrissie Lowe case, as we have no DNA evidence, we'll need to prove she was inside the house. All the men you interviewed insisted she didn't arrive at the party. If we can prove the opposite, with the samples I have of her stomach contents and the evidence from the vehicle, we can build a case. We have proof Jacobs was involved as his hair was a match to one found in the vehicle; now if I can match the other hair to one of these guys, we can at least implicate them in her rape. If you can pin them down and question them, we'll handle the search." He glanced back at the door. "I'll be collecting samples of everything that might be relevant to the case. If she was here, we'll find trace evidence." Wolfe handed Kane a plastic bag. "This belonged to Chrissie Lowe; see if Duke can pick up her scent."

"My gut tells me Lyons is lying." Kane took the bag. "If she was here, Duke will know."

"Don't forget to look for her shoes." Jenna led the way up the steps and banged on the door. A young man she recognized from their visit, Josh Stevens, gaped at them open-mouthed. Jenna held out the search warrant. "We have a warrant to search these premises."

"For what reason?" Seth Lyons appeared at the door and stood beside his friend, barring the entrance.

Jenna pressed the warrant to his chest. "The reason is listed, now stand aside." She pushed past them, walked into the family room, and surveyed the group all sitting around watching TV. The smell was the same: marijuana and beer with a hint of stale sweat. "Is anyone else in the house?"

"No." Lyons was looking over the paperwork. "You won't find anything here. I told you before, Chrissie was a no-show." He glared at Jenna. "I'm getting tired of you leaning on me, Sheriff. Maybe it's time I called my dad."

Annoyance at his veiled threat prickled Jenna's neck. "You can call Santa Claus for all I care, now stand aside. I want everyone in the dining room. Go sit at the table until we've completed our search." She stared at Lyons. "Non-compliance and I'll handcuff you to the chairs. Understand?"

When they shuffled to the table, giving each other worried looks, she nodded at Kane. "Give Duke the scent."

"Okay, Duke." Kane opened the evidence bag and held it out for Duke. "Seek."

The dog pushed his head into the bag then moved around the room, nose to the ground, tail wagging. Jenna watched him systemati-cally move from the front door across the carpet then head for the sofa. She kept a close eye on the men sitting at the table, and several were moving around as if they had ants in their pants. Of course, they had no idea what Duke was looking for, so she wondered if any of them had a stash of drugs.

A bark broke her thoughts and she turned her attention back to Duke. The dog was sitting on the floor at one end of the sofa. She glanced at Wolfe. "That's a positive response."

"Don't call him." Wolfe glanced at Kane. "I'll need to take a few shots for the record as we go."

"Sure." When he'd finished, Kane called Duke to his side, but the dog walked in circles and barked again. "He hasn't finished yet, he still has the scent." He rubbed the dog's ears. "Good boy." He reinforced the scent then gave the command again. "Seek."

As Duke continued his search, Wolfe came to Jenna's side.

"I'll take a look." Wolfe carried his forensics kit to the sofa, examined it in detail, and then took out a portable vacuum cleaner and went all over the chair. Next, he removed the seat cushion and collected all the detritus from below. He waved the seat cushion at the men around the table. "I'm confiscating this for evidence." He pulled a huge evidence bag from his kit and dropped the cushion inside. "I'll need to analyze the stains on the fabric."

Duke's barks came twice more, once in the hallway and again on the staircase, not on the step treads but halfway up the stairs on the handrail side. Jenna looked up as Wolfe examined the area closely. "What have we got?"

"Blood, as if someone spat it out." Wolfe took photographs then collected samples. His expression was ice-cold when he met Jenna's gaze. "Okay, I'm done down here. Now we move to the bedrooms." He turned to the group of men. "Which one is Pete Devon's bedroom?"

"First on the right, top of the stairs." Lyons snapped to attention when Wolfe looked at him. "He shares with Dylan Court."

After Duke's three positive reactions, Jenna's stomach tightened. She nodded at Wolfe. "You go ahead. I'm going to keep an eye on Mr. Lyons and his friends." She rested one hand on her weapon and noticed the somber reaction from the men at the table. The need to question them and drag out the information about Chrissie's last hours welled up inside her and she pushed it down. She wanted to split them up, question them about Chrissie, and have every word from their mouths recorded on tape.

Moving her attention from one man to the next, she made a mental note of those who refused to meet her gaze. Her skin crawled. Two or more of the men sitting a few feet from her could be serial rapists but she'd need a whole lot more evidence to prove it. For now, she'd concentrate on asking them questions about the Devon and Jacobs cases.

As Kane and Wolfe headed up the stairs to search the bedrooms, she pulled out her notebook and took down the names of everyone at the table. She had two possible homicide cases to solve and most of the people of interest were sitting in front of her. "Okay, I'm going to be asking you questions in relation to the deaths of your housemates." She looked at Josh Stevens. "When did you last see Pete Devon?"

"About an hour after dinner yesterday, he went to do his laps in the pool. He did the same thing every night since his injury." Josh shrugged. "Why?"

Jenna made a note. "It's just routine inquiries; we are trying to establish the time of death." She lifted her chin. "Which one of you would be his closest friend?"

"That would be me." Dylan Court gave her a discontented look.

The hostility toward her around the table was palpable, and she cleared her throat. "Didn't you think it was a bit strange when he didn't come home last night?"

"Nope." Court chuckled. "We come and go as we please. I don't give a f— fig if any of us stay out all night. I figured he'd got lucky."

The young men around the table chuckled in agreement. Jenna made a few notes. "Did he or Alex Jacobs have any enemies? Did he have a disagreement with anyone lately?"

"You do know we're on the football team, right?" Lyons gave her a condescending glare. "Of course they had enemies. Any member of the teams we beat last season could have a beef against one of us. If you're talking about enemies from college, sure. Some of the guys get angry when we steal their girls, but hey, we always give them back after."

Jenna wanted to wipe the smirk right off his arrogant face. "After *what* exactly, Mr. Lyons?"

"What do you figure, Sheriff?" Lyons looked her up and down. "I'm sure a fine lady like yourself has had her fair share of one-night stands." He shrugged. "None of us are planning to settle down; we're here to play football and have fun."

Jenna ignored Lyons' rudeness. "Anything else?"

"We don't walk away from fights on campus." Court gave her a long, steady look. "If some guy wants to cause trouble, we deal with it."

"Like the fight with Owen Jones?"

"Exactly." Court shrugged.

"That's why the dean asked you to leave the student hall, I believe?" Jenna stared back at him. "How about stepping up and giving me some names of these people with grievances against you?"

"Nope." Lyons frowned. "We don't throw people under the bus."

At that moment, Kane came down the stairs with Wolfe close behind. They had a number of evidence bags between them. Jenna turned to Kane and raised her eyebrows in question. "Are we done here?"

"Yeah." Kane held up an evidence bag stuffed with women's panties. "I found these in Seth Lyons' room. In a nightstand containing his belongings."

"So what?" Lyons barked out a laugh. "So I keep the panties of the girls I sleep with—big deal. There's no crime in that. I didn't steal them; they gave them to me for my collection."

"You ready to come clean about Chrissie Lowe being here the night she died?" Kane moved to Jenna's side.

"You hard at hearing or something? I already told you, she didn't show on Saturday night." Lyons waved a hand around the table. "Ask the guys or read my lips. She. Wasn't. Here."

"Well, Mr. Lyons." Wolfe leaned on the table and eyeballed him. "Our sniffer dog sure found her scent, and if I find her DNA on any of these items, we'll know you're lying."

Jenna wanted to grin but smothered it with a cough, then Lyons threw out a curveball.

"Ah, Sheriff." Lyons' face split into a wide grin. "I didn't say I'd *never* had sex with her or that she hadn't been here before. I said she wasn't here the night she died."

# CHAPTER TWENTY-SEVEN

It was dark by the time Colt Webber drove his truck along the winding driveway to Lyons' house. His headlights picked up a sign saying "Visitors' parking" and he pulled up on the gravel. His heart pounded with misgivings at the idea of walking into the lions' den—or should it be Lyons' den? He carried no weapon, and if Jenna's suspicions proved true, he might become the next victim from the football team the moment Lyons discovered he'd been a cop. A prickling sensation walked over his flesh as he looked around at the dense woodland setting. It was a perfect place for an ambush.

He gathered his courage and stared through the trees. In the distance, he could clearly pick out the house. Light shone from every window and he could see people moving around inside. The winding cement walkway to the front porch appeared to be new, but the lighting in the parking area and along the path to the house was zero. Trees formed a canopy and no moonlight was visible to offer a modicum of illumination. A shiver slid down his spine and he couldn't imagine anyone would enjoy walking through the spooky darkness alone. After gathering his iPad, he slipped from his truck and made his way down the dark walkway using the light on his cellphone to find his way.

A cool breeze rustled the trees and sent a swirl of golden leaves dancing at his feet. The smell of damp earth and pine enclosed him as if creeping out of the darkness to smother him. He missed the comfort of his weapon at his side. It had been a familiar friend and confidence booster in many unpleasant situations, and he'd hated leaving it in the compartment under his seat. As he walked, he glanced around at the foreboding trees cloaked in shadows and his imagination took flight. So many people had died in Black Rock Falls taking pathways just like this one and falling into the hands of a psychopathic killer. Deep inside he wanted to turn around and get the hell out of Dodge but remembered his mission and kept walking, his rubber-soled boots making little sound on the pathway.

An owl hooted close by followed by another some ways off, sending a warning that a stranger had entered their domain. A loud crack as if someone had trodden on a dry twig came from his right and, heart thundering, he turned his light to scan the trees. Red eyes, low to the ground, blinked and then something furry scampered in the opposite direction. A sudden burst of uncertainty gripped him and he quickened his pace, glad when the porch came into full view.

He ran up the steps and hammered on the door. It opened some moments later and a guy looked him up and down. Colt nodded to him. *Dylan Court.* He'd memorized every name on the football team. "Hi Dylan, I'm here to see Seth."

"He's in his room." Court's expression was none too friendly but he stood to one side. "Top of the stairs, last room at the end of the hallway." He waved him through the family room. "He said you planned to drop by. Nice moves today."

Colt nodded. "Thanks."

It was as if the temperature in the room had dropped. The sudden silence and cold, suspicious stares of the men sitting on the sofas unnerved him. One, maybe two he could handle, but four would be a problem. Ignoring the icy reception, he picked his way through the beer cans and takeout wrappers littering the floor and then ran up the stairs, taking them two at a time.

144 D.K. Hood

The house smelled like it needed a good clean, and he wondered how six or so grown men could live in filth. He reached the room. The door was open. The room was a stark contrast to the rest of the house and as neat as a pin. Seeing Lyons working at a desk, he paused and knocked. "Hey, are you busy?"

"This can wait." Lyons pushed away from the desk and stood. "The plays can't." He gave him a long stare and frowned as if evaluating him. "You're smart. I've been digging into your files. I hope you don't mind?" He dropped onto the foot of his bed. "You see, Colt, I can't figure out why a nerd like you wants to play on the team. You don't seem the type to want a career in football."

Colt smiled. "I don't." He leaned against the doorframe and met Lyons' perturbed gaze. "My future is in forensic science and one day I hope to become an ME."

"So why try out for the team?" Lyons clasped his hands together. "There's not much money in forensic science, and with your skills you could make millions if you made the draft."

"I won't make the NFL because I'm too old, but I need to keep fit and figured the team needed me." Colt shrugged. "Forensic science is a career that's going to take me into old age. I'd be washed up in football in two years."

"I guess that makes sense if you've no family money to fall back on. You don't seem the type to hang out with us jocks." Lyons stared at him for a long time. "If you do, we have a little initiation to prove you're one of the guys and that I can trust you."

Unease crawled over Colt but he grinned. "Oh, I've been through a few initiations in my time. What do you need?"

"Someone sweet and innocent." Lyons rolled his shoulders. "Like that blonde I've seen you talking to." A slow smile spread over his lips. "We like to share things here. Booze, women, you know the deal." His gaze never left Colt's face. "I need to know where you stand; are you in or out?"

*Emily.* He forced his mouth to remain fixed in a grin. "Oh, I'm in."

"Good, you'll have to prove it, but for now I'll give you a day pass." Lyons rolled over and grabbed a book from his bedside table. "This belonged to Alex. He had an accident at the gym and broke his neck." He stared at the book for a long moment. "We'd known each other for some time and now he's gone. How do you deal with working with dead bodies?"

It was obvious Lyons didn't trust him and he'd have to change his mind. What Wolfe had told him the first time he'd entered the morgue drifted into his mind. "I don't see a corpse. I see a person with a story to tell. I want to discover what happened to them."

"I'd see a corpse." Lyons shuddered. "So, you get to hang out with the sheriff as well?"

Colt barked a laugh. "Hang out? I don't think so. She's far too busy at crime scenes and barely looks my way. I keep out of her way."

"Let's get back to the sexy blonde I noticed sitting with you in the cafeteria." Lyons wet his lips as if savoring a memory. "How come she's hanging out with you?"

Of all the girls on campus, Lyons had picked out Emily Wolfe for his friends to rape. "Emily is interning at the morgue so our paths cross, is all."

"Emily, huh? Will she come to a party here if you invite her?" Lyons chuckled. "The boys need a distraction."

Searching for any excuse, Colt shook his head. "Not a chance. She's a little young for me and only sits with me at lunch to read over my notes from last semester." He cleared his throat. "I'm sure I'll be able to find you someone else if it's part of an initiation."

"But I have a hankering for *her*. I like them sweet and innocent." Lyons gave him a slow smile. "Introduce me and I'll make a move on her, but to prove you're one of us, you'll have to be involved." He sniggered. "Don't worry, they never complain."

*You won't have one chance in hell with Emily.* Colt swallowed the bad taste in his mouth. "I can't wait." He held his hand out for the book. "It's getting late, are you ready to go over the plays?"

"Sure." Lyons stood. "Come downstairs, we'll talk in the kitchen."


Two hours later, Colt stood and picked up his iPad and Alex's playbook. "I've got to go. My aunt bawls me out if I get home late and disturb her."

"That must make dating a bitch." Lyons frowned. "Maybe you should move?"

Colt shook his head. "I barely break even now. I share the food and utilities with my aunt."

"Ah, yeah, you're on a scholarship, I forgot." Lyons pushed to his feet. "Okay, I'll see you at practice in the morning." He led the way to the front door.

Colt followed and gave the guys in the family room a wave but none of them moved their eyes from the big-screen TV. He turned to Lyons. "Night."

"Introduce me to the blonde tomorrow." Lyons grinned.

*Over my dead body.* "Sure." He headed down the steps and pulled out his phone, accessed the light, and hurried along the dark pathway. The temperature had dropped considerably in the last few hours and the breeze had an icy chill straight from the mountains. Even in August, the night temperatures reminded everyone that winter was on the way. As he made the first turn, he heard a crunch behind him and stopped. Moving his light in an arc, he searched the path behind him and found nothing. The hairs on the back of his neck prickled as the feeling someone was watching him crept over him. He kept moving then the sound came again, like footsteps on the pathway behind him and the scrape of a shoe on the rough cement.

He wondered briefly if Lyons had set up a prank to scare him. Lyons wouldn't be aware he studied martial arts and could take care of himself to some degree, but the narrow, tree-lined pathway didn't offer him much room to maneuver. Added to the fact he had an iPad in one hand and a phone in the other, and anyone could be waiting around the next bend, it would be easy to get the jump on him.

His light made a tunnel before him, and as he walked, he slid the iPad under one arm, shifted the phone to his left hand, and then pulled his car keys from his jeans pocket. He hustled along, scanning the pathway in all directions and listening, but all he could hear was the sound of his deep breathing and the pounding of his heart in his ears. As the snaking pathway opened up to the parking lot, he heaved a sigh of relief then a slight buzzing broke the silence. He glanced up and caught a glimpse of the biggest insect he'd ever seen in his life. He stared into the darkness but whatever it was had vanished into the night.

Colt hit his fob key and climbed into his truck, locking the doors behind him. The walk had unsettled him more than he'd like to admit. He leaned back in his seat, glad when the engine turned over and music played on the radio. Feeling foolish for allowing his imagination to get the better of him, he stared into the darkness. Had the wind played tricks on his mind or had someone been lurking in the shadows?

# CHAPTER TWENTY-EIGHT

It had taken Kane some time to convince Jenna to take an hour or so to join him for dinner at the Cattleman's Hotel in town. They'd been too exhausted to cook by the time they'd returned to her ranch. He enjoyed her company and hated to dine alone.

Wednesday evenings weren't usually busy but with a festival in town, Kane had been lucky to secure a table later in the evening, not a prime position but not next to the kitchen either. After ordering, he took in the woman seated before him. She'd added a small amount of makeup, and the thin lines around her eyes made them appear huge in a face framed in glossy black hair. When she opened her mouth to speak, he shook his head. "No shop talk." He smiled and handed her the menu. "We deserve one hour away from murder and mayhem."

"My head is filled with theories and possible suspects. It's so much easier for Wolfe when people are shot or stabbed to death. So far, we have one possible suicide and two possible murders. It's hard to concentrate on anything else." Jenna moved her gaze slowly over him. "But I have to admit you're distracting dressed in a suit with your hair all slicked down." Her eyes twinkled with amusement. "I keep thinking any minute you're going to pull out your FBI creds."

It was so good to see Jenna's humorous side again. Kane chuckled. "I was going for the suave, sophisticated look." He paused as the waiter offered him a sample of red wine. He sipped, and then nodded his approval. His gaze went back to Jenna. "Didn't work, huh?"

"Trust me, you look just fine in blue jeans and a cowboy hat." Jenna sipped her wine and moaned. "Oh, this is good."

Kane lifted the bottle and showed her the label. "It's from Central Otago, New Zealand. It's a small area in the South Island. In my opinion, they produce some of the best Pinot Noir in the world." He met her gaze. "It goes real well with a nice thick steak and all the trimmings."

"I'm sure it will but you'll only have one glass, won't you?" Jenna shot him a mischievous grin. "Which means the rest of the bottle is mine."

Kane wagged a finger at her. "And you a sheriff and all."

They'd just finished their main course and had been waiting for dessert when Kane's phone pealed. He frowned and glanced at his watch. "I only wanted an hour's peace."

"Anyone we know?" Jenna leaned back in her seat as the waiter placed a slice of Black Forest cake before her.

Kane nodded. "Yeah, it's Webber." He answered the call. "Problem?"

*"Nah, just touching base."* Webber sounded a little anxious. *"I made the team and took up an invite to go over the plays with Seth Lyons at the house on Pine. Apart from the guys treating me as if I had the plague, I didn't receive any threats. I told him the truth about interning with Wolfe, so he won't be suspicious if someone remembers seeing me with him. He did ask if I knew Jenna. One thing: on the walk there and back along the pathway, I had the strangest feeling someone was watching me."*

Kane frowned and remembered the alternative entrance they'd discovered. "Next time you head out that way, go down the no-entry road; it leads straight to the front of the house." He glanced at Jenna. "The pathway through the trees has a silent alarm as well.

They obviously don't like unexpected visitors. Did you get any vibes from Lyons at all?"

*"He plays his cards close to the vest but he did invite me to a party on Thursday night, a wake, I figure, for Jacobs and Devon."* Webber cleared his throat. *"I'm angling for an invitation to move in. They've two spare rooms at the moment but it will be at a price."*

Kane leaned back in his chair and sighed. There always had to be a price. "How so?"

*"They want me to become involved in one of their parties. Lyons made it very clear they use procuring a suitable woman for group sex as an initiation. He was careful not to mention he planned to rape her."* Webber cursed under his breath. "I sure wish I'd been wearing a wire."

"Maybe we can find a local female cop willing to go undercover." Jenna glanced at Kane. "How long have we got?"

*"No time at all. Lyons has his mind set on one woman. I know it's a mind game to see if I'll defile a friend to make it into his inner circle."*

Kane blinked, his stomach clenching at the implications. "He's not got his sights set on Jenna, has he?"

*"No. Lyons wants me to introduce him to Emily."*

# CHAPTER TWENTY-NINE

## Thursday

The thought of speaking to Wolfe weighed heavy on Jenna's shoulders as she made her way into the morgue for Pete Devon's autopsy. After Kane had explained Webber's phone call the previous evening, the last thing she wanted to do was inform Wolfe one of his daughters could be in danger. Since moving to Black Rock Falls, both Emily and Julie Wolfe had come close to becoming victims. Although Wolfe was a consummate professional on her team, she expected a less than warm reception of her news, so seeing Webber and Emily waiting inside the morgue surprised her. "I wasn't expecting to see you here today."

"When there's an autopsy, we come to observe." Emily smiled at Jenna. "I hear you saved Owen Jones from the rapids."

Jenna shot a look at Kane as he stepped into the room behind her. "Did you have to tell everyone?"

"I never said a word, Jenna, but it's in my report." Kane looked abashed. "A good deal of college kids were there; I'm sure they couldn't wait to spread the news."

"It wasn't Kane." Emily frowned. "Everyone is talking about it, calling you Aquawoman and how you plunged in boots and all."

Jenna cast a glance at Kane. "Kane was there too, and if we hadn't gotten to Jones in time, he'd be here waiting for an autopsy." She frowned. "Can I have a word in private?"

"Sure." Wolfe led the way into the hallway and pulled down his mask. "What's up?"

Jenna explained the interest Seth Lyons had shown in Emily and the potential of her becoming his next rape victim, and then she waited with bated breath for his reaction.

"I'll talk to her." Wolfe's gray eyes held a flicker of worry and then it vanished and he smiled at her. "Thanks for letting me know, and don't worry—it's highly unlikely Emily would place herself in that position. She's aware of the Lowe case and this piece of information will keep her well away from anyone on the football team."

"And she has Webber in some of her classes to keep an eye on her." Jenna looked up at him. "Although, being undercover, I wouldn't encourage her to hang out with him anymore."

"I told her to keep her distance." Wolfe grimaced. "Anyway, she's more interested in college seniors at the moment." He shook his head in dismay. "She turns nineteen soon, it's a worry."

Jenna squeezed his arm. "I wouldn't worry too much. When any potential boyfriends lay eyes on you, they'll behave themselves." She waved a hand toward the door. "I guess we'd better get back to it." She led the way inside.

"Okay, are we all ready?" Wolfe followed her, went to the gurney and switched on the examination light, spreading a bright beam over the inert body. He turned on his recorder, made all the necessary references for the official recording of his findings, and then pulled down the sheet. "Let's get started."

Jenna breathed through her mouth to avoid the stench of decomposing flesh. The way Pete Devon had died intrigued her. "What is it about drowning cases that makes them so difficult to determine COD?"

"It's not so hard to determine drowning, it's proving if a person was *murdered* by drowning." Wolfe's eyes met hers over the body.

"We found Pete Devon submerged in water, his skin is wrinkled, and the amount of damage to the epidermis is a good indication of submergence for several hours." He indicated toward the skin on the hands and feet. "The diatom test I conducted yesterday on the sample of bone marrow extracted from the femur shows the same five algae present in the victim as in the pool water. So from that test, we know he drowned in the pool where we found him. This is more accurate than testing the water extracted from the lungs, but that was also a match."

Jenna moved closer. "So why is the cause of death so hard to determine if every result indicates drowning?"

"Emily, can you explain?" Wolfe took clippers and removed a section of Pete Devon's hair from the crown of his head.

"We know he drowned." Emily's eyes danced with enthusiasm over her face mask. "What we need to determine is if he slipped and fell or if someone murdered him. Dad is considering the latter but we need to prove it. He already pointed out the marks on the victim's ankles at the scene but now they are more pronounced." She moved to the end of the gurney and lifted one foot. "See here, the half-moon marks on each ankle? Dad said he mentioned them at the scene." She placed her hand around the pale ankle. "As if a larger hand than mine held on so tight they dug their nails into his flesh." She lifted the other foot for Jenna and Kane to examine. "Try your hand, Dave, and see if it's a closer fit."

Jenna stared in amazement as Kane lifted the leg then slipped one gloved hand around the ankle. His hands overlapped the nail marks. "So not as big as Kane's but close, so we'd assume a man?"

"With hands almost as big as mine, I'd say so." Kane replaced the leg on the gurney. "And from the positions of the nail marks, Devon was attacked from behind."

"Yes, or dragged off a woman by one of his friends." Wolfe cleared his throat. "If the damage was caused in the pool, I'd assume this man has considerable strength too." Wolfe turned his attention back to Jenna. "You'd figure attacking someone in water would be easy, but it takes quite an effort to pull someone down a ladder submerged in water." He touched Devon's nose. "This damage was caused by a sharp downward movement. The killer must have been in the water behind him, grabbed his ankles, and pulled." He looked over at Webber. "Why would I come to that conclusion, Webber?"

"If someone slipped on a ladder, they'd likely graze their shins or fall back into the water." Webber held out both his arms. "Climbing up a ladder out of the water, they'd be angled back not forward."

It didn't bother Jenna that Wolfe was making the autopsy a class for his interns and she was surprised at their knowledge. "So when the steps struck Devon and knocked him unconscious, he drowned?"

"I doubt it. Made him dizzy, yeah, but that doesn't look like enough damage to knock him out." Kane leaned forward and examined the body. "The impact hasn't pushed the nasal bones into the brain but it would've hurt like hell."

"This is why we don't jump to conclusions and search for the whole story. The fall could've easily rendered him unconscious." Wolfe waved Jenna to his side of the gurney. "During my initial examination, I noticed a discoloration of the scalp. As you can see, there is a distinct mark on the top of the head. I'll be opening the cranium later to determine the extent of the bruising, but at this stage I'd rule out a weapon. From the size of the injury, it's possible it was caused by a fist coming down from above." He re-enacted how a punch would come from above with force. "I've seen similar injuries in men killed in combat."

"I've seen similar injuries caused during football, even with a helmet." Webber shrugged. "He could've been injured in a tackle and not reported it to the coach."

Jenna flicked a glance at Kane. "If not a football injury, who are we looking at here? Someone trained in martial arts or hand-to-hand combat, boxing?"

"Yeah." Kane nodded. "A punch like that would subdue him."

"More than that." Wolfe turned to her. "Consider Devon is hurt, he's underwater, and no doubt disoriented and trying to get to the surface. The moment the top of his head breaks the surface, wham, someone lands one hell of a punch on his head. The first thing he'd do is gasp, and once water is in the lungs, it's over. He might have tried to fight back but his lungs would be bursting. Water is painful when it enters the lungs. He can't breathe, has no oxygen going to his brain. His body would be going into spasms and death follows pretty quickly."

Jenna leaned back on one of the counters. "So, suspected homicide?"

"I can't say until I complete the autopsy. I'll need to open him up and make sure he isn't suffering from anything unusual, but his medical record, apart from a recent football injury, indicates he was in top shape." Wolfe shrugged. "I'll do a toxicology screen as well but if someone murdered this young man, he sure tried to make it appear like an accident."

A horrible sensation of dread slid over Jenna at the thought of another killer in Black Rock Falls. Had the once sleepy town become a magnet for everyone with the itch to go on a killing spree? She lifted her gaze from the body back to Wolfe. "Okay, we'll head back to the office and try and hunt down some clues to get a jump on who is doing this and why."

"I'll send over a report when I'm through." Wolfe lifted a scalpel from the tray.

"Thanks." She waited a beat. "Did you match the ring we found in Jacobs' locker with the mark on Chrissie Lowe's arm, or the handprints?"

"Not yet." The scalpel in Wolfe's hand hovered over Devon's chest. "Later today I want to make sure that the bruising is more pronounced. I'll take more images and make a digital comparison but from what I can see with my naked eye, it looks like a match." He frowned. "It might be an idea to run down the design, just in case it's a team ring or similar."

"I'm on it." Jenna made a hasty retreat from the morgue. With Webber still officially a deputy, the need to have a law enforcement officer as a witness to the autopsy was satisfied.

As she walked out into the fresh air, she turned to Kane. "Dammit, seems like we've got another killer in town." She threw her hands into the air. "What is it with Black Rock Falls? It's as if someone is advertising it as a serial killer's playground."

"I wouldn't say that too loud." Kane grinned at her. "Someone will make it the title of a book."

# CHAPTER THIRTY

Kane met Rowley and Walters on the sidewalk outside the sheriff's department. He'd given Jenna a ride back to the office and then had gone to collect the food order for the meeting from Aunt Betty's Café. As Walters made his way inside, Kane stared at Rowley's disheveled appearance and raised one eyebrow. "Trouble?"

"You could say that." Rowley straightened his shirt and ran one hand through his hair before replacing his Stetson. "The usual fights breaking out all over town from the influx of cowboys, and this time they ran their mouths at an interstate MC having a few beers at the Triple Z Bar." He shook his head. "It wasn't pretty. We tried to calm things down without luck. I went back to my cruiser and pulled out the shotguns. I climbed onto the bar and the owner turned off the lights and then switched them on again. When they noticed us, they settled down."

Kane flicked a glance at Rowley's cruiser. "No arrests?"

"Finding out who threw the first punch would be like sorting my grandma's tangled knitting yarn." Rowley grimaced. "No one was talking, so I took down their names and gave them a warning." He indicated to the food in Kane's arms with his chin. "We having a meeting?"

"Yeah." Kane nodded. "Wolfe figures both deaths are homicides." He cleared his throat. "While you're here, Jenna wants to throw a birthday party for Wolfe's little Anna. You coming?"

"Wouldn't miss it." Rowley's cheeks pinked. "I'm seeing someone but it's early days yet. Sandy works in administration at the college. Can I bring her along?"

Kane smiled. "Sure." He headed up the steps and shouldered his way through the glass doors.

"Good, you're all here." Jenna stood at her office door. "Wolfe and Webber are still working on the Devon autopsy, so we'll have to go ahead without them." She went to her whiteboard and waited for them to sit down. "I've discussed the three cases with Kane and Wolfe. As the football team shares a link with these otherwise seemingly unrelated cases, I'll need to add the information to the whiteboard side by side so we can consider the whole picture. Kane, will you bring everyone up to date and I'll get the information onto the whiteboard?"

Kane scrolled through the files on his cellphone. "Okay, at first we believed we had three separate cases, so we'll take them one by one. Wolfe hasn't ruled out Chrissie Lowe's cause of death is suicide. She made a date with the quarterback Seth Lyons to go to a party on Saturday night but according to his friends at the house where they all live, she never showed. Duke thinks otherwise and gave positive results of her being there. We're waiting on blood samples taken at the scene to see if they're a match for Chrissie." He waited a beat for Jenna to write the information on the whiteboard. "Her roommate, Livi Johnson, gave us a statement confirming Chrissie left the building around nine and was last seen getting into a silver sedan. This sedan belongs to the janitor, John Beck, who leaves his car keys unattended in his office. Wolfe obtained forensic proof Chrissie was in that vehicle but Beck has a solid alibi, so we can only assume the person who gave Chrissie a ride to and from the house used his car." He frowned. "By all accounts Chrissie was intelligent and it's highly unlikely she'd take a ride with a stranger, which makes me believe Seth Lyons and perhaps one of his friends were in the car."

"As the football players living with Lyons are close-knit, we have Webber working undercover at the college; he's known there, tried out for the football team, and was accepted." Jenna turned to look at them. "So, if you see him on the street, walk on by, he'll understand. From conversations with Lyons, Webber believes he lures girls, usually freshmen, to the house and drugs them, and then he and a number of his friends rape them."

"Did Wolfe find any proof?" Rowley's mouth turned down. "Chrissie Lowe had been under a hot shower for hours; there'd be no DNA on her body and I doubt anyone who planned a rape would forget about protection."

Kane shook his head. "No trace DNA evidence was found but she does have handprints on both arms, and one bruise is quite distinct and in the shape of a ring. Wolfe has a ring owned by Alex Jacobs and will update us if he considers it a match."

"Walters, I need you to run down the ring design." Jenna looked at the elderly deputy. "Make sure it's not a school ring or whatever and everyone has one."

"Sure thing. So why wouldn't the girl come and tell you about the rape, Sheriff?" Old Duke Walters scratched at the white stubble on his chin. "Why kill herself? From what I've found out about her, she was a straight-A student. Makes no sense, no sense at all."

"We'll get to that later." Jenna continued to add the facts to the whiteboard. "Our first assumption was it was murder, and until Wolfe makes a decision that still must be a consideration. She didn't leave a note but maybe she tried to reach out to someone before she died." She frowned. "We couldn't find her cellphone, although from her records she sent a short message at two thirty on Sunday morning."

"To who?" Rowley leaned forward in his seat. "This could be the key."

Kane shook his head. "We don't know. When Wolfe backtracked the number, the military shut him down. I figure she wanted to reach out to someone and the only person we can link to her is her brother. We know the Navy deployed him some weeks ago. His status is unknown, which means he is MIA. The Navy informed the family in the week before Chrissie died." He sighed. "There's no way of knowing what was in the message."

"So she knew her brother was MIA?" Walters shook his head. "Poor kid. That might have pushed her over the edge."

"Or she wanted to say goodbye." Rowley frowned. "So, she lost or dumped the cellphone between the party and her dorm. She could've thrown it anywhere—oh, shit… you don't think her rapists could've sent the message?"

Kane grimaced at the thought. "Anything is possible, and sending disgusting images to her brother could sure push her to suicide."

"One thing: even if Wolfe rules her death as suicide, we need to find evidence and bring charges against her attackers. Seth Lyons is our main suspect." Jenna's face had become stone. "There is no consent issue here. Read the autopsy report. This girl had enough date-rape drugs in her system to render her unconscious for hours. I want these men found and charged."

Kane met her gaze. "That's a given."

"So why focus on Seth Lyons?" Rowley lifted his gaze to Jenna. "He asked her to the party, but any one of the men at the party could've been responsible. She might have been part of an initiation like Webber suggested."

"Not this time because Lyons was running the show. He invited her to the party and has a motive." Jenna added the word to the whiteboard beside Seth Lyons' name. "The guy she broke the date with, Phil Stein, had a fight with Lyons in the cafeteria at the college and flattened him with one punch. From an eyewitness account,

Stein humiliated Lyons. It was no secret Stein was seeing Chrissie, so it gives Lyons a motive. Raping his girlfriend would be payback and we know Lyons and his friends don't give an inch."

"But we have no solid evidence to charge Lyons with rape." Kane glanced down at his notes. "As you know from the files, the guys living at Lyons' house all gave each other alibis for the night of the rape and they've sterilized the room we considered as the possible scene of the crime; however, they didn't do the same for the rest of the house or the vehicle. Wolfe has hair samples from Jacobs and Devon but needs samples from the other people living at the house to see if they match those collected from the vehicle."

"Also, her shoes are missing." Jenna turned to look at Kane. "There's a description of them in the file. The shoes might give us some trace evidence. It's something I'll add to a press release. Kane, I want you to contact the college to see if they've been turned in to lost-and-found."

"Yes, ma'am." Kane made a note.

"Next, we had the unusual death of Alex Jacobs." Jenna wrote his name on the whiteboard. "Wolfe is not convinced his death was a homicide; he thinks maybe a tragic accident." She turned to face them. "The autopsy report will give you the reasons we are looking into this case as a possible homicide, and our investigation will center on the motive for killing him. Jacobs was a pivotal player on the football team, admired and liked as far as we believe, and then the janitor gave us some interesting information about Jacobs and some of the other members of the team. The group took part in a plan to remove Owen Jones from the team. Jacobs went to the coach and told him that Jones had attempted to sell them drugs. After a fight broke out between Jones, Lyons, and Jacobs, the coach benched Jones. Security carried out a search and found a crack pipe; Jones insists someone planted it, but the dean removed him from college for the entire semester." She shrugged. "He's back now, so I figure he has a motive for killing Jacobs. Don't forget the fight at the rapids."

"Then you should add Phil Stein as well." Rowley gave Kane a direct look. "If he believes Jacobs was involved in Chrissie's rape, he has a motive as well."

Kane smiled. "You're echoing my thoughts. We have another possible as well: Chrissie's cousin, Steve Lowe. I figure as she was family, he has motive too, and we'll need to discover his whereabouts during both TODs."

"Yeah, but let's stick to Jacobs' death first or it gets confusing." Jenna added the names to the list and the motives. "Lowe is a big guy and works part-time at the local feed store, so he will be lifting heavy weights all day. Both Jones and Stein are strong, muscular guys too; both are capable of holding the weight Jacobs was lifting, but I figure Stein is perhaps the only spotter Jacobs would trust. Lowe is an unknown quantity at the moment."

"I'm not so sure." Rowley shook his head. "You'd have to be part of a college football team to understand. Yeah, there might have been hard feelings between them but Jones is part of the team now, and if I planned to kill someone I'd make sure to get closer to my target and gain his trust."

"Good point." Jenna nodded in agreement and added Jones to the board. "Jones doesn't have a solid alibi for the time Jacobs died." She glanced at Kane. "We'll go see Stein, Jones, and Lowe later and see what they have to say."

Kane reached for his cup of coffee and took a sip. He glanced down at his notes again. "Okay, Wolfe hasn't sent an autopsy report for Pete Devon yet because there are too many inconsistences for him to determine cause of death."

He ran through the preliminary findings and then glanced up at Jenna. Seeing she had added all the pertinent information to the whiteboard, he turned to Rowley and Walters. "Here's where it gets interesting. Both Jacobs and Devon died around the same time of night, in the same building, and the CCTV cameras went down at the same time both nights. Unfortunately, there's not enough footage to discover if this is a regular occurrence, and the college security guards haven't noticed anything unusual, so they are useless."

"We've determined that if someone killed both men, they would've needed to have a considerable amount of strength, which again targets our suspects." Jenna looked back at Kane. "Wolfe figures we should think out of the box with these cases. For instance, we're including Chrissie's rape in the two suspected murder cases because of the football team link and also looking at any enemies of the team or the coach."

"Yeah." Rowley nodded in agreement. "The coach has made a zillion enemies over the years. He's tough and unforgiving."

"I'd say there'd be a few people out to get his job too." Walters' gray brows furrowed. "If the team fails, the college will be looking at replacing him. It's a matter of pride."

"Which brings us back to our suspects." Jenna sat in her office chair and leaned back. "All have a problem with the team. All want to get even. They may have different reasons but it's the same result."

Kane nodded. "Seems open and shut to me. Three suspects? My gut tells me there's more to this and we're missing something." He pushed a takeout bag toward Jenna, noticing she hadn't eaten anything or touched her coffee. "Do any of these guys know how to disable a CCTV camera, for instance? Has anything else happened with the team or the coach we're not aware of?"

"Okay, Rowley, I'll need you to run things here, but if you get any downtime, see what you can find out about rival teams, anything that could point to someone trying to destroy the team or any dirt you can dig up on the coach." Jenna took a sip of her coffee and sighed. "That's all we have for now." She waved at the bags of food. "Grab what you want and we'll all get back to work."

Kane waited for them to go and looked at her. "You know what's bothering me about all this?"

"What?" Jenna raised one eyebrow in question.

"If it's payback against the team for whatever reason, why take out the lesser players first? All can be replaced by players on the bench." Kane reached for a bag of sandwiches. "If it was me, my target would be Lyons, the star quarterback."

"Hmm." Jenna leaned back in her seat. "Maybe whoever staged the accidents is planning something special for Lyons?"

# CHAPTER THIRTY-ONE

For Jenna, writing out the facts in a case on the whiteboard centered her mind and put the priorities in order. She stared at the board. The three cases revolved around the football team but if they turned out to be murder, she needed to know what would trigger someone to kill the players? She finished her sandwich and took a sip of coffee before dragging her attention away from the whiteboard and looking at Kane. "What if I go left field and make a crazy assumption about these cases?"

"Give it to me." Kane leaned on the desk and met her gaze.

Jenna nodded. "Okay, what if we're looking at this all wrong?" She drummed her fingers on the table. "These college football teams are rivals and do weird things, like stealing each other's mascots. I know there was some trouble with the team from Louan a couple of years ago."

"Where's this going, Jenna?" Kane lifted his cup and sipped.

"Say it wasn't Lyons and his friends who raped Chrissie—what if it was members of a rival team? Maybe they figured we'd haul in Lyons and his friends for Chrissie's rape. When that didn't work, one or more of them went postal and decided to kill the players."

"Uh-huh." Kane rubbed the back of his neck. "I guess if we could prove someone else overheard Lyons asking Chrissie to the party, it might be possible. We know Lyons lures girls to the house to rape them and has been doing so for some time."

Exasperated, Jenna stared at him. "Yeah, you're probably right, I'm just grabbing at straws—and from what Livi told me, it's not a secret. Guys like him, who have fathers to make their mistakes go away, often brag about breaking the law, and it's not too far-fetched to believe the other teams are aware of his deviate behavior. Think about it. Lyons has just scored. He's found an innocent young girl willing to go to the party alone. Do you honestly believe he'd keep the news to himself? No way, he'd be crowing to everyone involved in his dirty little games." She tossed the bangs out of her eyes. "They'd all be in on the plan, wouldn't they? Anyone could have overheard them."

"So why bleach the room? We know Chrissie was there, it had to be them. Duke picked up her scent." Kane leaned back in his chair. "Unless the other players dropped her at the house and she staggered inside for help." His mouth turned down at the edges. "Lyons and his gang are sick enough to use the situation to their advantage—like I've said before, rape is violence, not sexual gratification." He sighed. "Then there's the vehicle. We know it belongs to the janitor and we have positive proof Chrissie was inside."

"But *when* was she in the car?" Jenna stared at the whiteboard. "We *know* she was given a ride home in the silver sedan but that doesn't prove it was the same vehicle that she was seen getting into by Livi. It was dark and she wasn't sure of the color." She threw her hands in the air. "We sure haven't gotten much to go on up to now, have we?"

"You mentioned chasing down Stein, Jones, and Lowe—that's a start." Kane finished his coffee, collected the empty bags, and stood to throw them in the trash.

Jenna looked up at him. "Okay, make a call to the college security; if they are on campus, we'll go see them. And call the office at the college as well to find out if someone has turned in Chrissie's cellphone and shoes. I'm going to write a press release about the missing items and hope someone in town has found them." She frowned. "I might mention a reward with no questions asked for their return. With any luck, we'll get a break in this case."

*

Moments after Jenna had disconnected from her local media contact, her cellphone chimed. She glanced at the caller ID. It was Wolfe. "Hi Shane, do you have any good news for me?"

*"Some. I have nothing to add to my conclusion of Devon's death. His autopsy showed nothing of interest but the cranial autopsy did show a hematoma below the scalp, which only means he was alive after the blow to his head. So it could have occurred during football practice."*

Jenna pushed away the awful memory of the autopsy and cleared her throat. "What about the evidence from the janitor's vehicle?"

*"I've identified two of the foreign hairs in the janitor's sedan as belonging to Jacobs and Devon."* Wolfe took a deep breath. *"Jacobs could have been responsible for the bruises on Chrissie Lowes' arms; his hands fit. I've made an impression of the ring and compared it to the mark on her skin. And I was able to extract a small amount of DNA from the ring. I'm testing it now. If it comes back as a match for Chrissie, we'll know he was involved. The DNA traces I found were blood, caught around the stones in the ring. He might have been the one who hit her and split her lip. The blood we found on the stairs is her blood type, and alcohol is in the sample. It will take a few more days before we know for sure if it's Chrissie's."*

A wave of relief swept over Jenna. At last some headway in the case. "Anything on the blood trace in the car?"

*"Yeah, it's a match for Chrissie's blood type."* Wolfe sighed. *"I hope the DNA test will prove beyond doubt Chrissie was in the house and in the janitor's vehicle after the rape, but we have no evidence to prove it was the same car she got into on Saturday night."*

"Thanks for rushing this through. I really appreciate it, Shane."

*"It's my job but I appreciate an ego stroke from time to time."* He chuckled. *"I'll write up my reports and bring them over to you in the morning."*

The line went dead and Jenna smiled. "I'm sure lucky to have such a great team."

She stood, grabbed her jacket, and headed out the door. She met Kane at the front counter. "Any luck with the lost-and-found?"

"Nope." Kane straightened from leaning on the counter. "Both items are distinctive, so it didn't take too long. Security will be looking out for them in case they're turned in." He handed her a go-cup of coffee. "And we're in luck, Stein and Jones are in the library, so we can go and speak to them now."

"We'll stop by the feed store on the way back and speak to Lowe."

"I sure hope nothing else happens while we're out." Kane slid his Stetson on his head and made his way to the front door. "We're getting snowed under now."

Jenna grimaced. "This is Black Rock Falls. If it's gonna happen, it's gonna happen here."

# CHAPTER THIRTY-TWO

The sky seemed to go on forever above a million pines, and fluffy white clouds nestled over the mountaintops like cotton candy wigs. He hadn't been at peace for a long time. Of late, his mind had muddled events into streams of images frayed at the edges or incomplete like the faded color of an old photograph, but all this had changed the first time he'd lain down on the college roof. On his back, hidden between two huge air conditioning units, the gritty cement was hard against his spine as he stared at the screen watching a live feed from the drone.

It was like watching a reality show, the weird and entertaining daily lives of the students and faculty. All had secrets and stories to tell. Most people lied or exaggerated happenings in their lives. It was as if there wasn't enough excitement in their humdrum existence, so they had to make up stories to impress their friends. The gossip reminded him of the kids' game where a story is told to one person at the beginning of a line and asked to pass it on. By the time the story arrives at the final person, it's a different story, with so many embellishments and add-ons it doesn't come close to the truth.

He'd come to the conclusion people acted like ants, all with a job to do or a place to go. Some so predictable he could set his watch to them. Take Emily Wolfe, for example: this semester, each afternoon at four, she'd drive to the forest, park in the parking lot, and then run up the path alongside the rapids. But did she take the switchback and come back down like everyone else? Not Emily. She jogged past the top of the rapids and weaved her way along an old trail that eventually led to the top of Black Rock Falls—the actual place the founders had used to name the county and the sprawling town.

Once there she would stand staring out across the wide-open vista, to the town spreading out way below and the miles of grasslands stretching into the next county. After a short break, she'd turn back around and then head down the winding pathway, past the old dilapidated bridge spanning the river, and then follow the trail down to the parking lot.

In fact, he'd discovered many secrets of late. The tiny drone had offered him the opportunity to eavesdrop on just about any conversation. If he didn't find a convenient window, most people were too busy checking out their cellphones to notice his tiny machine hovering above their heads. His drone had been close by when Emily had told Webber about jogging to the top of the falls at four each day. It made sense: she'd chosen the most popular time, as usually there would be a number of other students on the lower trail. Nice and safe.

*Nowhere is nice and safe, Emily. Nowhere.*

# CHAPTER THIRTY-THREE

The noise and smells of the college surrounded Jenna as she followed the security guard to the library. She waited with Kane outside the door for the guard to go and find Stein. She turned to Kane. "Isn't it strange how the smell of a place brings back so many memories? The moment I walked in here, the smell of books and body odor made me remember a day a security guard came to the library for me." She pushed the memory back into the recesses of her mind. "Before you ask, it's old news, okay?"

"Sure." Kane took her hand and squeezed. "I'm here for you if you need me. Any time, you know that, right?"

She turned and smiled at him. "Yeah, and it's good to know." She reluctantly let go of his hand, pulled out her cellphone, and searched for a file. "We've got zip on Stein. No priors of violence; a few fights on his school record but he's never been charged with anything."

"He admitted to having feelings for Chrissie, so he has motive." Kane shrugged. "It doesn't take too much to push people over the edge. Gang rape and then if he figures she committed suicide because of it, it's one hell of an inducement."

"Yeah, especially as Livi and likely most of the women living in her dorm are saying that's how she died." Jenna peered through the glass door at Stein, heading in their direction with a confused expression. "He's on his way." When he walked through the door and looked at her, she indicated toward the doors to the garden. "Can we talk outside?"

"Sure." Stein walked beside her. "Have you charged the men who raped Chrissie?"

Jenna shook her head. "Not yet. Her cause of death is inconclusive."

"So, what do you want with me?" Stein looked perplexed. "I sure as hell didn't hurt her."

"I didn't say you did." Jenna let her gaze move over the young man. He had the chiseled muscular frame of an athlete, yet he was unshaven and dark circles ran under his eyes. "You keep in good shape. Do you lift weights, swim? Martial arts?"

"I do track, weights, and swimming, and I run most afternoons. Yeah, I've studied martial arts. It's good for my flexibility." Stein gave a snort. "Good Lord, you think I'm involved in the accidents of Alex Jacobs and Pete Devon, don't you?" He shook his head. "Those two boneheads wouldn't be worth my time. Now, Seth Lyons…" He punched the palm of his other hand. "I'd like to take him apart piece by piece, but if I laid one finger on him, his old man would have me in jail for ten to twenty. I'm not that stupid."

Jenna nodded. He might be smart but he hadn't convinced her of his innocence. "Where were you on Tuesday night, the day Pete Devon died?" She waited for a reaction but his blank expression meant either he couldn't remember or he was remembering just fine and trying to come up with an alibi. "Around nine thirty?"

"I'm not sure." Stein scratched his head. "I usually spend time in the library after dinner. I could've still been there or in my room. I'm not sure, things have been a bit muddled"—he tapped his head—"in here since Chrissie died."

Jenna made a few notes then looked back at him. Maybe he was taking her death harder than she'd thought. "Are you sleeping?"

"What, are you a doctor now?" Stein snorted in resentment. "How do you figure I'm sleeping? My friend was pack raped and then committed suicide. Everyone knows what happened, so I'm not sure how you came up with an inconclusive verdict. How do you think I feel knowing the men that hurt her are out there laughing about it?" He took a step closer, his fists clenched. "You know Seth Lyons is responsible, why don't you arrest him?"

"Take a step back, Mr. Stein." Jenna rested her hand on her weapon. "You can be assured we're doing everything in our power to find out who assaulted Chrissie."

"I've told you." Stein's face contorted with rage. "It has to be Seth Lyons and his football buddies. No one else lured her out alone."

"We have no proof it was Lyons but you can be assured we're hunting down suspects." Kane laid a hand on Stein's shoulder. "With three deaths within a week, we'll be asking everyone questions. We're tracking people's movements, and right now, we need to know who was seen in and around the swimming pool the night Pete Devon died."

"I don't remember being in the area." Stein glared at Kane. "My roommate might remember. Why don't you ask him? His name is Paul Brown. He's in the library studying. Want me to go get him?"

*What, and ask him to give you an alibi?* Jenna closed her notebook and looked at Stein. "No, you wait here with Deputy Kane and I'll speak to him." She turned to the glass door. "Where's he sitting?"

"Over by the window." Stein led the way back inside and pointed through the glass door to a man with auburn hair. "Black T-shirt."

"Okay, thanks." Jenna walked to the door, and the security guard who'd accompanied them went to meet her. "I haven't finished with Stein yet but I need to speak to Paul Brown." She pointed to the man at the desk. "It will only take a minute."

She hurried over to the man and lowered her voice to introduce herself. She asked him about the night Devon died. "Do you recall seeing Phil on Tuesday night around nine thirty?"

"He's been a bit crazy since Chrissie died." Brown rubbed his chin. "We studied for a while after dinner, we do most nights, but he said he needed some fresh air and alone time. I went back to our dorm and watched TV with some of the guys. He came back around ten thirty. The show had finished and I was heading back to our room when he came in through the front door."

The next question stormed into Jenna's head. "Was he acting normal? Was his hair wet or perhaps his clothes?"

"Not that I recall. He was wearing a baseball cap, so I didn't see his hair. He acted normal, I guess. I didn't take much notice." Brown frowned. "Sorry I can't be more helpful."

Jenna stood. "You've been very helpful. Thank you." She walked to the security guard. "When Stein returns, we'll be ready for Jones."

Out in the hallway she went to Kane's side and looked at Stein. She hoped that in her absence Kane had gotten more information from him. "Do you remember taking a walk on Tuesday night after studying with Paul?"

"Not really." Stein stared into space. "Oh yeah, I came out of the library and turned toward the stadium. I'm not sure where I went. I had a lot on my mind."

"Did you speak to anyone or see anyone who could verify your whereabouts?" Kane narrowed his gaze. "Don't you think it's a little suspicious that a person you had a problem with died on campus and you don't have an alibi?"

"I'd say I'm not the only person who had a beef with those guys." Stein stared back at Kane, nonplussed. "Or who can't prove where they were on campus at the time they died. My friend just committed suicide and I can't stop thinking about her dying alone. It's eating me up inside. So, no, I don't remember seeing anyone. If that's not good enough, arrest me for whatever you figure I've done, and we'll let my lawyer sort it out."

Jenna nodded. "Okay, that's all for now. Thank you for your time."

She waited for Stein to make his way back inside the library. "The guard is finding Jones for us now. What do you think?"

"He's got motive and you can see how disturbed he is about Chrissie's death." Kane leaned one shoulder against the wall. "Problem is we haven't got much to go on. I looked at his fingers: his nails are short and he has large hands. If both men will let Wolfe make a casting of their hands, he could match them against the marks on Devon's ankles."

"It would be a long shot and I'm not sure if it's admissible in court. Even bite marks are inadmissible now." Jenna nodded. "Just a minute, I'll catch up with Stein and ask him. If he's got nothing to hide, he'll cooperate." She pushed through the library door.

It took a few seconds to catch up to Stein. She beckoned him away from the other students and kept her voice to a whisper. "Would you be willing to give the medical examiner an imprint of your fingers?"

"Why?" Stein frowned down at her.

Jenna lifted her chin. "To remove you from my list of possible suspects in a homicide."

"You saying someone murdered Chrissie?" His eyes darkened. "I loved her. I'd never hurt her."

"No, not Chrissie." Jenna had no choice but to reveal Wolfe's findings. "The ME has reason to believe someone was involved in Pete Devon's death."

"Involved how?" Stein's eyes narrowed.

Jenna straightened and stared him straight in the eyes. "It's an ongoing investigation."

"Okay." Stein shrugged. "I'll give you my number—call me and set a time." He bent over to look deep into her eyes. "Trust me, if I'd wanted to kill Pete, I'd have picked something more painful. Drowning would've been too easy for that SOB."

Unsettled by his encroachment into her private space, she took down his number and stepped away. "Thank you for your time."

She hurried back to the hallway. Jones was already with Kane. His face showed the aftereffects of the fight on the mountain trail and his fall into the rapids. She moved closer to listen.

"No, I don't like Coach." Jones shook his head. "All he thinks about is winning. He doesn't consider the health of the players. Take Pete Devon, for example. Instead of making him do laps in the pool every night, he should've gotten him to the physio for ultrasound treatment. The man is a sadist." He indicated to his face. "Look at me, I had a possible concussion after the trip down the rapids and he still had me out training. The man's an idiot."

"So, you were aware Devon would be at the pool?" Kane made notes and acted as if speaking to him was a chore. "Did you see him there, the night he died?"

"Nope." Jones lifted his gaze to Jenna. "Ma'am. You wanted to speak with me?"

Jenna waved a hand toward the garden. "Would you prefer to speak outside?"

"Here's just fine." Jones rolled his muscular shoulders. "Who's made a complaint against me this time? Lyons again?"

Jenna took in his arrogant pose and self-assured stance. "I haven't received any complaints, Mr. Jones." She unfolded her notebook. "You were speaking about Pete Devon when I arrived. When did you last see him?"

"At the rapids." Jones grimaced. "We don't move in the same circles. I'm studying engineering and let's say his ambition doesn't go to great heights."

"I see." Jenna glanced at his hands. "Would you be willing to have an impression made of your fingers by the medical examiner?"

She looked up at him. "We're using the information to clear people who knew Devon from his possible homicide."

"Sure." Jones chuckled. "I wouldn't have drowned him. I'd have strangled the lying piece of crap." His expression turned to grim as he looked at her. "Him and the rest of Lyons' followers."

"Really?" Kane straightened from leaning against the wall. "We've two potential homicides and you've admitted before two law officers to wanting to kill them. Do we assume this is an admission of guilt?"

"Nope." Jones frowned. "It's a statement of truth. In case you've been living in a dream world, it's common knowledge around here that Lyons and his friends have no respect for women." He looked straight at Kane. "I explained the reason to Deputy Kane the last time we spoke and I'm not discussing it again."

Aware that Jones's anger was escalating at an alarming pace, Jenna lowered her voice to calm him. "Did the fight at the rapids have anything to do with Chrissie Lowe's suicide?"

"Nope." Jones looked away. "Lyons and his friends were making remarks about some of the girls running up there is all." He shrugged. "Things like 'get that fat ass moving' or 'great legs, shame about the face.' I told them to shut up and they took it real personal." He snorted. "I'd have gotten in a few punches but Court had me by the arms." He looked sheepishly at Jenna. "Thanks for helping Deputy Kane to save me."

Jenna nodded. "It's all part of my job." She cleared her throat and took a chance. "So, your martial arts didn't help too much with the three of them?"

"Obviously." Jones pointed to his face. "Dylan Court grabbed me from behind and Devon and Lyons had gotten a couple of punches in before I had time to react. I figure they planned the whole thing."

*So he knows martial arts as well. Interesting.* "Did Lyons push you over the falls?"

"Like I said before, I'm not sure, but one of them did." Jones snorted. "I didn't jump into the rapids for fun."

"That's a shame, we could have charged one of them for attempted murder." Jenna met his angry gaze. "Moving on, can you remember where you were between, say, eight thirty and eleven the night Devon died?"

"Hmm. I went for a drive into town, collected some takeout from Aunt Betty's Café. I came back here and studied. The security guard asked me if I wanted the library left open around eleven, I guess. I had training in the morning, so I left and went to my dorm."

He'd mentioned times and places that could be easily checked. Jenna folded her notebook and smiled. "I think that's all for now. If you'll give Deputy Kane your number, we'll be in touch to arrange that impression of your fingers."

"Sure." Jones gave out his details then headed back inside the library.

Jenna sighed. "Hmm, I'm not too sure about him, and Stein really unnerved me before. For a guy who acts gentle, he tried the stand-over tactic with me."

"And Jones is volatile." Kane pushed his notebook inside his pocket. "It will be interesting to see if either of them matches the fingernail marks on Devon's legs. One thing's for sure: they're both strong enough to be the killer of Jacobs and Devon."

Jenna led the way back to the college entrance. "They are both more than capable of killing both men, they both have motives, and neither has a solid alibi for the TOD." She sighed. "We'll see if anyone remembers seeing Jones at Aunt Betty's, but with the visitors in town for the Fall Festival, the chances will be slim."

"As Rowley hasn't called, I'd say he hasn't found any standout enemies of the team or the coach, and no one has called in about Chrissie's missing items." Kane slipped into step beside her. "We need to know if Walters has hunted down the design of Jacobs' ring. It would be a problem if everyone living in Lyons' house owns one."

Jenna frowned. "I'll call Walters and find out. Then we'll talk to Lowe." She glanced at her watch. " It will be getting late by then, so we'll leave Rowley to close up. I figure as we have to drop by Aunt Betty's, we might as well stop for an early dinner."

"That sounds like a plan." Kane grinned at her and rubbed his belly. "Thursday's early-bird special is bison short ribs, mashed potatoes, and buttered carrots."

Jenna couldn't stop smiling at Kane's expression of absolute bliss. "That good, huh?"

"Oh, yeah."

# CHAPTER THIRTY-FOUR

Kane eased his truck into a space behind the feed store and glanced over at Jenna. "I guess we tread easy with this guy as he's just lost a relative."

"You take the lead, I'll take notes." Jenna rubbed her forehead. "I've a headache straight from hell."

"Sure." He slid from behind the wheel and headed toward the back of the store.

The door resembled the entrance to a barn. It had a ramp up into the main store and roll-down shutters over a wide entrance. The smells coming from the feed store had their own unique flavor. He'd recognize a feed store blindfolded by the mixture of hay and pony pellets with a dash of leather. Chaff and hay littered the parking lot, making patterns in the dust as the wind moved them in different directions. All around him, men moved back and forth. The next moment a forklift zoomed down a ramp carrying bales of hay. Soon after a tall man with a buzz cut and dark stubble, wearing blue jeans and a plaid shirt, carried a sack of feed out to a truck and dumped it in the back.

Kane sidestepped a hunting dog curled asleep among the commotion and looked at Jenna. "Busy place."

"Looking for anyone in particular, Sheriff?" Plaid shirt headed toward them.

"Yeah." Jenna looked toward the open space into the store. "Steve Lowe."

"Then you've found him." The young man smiled at Jenna. "Need to change the feed order for your ranch?"

"Not this time." Jenna sighed. "We're sorry for your loss."

"I am too but I figure you've got something else on your mind." Lowe flicked a glance at Kane. "What else has happened? Is it Jack?"

Kane stepped forward. "No, his status is still unchanged. We came to ask you a few questions about Chrissie. Is there anywhere private we can talk?"

"There's a room out back." Lowe headed up the ramp, past the sacks of various feeds, salt licks, and barrels of molasses, to a room. "In here. We use it for breaks."

Kane followed him inside with Jenna on his heels. The room was sparse, containing a table with chairs, a refrigerator, a coffee pot on a bench, and a sink.

"Okay, what's the problem?" Lowe leaned against the bench and turned to look at them with a worried expression.

Kane pulled out a chair. "Why don't we take a seat?"

"Sure." Lowe glanced at the door. "But can we make this quick? My grandpa will be back soon and he don't like unofficial breaks."

"Did Chrissie make contact with you the day she died?" Kane waited for a reaction. "Did she send you a message late Saturday night?"

"No, but I did see her on campus on Friday around six." Lowe leaned back in his seat. "She didn't seem suicidal to me."

Kane's interest piqued at the mention of the college. "Why were you on campus?"

"I work here part of the time." Lowe raised an eyebrow. "I attend classes at the college and take a few night classes as well. Where's this heading?"

Kane smiled. "It's just routine questions. We're looking for witnesses on certain days. When are you usually at the college and at what times?"

"Most mornings, and I take night classes three times a week: Monday, Tuesday, and Friday. I'm studying business management. I'm planning on taking over the store when my grandpa retires." Lowe drummed his fingertips on the table in an agitated manner. "I usually have dinner at the cafeteria to catch up with friends. Classes go to about eight thirty."

The timeframe fit but the man before him had volunteered the information a little too easily. "You always leave around eight thirty?"

"No." Lowe spread his hands. "There are some nice girls in my classes; sometimes I stay later and we have coffee and chat."

"I see." Kane nodded. "Did you use the gym or pool this week?"

"Nope." Lowe glanced at Jenna and then moved his gaze back to Kane. "I'm lifting heavy weights most days, and I'm usually tuckered out by then."

Kane noted the man's well-muscled frame. He was the third man they'd interviewed who was well capable of killing Jacobs and Devon. "Do you know Alex Jacobs or Pete Devon?"

"I know who they are but they're no friends of mine." Lowe snorted. "Their friends are all from money."

"Did you see them at all on campus, Monday or Tuesday evening?"

"Maybe. On Monday, some of the team got off a bus as I walked past. Those two should've been with them but I couldn't swear to it." Lowe sighed. "Tuesday, I don't recall seeing them."

Kane noted the repressed agitation coming from this man. He needed a few more answers. "Were you in the vicinity of the pool and gym on Monday or Tuesday evening?"

"Yeah. I walk past there to get to my truck." Lowe narrowed his eyes to near slits. "What is all this about?"

Sometimes bluffing a suspect worked wonders. Kane cleared his throat. "We're trying to identify the people on the CCTV footage collected on the night Alex Jacobs accidentally died as we need to establish his time of death. We're speaking to people who may have seen him arrive at the building."

"I see." Lowe shrugged. "I don't remember seeing either of those football players. Or anyone in particular."

"Do you remember the names of the girls you had coffee with on those nights?" Kane rested his hands flat on the table. "They might recall what time you went back to your vehicle."

"Yeah, one girl, Stella." Lowe pulled out his cellphone. "I'll give you her number and you can call her." He read out the number and Jenna took it down then stood and walked out of the room.

Kane needed to know one more thing. "Do you know the name of the man Chrissie was meeting the night she died?"

"Yeah." Lowe grimaced. "Seth Lyons, the Teflon quarterback. If he's the one who raped her, you'll never make it stick. His father will buy him out of trouble, same as all those dogs living in the house on Pine."

Kane pushed to his feet. "No one is above the law. If Lyons is responsible for raping Chrissie, we'll charge him."

"Good luck with that." Lowe stood. "Are we done here? I've gotta get back to work."

"Yeah, for now." Kane handed him his card. "If you remember anything that might assist us in chasing down the men who hurt Chrissie, give me a call."

"Sure." Lowe pushed the card into his top pocket.

Kane headed for the door and met Jenna outside at his truck. "Did you call Stella?"

"Yeah, and she says Lowe left around nine, nine thirty, which puts him in the vicinity of both crime scenes around the time the CCTV cameras went out." She sighed. "Three suspects and not one solid shred of evidence to pin a murder on any of them."

Kane opened the door of his truck. "Then we'll have to look harder."

"I figure we need to expand our net and look closer to home." Jenna stared into the distance, thinking. "Maybe start looking at the guys living in the house. We don't know what happens behind closed doors. A students' hall like Lyons runs has rules, and breaking the rules has repercussions. We know he encourages rape, so maybe he uses murder as a punishment as well."

# CHAPTER THIRTY-FIVE

As he climbed out of his vehicle and ran up the steps of Lyons' house, the mingled smells of beer and weed drifted out the door like a living entity, catching the slight breeze and whisking away. A cold chill raised the hairs on his arms as if the ghosts of Jacobs and Devon had passed straight through him. He raised his voice so Court could hear him over the loud music. "Don't wander off. I have something to show you."

"Sure." Court barked a laugh. "I'm not going anywhere but I have to go down to the cellar later."

"Okay." He shrugged.

He peered around Court's large frame, scanning the immediate area. The lights inside were dim and guys stood in twos or threes talking. He figured that maybe ten or twelve people had showed.

"Were you expecting someone?"

"Yeah." Court's mouth turned down. "It looks like the freshman I asked to come by is a no-show. Dammit, we need something to take our minds off what's happened."

"I might be able to ease your pain a little when I show you what I have." He motioned to a quiet corner and they moved away. "Not everything happens here."

He glanced over Court's shoulder to see Webber deep in conversation with Josh Stevens. He opened one hand to display a couple of loaded syringes. "I'll need to hide these." He pushed the drugs back inside his jacket pocket and then took out his cellphone and wiggled it in front of Court's eyes. "This girl is real hot." He wet his lips. "Last week, Alex and me took her out to an old barn and tied her down—but if you're too squeamish…"

"You tied her down?" Court's expression turned from worried to interested. "Okay, give me a taste."

Dropping his voice and moving closer, he opened the file and then glanced around. "This vid will blow your mind but it's real noisy." He waved a hand at the others in the room. "I'm not showing this to everyone—not yet anyway. I'll come and find you in a bit."

"Sure."

# CHAPTER THIRTY-SIX

Colt Webber turned to face the door, leaned his back against the wall beside the fireplace, and listened to Josh Stevens talking about his truck. The moment Lyons walked into the room, Stevens melted into the crowd and Lyons took his place as if they'd planned to keep him in their sights all night. The thought unnerved him; if Lyons took it into his head to drag him into the cellar and murder him, he wouldn't stand a chance. With effort, he kept his expression neutral as Lyons went on and on about the trillion games he'd played and won because he was so great. In truth, Lyons did have talent as a college quarterback, but to make it to the big time was something his daddy couldn't buy for him. He wondered how many other budding quarterbacks had sat on the bench for years hoping Seth Lyons would break a leg.

"Why are you staring at the door?" Lyons turned and followed Colt's line of sight and then turned back. "Waiting for someone? Ah, don't tell me, you invited Emily along?"

"Nah, but I hoped you'd have lived up to your reputation and organized some entertainment." Colt snorted. "Emily wouldn't come. She finishes classes and then jogs every afternoon before heading home. Apparently she lost her mom some time ago and helps with the other kids."

"Hmm, shame, but she must get some downtime." Lyons puffed out a sigh. "I haven't gotten close enough to speak to her yet but I'm working on it." He grinned. "I'm inclined to meet up with her this Friday."

Colt's stomach cramped at the idea of him alone in the forest with Emily. "I think you're wasting your time. I tried to get close but she shut me down. She made it clear she's not interested in getting involved with anyone until she's through college."

"Well, she hasn't come up against the Lyons charm yet. Actually, Dylan planned some entertainment for tonight but the girl he invited is a no-show. I gather she insisted on driving herself too, which is another strike against him. He should know better, but I guess he didn't have a choice." Lyons shook his head. "I like to get one of the guys to give them a ride here. Then they get offered a drink along the way, and by the time they arrive, they're starting to mellow." He rolled his shoulders. "I don't have time to sweet-talk them. They know why I've asked them here."

Colt frowned. "Do they? You only invite them here for sex?"

"Yeah." Lyons sipped his beer. "I have a girl back home, we're engaged. When we marry, we'll join two companies together."

Colt had no idea such archaic practices happened anymore. "You mean it's an arranged marriage?"

"Kinda." Lyons shrugged. "I don't love her if that's what you mean, but she's old money. She looks okay and I'll have my own life. Once she produces a couple of heirs, she can take a lover if she wants. We've discussed everything and she's down with it."

"Nice deal." Colt grinned. "One of the benefits of being on the football team is the women. Man, I got laid nightly the last time I played, and I've really missed being on the team. We knew how to party, if you know what I mean?" He scanned the room again, noticing Court ushering a guy through a door at the end of the hallway.

"I figure we do too." Lyons tipped his head to one side as if examining him. "But most guys are just talk." He snorted. "Are you just talk, Colt?"

"Need proof, huh?" Colt pulled out his cellphone, glad Kane had moved a few confiscated images from past crimes into his files. He waved his screen in front of Lyons' eyes then pulled it back. "Still figure I'm talking shit?"

"I somehow knew you and I would fit together." Lyons smiled. "You're what we need on the team—a man after my own heart."

Colt continued the talk about women with Lyons to discover if Lyons and his friends could be the serial rapists who'd attacked Chrissie Lowe. Phrasing his questions without causing suspicion wouldn't be easy. He dove in, hoping he hadn't pushed his luck too far. "I can't believe I came this close to sharing the girl you invited last week." He held his thumb and forefinger an inch apart.

"There'll be more." Lyons shrugged. "I'll ask the guys if they want you to join in. We'll need to be careful." He gave him a long look. "Everything that happens here stays here."

Colt frowned. "The women agree to party, don't they?"

"You've never heard a complaint, have you?" A slow smile crept over Lyons' face. "Yeah, they like to party with us and come back for more. The freshmen in particular come across all sweet and innocent, and once they have a few drinks they turn into nymphomaniacs. The guys are more than happy to oblige."

Colt took a long drink then met Lyons' gaze. "They also tend to change their minds once they're sober. It's hard to believe none of them have complained."

"That's because I have insurance." Lyons chuckled and pulled a cellphone out of his pocket. Colt noticed it was a cheap burner and not the one he usually carried. "I'll show you a few images but we have a library of these and they're well-hidden. No one could find them, and if anyone went to the cops and complained, I have a few cut versions to show them. The way I've edited them, they prove the girls were into everything we did to them." He opened the file and passed him the cellphone. "Take a look for yourself."

A wave of disgust hit him like a tsunami at the sight of Chrissie Lowe in indecent poses. He zoomed in on her face. Her hooded eyelids hadn't disguised her huge, dilated pupils and the blank, slack expression told him she was barely conscious if at all. He kept his eyes lowered as if taking in the images and tried to control his rage. He'd blow his cover for sure if he wasn't careful. How he handled his response now was crucial to catching this SOB. He took a deep breath and let it out slowly. "Oh man, this is hot. Ever had two at the same time?" He forced a chuckle. "Now that would be fun."

"Oh yeah, and we've got videos too." It was a boast and now Lyons' eyes were dancing with delight. "Although watching reruns is a turn-on, it's nothing like being there."

Colt went in for the kill. "When's the next party?"

"Hmm." Lyons shrugged. "I'm not sure, maybe Saturday. The guys need to come down from the game. I'll see what I can arrange but I'm going to have Emily one way or another. I can't resist a challenge and I always win." He gave him a long look. "If you want to earn your way into our group, you'll have to hook up with a girl after the game. If the guys know you've supplied one of them, they'll agree to you joining us." His mouth raised at the corners. "Look, I'll make it easy for you. If we work together, the girls won't be able to resist, and they'll believe there's safety in numbers. Don't worry, the guys can easily handle three at once."

*Woah, this plan is going way too fast.* Colt frowned. "Sure, but three, isn't that risky?"

"Nah." Lyons chuckled. "Don't worry, the moment the jet hits their systems, they'll be demanding to get laid."

Colt wished he'd been wearing a wire. The confession that Lyons used a date-rape drug on his victims was all the proof he needed.

*Dammit, everything he says to me is hearsay.* He'd recognized the street name for ketamine, a date-rape drug, and forced a smile. "Count me in."

"We'll see, my eager friend." Lyons chuckled. "Wait here and chat with some of the guys." He motioned to a group of men chatting close by. "I need to use the john." He strolled toward the hallway.

Surrounded, Colt had the weirdest sensation of drowning. The men's faces all had the same suspicious expression and looked at him, saying nothing as if he'd become the enemy. It was obvious Lyons didn't fully trust him yet if he had to run his presence past his boys. He glanced casually at his tracker ring and calculated how fast backup would arrive if they decided to kill him. *Not fast enough.*

# CHAPTER THIRTY-SEVEN

Dylan Court used his key to open the door to the cellar. He glanced around, making sure no one had followed them. "I'll get the light. I need to stash my flash drive in the safe." He stepped inside the room and flicked the switch to turn on the lights.

"Something I gotta know." His friend paused in the doorway. "Where else have you been keeping your copies?"

"Nowhere, only in the safe." Court's gaze slid around the room. Big, comfortable sofas surrounded a gigantic flat-screen, and it seemed every time he came down here he found another luxury. The fully stocked bar and coffee machine were new additions to their special room. He walked toward a framed picture of the team, pressed a button hidden under the mantel, and the picture flipped back to reveal a safe. "See, I'll lock it away, safe and sound. I just needed to add a few things."

"That's good." His friend pulled out his cellphone and offered Court a few seconds of video. "This is what I have—like it?"

Court had never seen anything so professional filmed on a phone. "Man, that's almost porno quality." He looked into his friend's eyes. "Can we put it up on the screen?"

"Later. I want to see what you're hiding on your flash drive first." His gaze became intense. "Give me a look." He waved his cell. "And I'll download a copy of this right now, for your personal collection."

Unable to resist the chance to see the rest of the footage, Court dove into the safe and found his flash drive. He led the way to a desk at the back of the room, booted up the computer, entered his password, and then inserted the drive. "There, now can I see the damn video?"

"Thanks, I'll transfer the files now." His friend smiled at him. "It will give you something to do while I look at these."

Moments later, Court's cellphone chimed with a message. He waited for the file to download then dropped onto the sofa to play the files. Engrossed, he didn't notice his friend until the sofa dipped as he sat beside him. He paused the clip, slightly annoyed at being disturbed, turned, and looked straight into the muzzle of a gun. "W-what the heck?"

"Push up your sleeve, the left one." His friend's expression had hardened to granite. "That's right. Now take the rubber tubing and tie it around your arm. I wanna see those veins popping. Then use the syringe." He nudged him with the cold muzzle of the gun. "You know how to do it, don't you, Dylan?"

Court stared at the two syringes. "What is it?"

"Something just for you." The man's lips curled in a sinister smile. "You'll enjoy the ride. You should thank me." He jammed the muzzle harder into Court's temple. "Hurry up, I don't have much time."

Panic made his hands shake but he took the rubber tubing, tied it around his arm using his teeth to assist him, and then pulled it tight. "You know this will show up on a drug test? I'll be off the team for sure." Court pressed the needle into his vein. "Is that what you want?"

"Yeah." His voice had become a low growl. "Do it."

The moment the drug hit his vein, Court became drowsy. It was a good feeling, like floating away. He could deal with being high. It wasn't the first time. At least he wouldn't remember much about his ordeal, and he'd been smart and only squeezed a small amount into his arm. He'd be awake in an hour or so, and once he told Seth what had happened, they'd make this SOB pay for what he'd done. The next moment, leather-covered fingers closed around his hand and a rush of cold liquid shot up inside his arm. The high dose would kill him if he didn't get help. Sheer terror had him by the throat. *I'm going to die.*

Disoriented and trembling, he forced his heavy eyelids open and stared at the syringe hanging out of his arm. His friend was loosening the rubber band but hadn't removed it and watched him with dark, stone-cold eyes. He wanted to say something, plead for his life, but his mouth went slack and he couldn't speak. His heart pounded and then slowed, missing beats as if fighting to pump the blood through his veins. Sweat poured into his eyes, stinging but not for long. As he slipped into oblivion, he heard him emptying the safe. The room plunged into darkness and the last sound he made out was the door clicking shut as his killer left him alone to die.

# CHAPTER THIRTY-EIGHT

## Friday

It was going to be one of those days. Jenna could feel it in her bones. Dashing to the office without stopping for breakfast was affecting her thought processes. She stared at the whiteboard and shook her head. They had made little headway on any of the cases and the reports she'd ordered had not arrived. When Rowley knocked on her office door, she waved him in. "Have you found anything we can use?"

"Not specifically, no, I'm afraid, ma'am." Rowley dashed a hand through his unruly curls and sighed. "Seems just about every man and his dog has a beef against the college football coach. He has a string of complaints against him from other teams, and players who he benched over the years are all out for his blood."

Baffled by Rowley's information, she cleared her throat. "How the heck does he keep his job?"

"I guess because every team he coaches wins." Rowley frowned. "It's all about reputation, ma'am. The college holds football in the highest esteem. You see, Black Rock Falls is one of the first places the scouts come looking for suitable players for the NFL." He smiled at her. "That's why we get kids from all over wanting to join the team."

Jenna nodded. "Okay, so we could have a disgruntled parent, ex-player, or any number of people intent on destroying the team?" She sighed at Rowley's apologetic shrug. "No one in particular? Or have there been any recent threats?"

"Yeah but I spent most of last night and this morning chasing down everyone involved and none of them came anywhere near here around the time Jacobs or Devon died. Another thing: Wolfe called and said the casts of the suspects' hands were inconclusive. He couldn't prove either of the suspects' nails made the marks on Devon's ankles." Rowley met her gaze. "I've more bad news."

Jenna's stomach dropped. "Okay, give it to me."

"Walters chased down the design of Jacobs' ring." Rowley frowned. "The team made it to the National Championships last year and all the players on the team have one." He frowned. "Which means every resident of Lyons' house, with the exception of the guy with epilepsy. He's the brother of Seth Lyons' fiancée, so he lives in the house."

Astonished, Jenna stared at him. "Lyons has a fiancée?"

"Seems so." Rowley shook his head. "Not for long, I guess, once she finds out what he's been doing."

"Unless she plans on visiting him in jail." Jenna rolled her eyes. "I hope Kane has found something or we're back to square one."

"Did I hear my name?" Kane hung in the open doorway, hands on both sides of the doorframe, his jacket hanging open like the wings of a bat.

Jenna smiled at him. "You did. Have you checked Jones's alibi?"

"Yeah." Kane nudged Duke into the room. "Give me a second, I've left some takeout in the truck." He glanced at Rowley. "Wanna give me a hand?"

"Sure." Rowley followed him out the door.

Jenna stared after them. She somehow knew Kane would come back from Aunt Betty's Café laden with food for breakfast. A few moments later, they reappeared carrying takeout bags and go-cups of coffee. "Okay, sit down and tell me what you've found."

"Jones was in the library, and since Aunt Betty's installed a CCTV system, I was able to look over the tapes. He did drop by for a burger

at eight thirty, but I spoke to college security, and they have him
scanned back in the library at ten. He had plenty of time to eat and
then go kill Devon."

Jenna stood and added the information to the whiteboard. "Hmm,
seems all our suspects went missing around the time of Devon's
death." She glanced at Kane. "If Stein went for a walk, would he be
picked up on any other CCTV cameras?"

"Not likely." Rowley frowned. "They're in the parking lot and
around the entrances mainly. You might be able to pinpoint the time
Jones arrived back on campus and when Lowe left."

"Already looked." Kane sipped his coffee. "When Jones arrived at
nine, he walked out of the parking lot and wasn't carrying anything. I
figure he ate his burger in the vehicle. I couldn't pick him up anywhere
near the pool because, as you know, the CCTV cameras were down."
He shrugged. "Lowe left at nine fifty, so he had time as well."

"Okay, so Jones arrived back at nine and wasn't seen again
until ten at the library. From the scanner records, Stein and Jones
arrived at the library at ten. How strange." Jenna shot a glance at
Kane. "You don't think they're both involved in these accidents,
do you?"

"It's possible." Kane shrugged. "They both have different motives
but could be working together." He put down his cup and frowned.
"One thing about Jacobs' death still bothers me and it's been mentioned before. Both Jones and Stein argued with him recently; sure
as hell Jacobs wouldn't trust either of them to spot him lifting that
amount of weight." He met Jenna's gaze. "Devon, maybe. If they
both jumped in the pool, grabbed a leg each, and hauled him under
the water... but standing over Jacobs when he was that vulnerable?
Nah, no way."

"What about Lowe?" Rowley was scanning the case file. "Does
he use the gym?"

"No, he said his job involves a lot of lifting." Jenna sat down and dropped her head into her hands. She lifted her gaze to her deputies. "Who did Jacobs trust above all others?"

"Lyons." Kane leaned back in his chair. "What if he knew Jacobs had left distinguishing marks on Chrissie? Perhaps we're looking at this all wrong. Maybe Jacobs became a liability."

"And Devon had image files on his burner." Rowley frowned. "If he'd broken the rules, maybe Lyons decided to eliminate him as well."

Jenna looked from one to the other. "So we'll need to find out where Lyons was at the time of both deaths. I figure if he is capable of rape, murder would be second nature to him." She made a note in her daybook and then leaned back in her seat. "We still need more than circumstantial evidence to prove Lyons and his friends were responsible for raping Chrissie. Has anyone heard from Webber? I was expecting a report from him by now."

"He was heading out to the house last night." Kane reached in a bag for a sandwich. "They had a wake for Jacobs and Devon. Maybe he stayed over, and he'd be training this morning. I doubt he'd have found any alone time to contact us. He wouldn't risk sending a message in case Lyons got suspicious and checked his phone." He blinked then stared at Jenna. "See if he logged into the files last night."

After scanning the files and finding an entry Webber had made in the early hours of the morning, Jenna's heart pounded. She read the report aloud and looked up at her deputies. "Webber is close to getting the proof we need. I agree with him: Lyons having the images is one thing, but if they don't prove he or any of the others are involved in Chrissie's rape, they're useless. We can't prove when they took the images, so it won't hold up in court. It's not a crime to have explicit images of women over the age of eighteen." She turned to Kane. "Nice touch adding those files to Webber's phone. It seems like he needed them. I don't envy him. He is taking one hell of a risk."

"I was just covering all the bases." Kane rubbed his chin. "If Lyons is a killer, he won't think twice about taking him out." The nerve in his cheek twitched and his agitation was palpable. "As Lyons has Emily in his sights, it's going to make life difficult if we have to watch out for her as well. Webber is going to be in trouble if Lyons expects him to procure girls for their party and participate."

Jenna shook her head. "That is so not gonna happen." She drummed her fingers on the desk. "We could raid the party for drugs. Surely Webber will give us a heads up if he discovers how Lyons is administering them."

"We know how." Kane frowned. "They slip something into their drinks. Pinning it on one person would be difficult, especially if they have a punch bowl, for instance."

"Do people make punch anymore?" Rowley pulled a face. "Maybe ten years ago but not now."

Jenna rubbed her temples. "Seems to me we have to be at the game on Saturday, and I suggest we have eyes on Emily as well. She runs each afternoon around four; we'll make sure we have someone in the area just in case she has any problems with Lyons."

Jenna's cellphone chimed and she looked at the caller ID before answering the call. "Morning, Shane. How are you?"

She listened and then put the phone on speaker. "Okay, you're on speaker, and Kane and Rowley are here."

*"A cleaner, Doris Beachwood, at Lyons' house called the paramedics around eight thirty this morning. She found the body of a man, since identi-fied as Dylan Court, in the cellar. Before you ask, the cellar is more of a man cave, big-screen TV with a theatre-type set up. It looks like they like their privacy—I noticed some porn DVDs beside the TV."* Wolfe paused a beat. *"The paramedic who called said Court was DOA—possible drug overdose."*

A shiver of dread ran up Jenna's back. Kane had drug-tested all the men living at the house and they'd all come up clean; and after the fiasco with Owen Jones, the coach had implemented random drug testing. "He wasn't a user. Kane drug-tested them all the night we found Jacobs."

*"Yeah, well, a couple of things don't look right about the scene either. You should come and take a look before I move the body. This man was sharing a room with Pete Devon."* Wolfe cleared his throat. *"I'm not convinced this is an accidental overdose. Apart from the cleaner and the paramedics, no one else but me has been in the room. Seth Lyons is on his way, and I called in Webber to make everything appear normal. I'll explain my concerns when you arrive; I could be overheard here."*

Jenna exchanged a worried look with Kane. "We're on our way." She disconnected and stood. "Rowley, find out what you can about Dylan Court. I'll need his next of kin and if he had any prior drug problems."

"What about Emily?" Rowley got to his feet. "It's usual for Wolfe to call her in to assist at a scene, and I figure we're just handing her to Lyons if she's there."

"No doubt. I'll call him and make sure she doesn't show." Jenna waited a beat to think. She had so many things to juggle and so few deputies. "Ah, and if you have any trouble with the rodeo crowd in town, call Walters in to run the place while we're all out on a call. I've asked the Blackwater sheriff to send over more deputies to handle the crowd at the showgrounds over the next few days, so they'll have things under control while we're busy with our caseload." Jenna shrugged into her jacket and then headed for the door. "Okay, Kane, you're with me."

# CHAPTER THIRTY-NINE

Kane sidestepped a couple of kids on skateboards flying along the sidewalk and followed Jenna to his truck. People milled around town dressed in fringed shirts and cowboy hats; they seemed to go all-out when the rodeo came to town. He glanced up, catching sight of a red balloon trailing its string as it escaped above the trees on an updraft of wind. As he pulled open the door to his truck, the tempting aroma of hot dogs and onions drifted from one of the street vendors. At his feet, Duke lifted his nose in the air and whined. He lifted him into the back seat of his truck and strapped him in. "I'll buy you one when we get back."

"You'll buy me what?" Jenna climbed in and clicked in her seatbelt.

Kane slid behind the wheel and started the engine. "A hot dog for Duke. I figure he's becoming addicted to them."

"They can't be good for him." Jenna frowned and glanced over at the dog. "You spoil him."

Kane backed out and turned his truck toward Stanton Road. "Nah, he's good. I only give him the sausage to eat."

"Well, I figure it's just another excuse for you to eat." Jenna chuckled. "You're a bottomless pit."

Kane smiled at her. "I've never been called that before. Annie used to say I was like a teddy bear." Memories of his dead wife flooded over him. "With my stomach growling and all."

"She's still with you, isn't she?" Jenna stared straight ahead. "My folks sure are. I think about them all the time."

Annie's smiling face drifted into his mind but the scent of her had vanished, and her soft laughter no longer tormented his dreams. He closed his fingers around Jenna's hand and squeezed gently. "She'll always be a part of me, Jenna, and I'm trying to move on but it's difficult."

When a slight tremor went through her, he glanced at her, meeting her gaze and seeing a dampness in her eyes. He had to force his concentration back to the road and dropped her hand to grip the wheel. She'd been very patient with him and never demanded any type of commitment. Yet he figured she wanted more and was allowing him time to grieve his wife. Hell, she was his best friend and he cared for her. "Jenna, I guess I shouldn't talk so much about Annie."

"No, don't ever think that, Dave." Jenna cleared her throat. "It's good you trust me with your past." She turned in her seat to peer at him. "You play your cards very close to your vest."

Unsure of what to say, he smiled. "After my injury, you told me we'd take it one day at a time. I know you don't want to get burned, Jenna."

"You don't know too much about fire, do you?" Jenna snorted a laugh. "A slow burn can turn into a wildfire without warning."

"It sure can." He smiled and turned onto the driveway. He ignored the no-entry sign and took the direct way to the front door. "And as much as I'd like to discuss this topic further, I figure we'd better put our game faces on."

"Yeah, but with people getting murdered around us all the time, we need to step away for a few minutes and think about something nice or we'd lose it." Jenna sighed. "Then we'd have to quit and join the rest of the crazies off the grid."

"Yeah, but I figure I could handle complete isolation. Fishing, hunting, and sleeping rough." Kane nodded in agreement and parked beside Wolfe's van.

"Maybe not the sleeping rough bit... You can sleep rough if you like but I want a nice log cabin in the woods, with power and internet." Jenna giggled. "I'd post no-trespassing signs and people would leave me alone."

"Uh-huh." Kane turned to look at her and smiled. "Or maybe we should stay here with all our friends and take another vacation—Hawaii next time?"

When Wolfe appeared on the porch and waved them inside, Kane took in his serious expression and all thoughts of another vacation with Jenna evaporated. He turned to Jenna and frowned. "He doesn't look too happy."

"Let's hope this isn't a homicide." Jenna slid from the truck and headed toward the house.

Kane hurried up the steps with Duke at his heels. Inside, a middle-aged woman sat on the sofa in the family room drinking a glass of water. Seth Lyons and Colt Webber stood talking to Wolfe, who was making notes. Jenna stood beside Wolfe, notebook in hand. Kane walked to her side and listened to the conversation.

"When was the last time you saw Dylan alive?" Wolfe stared at Lyons with a strange intensity.

"I'm not sure, last night sometime, maybe around eight, I'm not sure." Lyons turned to Webber. "I was talking to Colt for most of the evening, well until late, and I headed to bed around one thirty, I guess."

"Webber will be assisting me with the autopsy. You *do* know he's one of my interns?" Wolfe moved his attention away from Lyons and looked at Webber. "Unless, of course, you're one of Dylan's friends?"

"I've seen him at practice but, no, I'm not one of his friends. I'll be there, sir." Webber's gaze slid to Kane then back to Wolfe. "I noticed him last night. He was heading down to what I now know is the cellar. I'm not sure of the time. He was with another man but I didn't get a look at his face. He had a hoodie pulled up over a baseball cap and I only saw him in profile. He was about my height. Broad shoulders. That's about all I noticed. He could've been any one of the guys on the team."

"I'll want a list of everyone at the party." Jenna handed her notebook and pen to Lyons. "Did you invite anyone new?"

"Nope, only Colt, and he was with me most of the evening." Lyons narrowed his gaze. "Why?"

"I want a list while it's fresh in your mind, just in case we need to speak to them later." Jenna frowned. "Was Dylan a habitual drug taker?"

"Heck no!" Lyons shook his head. "We're tested regularly and he'd never do anything so stupid. He's not that kind of guy."

Kane moved his attention from one man to the other and acted as if Webber was a complete stranger. "So, this guy you claimed you saw could've been a dealer? Maybe after losing his roommate, Dylan needed something to get him over the shock. Losing two friends in a week can push people over the edge."

"I don't know anyone dealing drugs, sir." Webber raised one eyebrow then turned to Lyons. "Do you?"

"If I did, I wouldn't be stupid enough to rat them out to the cops." Lyons snorted. "Getting my legs broken or worse wouldn't be a good career move."

"Why didn't you check the cellar when Dylan went missing?" Kane stared at Lyons.

"I didn't know he'd gone missing until Mr. Wolfe called me. Look, man, things happen, people die. It's life. No good getting all tied up in knots about it." Lyons shrugged as if he was used to losing his friends. "We're adults. We don't have to check in and out or be home for dinner."

"What else have you got for me, Wolfe?" Jenna looked up at him.

"I've taken a statement from the cleaner; she found the body. She has a key to the cellar and said it's usually locked but she found it unlocked this morning. I'll email you a copy." Wolfe tapped away on the device in his hand. "I figure she's in shock. Her husband is coming to collect her soon."

"Okay." Jenna's cellphone signaled a message. "Show me the body." She turned to Lyons. "Stay here and work on that list. I may have questions for you later."

"Webber, come with me. I'll explain the procedure for this type of situation." Wolfe led the way down the hallway to the open door to the cellar.

Kane followed and, once inside, turned and locked the door behind them. He needed to speak to Webber without Lyons walking in on their conversation. Beside him, Duke let out a mournful howl that made the hairs on Kane's arms prickle, and as he moved down the steps, the unmistakable smell of decomposition wafted toward him. At the bottom of the stairs, he instructed Duke to sit then pulled out his scanner, attached the earbuds, and swept the room for cameras or a listening device. He made a grid in his mind, taking in every possible aspect. "It's clean."

He glanced around the room. A vacuum cleaner lay on the edge of the rug, no doubt discarded when Doris Beachwood spotted the discolored face and empty, staring eyes of the corpse. Taking in the scene, he noticed a picture hanging on the wall was askew. He pulled on latex gloves and looked behind it to find an empty safe with an unlocked door. For a bunch of messy guys, this room was out of place, much like Lyons' bedroom, which made him suspicious. He looked closer but found no signs of a struggle. It was tidy and the rugs hadn't been disturbed. He moved to Jenna's side and pointed to the safe. "We might have a motive."

"Yeah, I spotted that too. It was wide open when I came down. I took some photos and then pushed it shut to get past. It's been cleaned out." Wolfe walked to his side. "So, we could assume Court brought someone down here to show him something in the safe. The person waited for him to shoot up, took the contents, and left. If he was a dealer, and decided to rob him, maybe he killed him to hide his identity."

"Killed him?" Jenna moved closer to the body and shrugged. "What makes you think this is a homicide?"

"This." Wolfe carefully turned the victim's head to show her his cheek. "That could be the mark from a gun muzzle." He laid Court's head down respectfully and looked at her. "It's possible someone held a weapon to his head and made him shoot up."

"Or it's a mark from his helmet after a hard tackle." Kane scratched his cheek. "I wonder what was in the safe." He dropped his kit on the carpet. "I guess I'd better dust for prints."

"Don't bother." Wolfe pointed to a slight mark on Court's thumb. "See that? Looks like a pressure mark; it's got a slight ridge to it, like the stitching on a leather glove."

"I figure we can place the time of death between around ten and twelve last night." Webber peered at the body. "That's when I saw him head this way with the guy I mentioned before; problem is I didn't see him leave. I was too interested in what Lyons was saying and showing me." His expression darkened. "He is one sick puppy."

"I thought he was the organizer all along." Jenna shook her head. "We'll need that phone." She frowned. "Did he leave you at any time during the evening?"

"Yeah, when he went to the bathroom." Webber cleared his throat. "I went to the bathroom as well during my time here, so I wasn't watching him the entire time."

"How long was he gone?" Jenna lifted her chin. "Long enough to kill Court?"

"Yeah, I guess." Webber shrugged. "I couldn't swear in court how long. I figured he had his boys surround me to keep me in line. I had concerns they might cause trouble."

"Okay, I want details of what was said between you." Jenna narrowed her gaze. "Don't leave anything out."

Disgust and anger dropped over Kane as Webber gave them a rundown of the conversation he'd had with Lyons the previous night. "If you couldn't make out anyone else with her in the pictures, he's smart enough to crop the images he shares. For sure, he won't be carrying the burner on him."

"I don't figure he cropped the images I saw of Chrissie Lowe." Webber rubbed his chin. "They were erotic poses, possibly after the rape, but I could see her eyes. She had dilated pupils even though the room was bright. I figure she was heavily sedated."

"Can you think of anything else he said?" Jenna looked at him with interest. "Anything else about the images?"

"Yeah, I can." Webber flicked a glance to the open safe. "He mentioned they had a ton of uncut images and video files locked away."

Kane exchanged a knowing look with Wolfe. "You thinking what I'm thinking?"

"Yeah." Wolfe frowned. "This takes the supposed accidents to a whole different level."

"How so?" Jenna looked from one to the other.

The pieces of the puzzle seemed to drop into place. Kane met her gaze. "Blackmail. Just as we figured." He waved a hand toward the safe. "Lyons uses the files to prevent the girls he rapes from informing the cops. He has images and videos, and I'd bet that computer over there"—he indicated to a desk set against the wall—"has editing software. He threatens his victims to make sure they'll keep quiet. As sure as hell, he makes them look as if they're willing."

"I'll take a look." Wolfe went to the computer and in seconds had bypassed the password. He scanned the screen and his mouth turned down. "Yeah, he has all the necessary software but no image files. He must delete them after copying them." He turned off the computer and stood.

"So, do you believe it could be one of the rape victims, seeking revenge?" Webber nodded. "Possible, I guess, but I didn't see any women at the party."

"No. We know it was a guy who came down here with Court, and Lyons went missing for long enough." Jenna frowned.

"He seems too obvious a suspect. Say Lyons invites other men to his lurid parties to blackmail them. He's already invited Webber, and I find that suspicious as they've only just met." Wolfe straightened from examining Court's body. "If we assume all the accidents are murders, then the killer had to know the safe contained some of the uncut video versions. He might've cut a deal with Court to get his file. While he was here, he grabbed the evidence and then killed him." He glanced at Jenna. "If this is vengeance, it makes sense for him to take out everyone involved in blackmailing him."

"Yeah." Jenna nodded in agreement. "Revenge would be a solid motive and would account for the almost clean way of killing. Hate kills—where a person has been physically abused, for instance, or humiliated—are usually overkill."

"That idea has credence." Webber rubbed his chin. "The killer likely worked his way down the list until he found someone who would deal with him. Those who didn't, he killed."

Kane allowed the ideas to filter through his mind. "Hmm, makes sense. It's doubtful Lyons would fold and give him the files; he likes to be in control. He's blackmailing for a reason. The men he chooses must have something he can use, or he's using blackmail to keep them under control."

"This theory opens up a can of worms." Wolfe's eyebrows knitted. "It doesn't fit any of our suspects, especially Steve Lowe. The other two are athletes and have prominent families."

Kane shook his head. "I'm not so sure. What we didn't have is a clear motive. How do we know Jones wasn't supplying the drugs to Lyons and came by for a taste of the action?"

"Go on." Jenna stared at him.

"We know Jones was angry about being dropped from the team but being set up could've been Lyons' idea of a lesson, same with the beating he took up near the rapids." Kane glanced at Jenna. "Same with Stein. How do we know Stein wasn't involved in past rapes? Maybe Jones and Stein wanted out. How could Lyons punish both of them? He'd make Stein agree to stand down and say nothing when he invited Chrissie to the party. I figure Lyons may have raped Chrissie as a punishment and a taste of what he was capable of doing."

"It's all possible." Webber sighed. "Stein didn't seem too worried about Chrissie going to the party with Lyons."

Kane nodded. "Yeah, maybe things weren't moving along fast enough for him and he figured he'd be a shoulder to cry on for Chrissie after the party." He cleared his throat. "Seems to me there's a deal of threatening going on after these rape parties. I figure Lyons has everyone under the thumb."

"We'll never arrest anyone at this rate. We've all got different ideas on the suspects and motives." Jenna stared at the open safe. "It's been hours and whoever took the files would've destroyed them by now."

"Unless he tries to take out Lyons in a freak accident." Wolfe's gaze moved over them. "It would tie up loose ends to take out the ringleader."

"Then find out what Lyons' plans are for the next few days." Jenna turned her attention to Webber. "The team doesn't train on

Saturday mornings, do they? So find out where he's planning to be. Sure as hell, the killer will know and go after him."

"I already know some of his movements." Webber crossed his arms over his chest. "He's planning on running this afternoon on the rapids trail. He's been going up there regularly and just about made an announcement in the cafeteria yesterday he's going at four. He told me at the party he plans to follow Emily up the mountain. He figures if he gets her alone, she'll agree to come to a party here tomorrow night. He also figures, if that fails, he'll have time to hit on a couple of girls after the game, but I doubt he'll have any luck. There's the rodeo on Saturday and then the dance. The Fall Festival dance is a big deal, and I figure most girls already have dates."

"If I see that animal near Emily…" Wolfe's expression had turned dangerous. "I'll break him in half."

Although the idea of Emily being in the crossfire angered Kane, he could see an angle they hadn't considered. He moved to Wolfe's side. "Emily knows the deal with Lyons, and if he causes trouble, he won't expect to be coming up against a girl with her level of close combat training." He gave him a long look. "Explain the situation and tell her to run as usual. I'll shadow her with Jenna. I'm betting if the killer isn't Lyons, then he'll know he's heading to the secluded part of the mountain where Emily usually runs. I figure he'll wait for her to pass and then grab Lyons." He shrugged. "It's what I would do, and this guy certainly seems to know everyone's movements, and he plans his kills. He has eyes on his victims so is closer than we think."

"You mean, use my daughter as bait?" Wolfe shook his head. "No way. I'm over my daughters getting mixed up with serial killers."

Kane frowned. "Emily won't be bait for the killer. She'll be the lure to get Lyons alone on the mountain. There's no reason the killer would target her—even if he shows." He stared at Wolfe. "It's a win-win situation. If Lyons makes a move on Emily, we'll have him; if the killer tries to take out Lyons, we'll arrest him." He sighed. "If none of the above happens and Lyons just asks her to the party, then we'll have her on scene with Webber as backup. She knows the score. The moment Lyons offers her a drink, all she has to do is walk out the front door. We'll be right outside, and if the drink contains a date-rape drug, we'll arrest him for Chrissie's rape and anything else we can throw at him. His fingerprints will be on the glass and we'll have Webber as a witness."

"She'll want to do it. She's part of the team now. With both of us as backup, and Rowley and Walters close by, what could possibly go wrong?"

"That's what I'm afraid of." Wolfe's expression resembled the sky just before a storm. "When does anything ever go right in Black Rock Falls?"

# CHAPTER FORTY

He'd spent a leisurely morning sitting under a tree outside the library at the college. He tipped his head back and stared into a cloudless blue sky. A light breeze blew down from the mountains, bringing with it the unmistakable smell of snow. It wouldn't come yet, not for some weeks. He needed the weather to cooperate and not interfere with his plans, and as luck would have it, Mother Nature was still in the last throes of summer and only a few of the signs of fall were evident. It was spectacular this time of year; some might see the bloom of summer fading, but in his eyes, it was a feast of color. The spectrum changed as did the unique smells of an alpine town. The pines would always be there, tall and majestic, but as the green faded from the undergrowth and wood smoke filled the air, it was as if nature had replaced the summer scenery across the forest and grasslands.

The time he'd taken of late to observe human behavior had fascinated him. The students moved from one class to another like ants, all with a purpose, all following their set path, programmed to move, eat, and leave at the sound of a bell. They walked in orderly lines, carrying their media devices and books. It seemed the brainwashing of people to obey anyone in authority came at an early age. Get a group together and ring bells or issue a few orders and they'd do just about anything. Heck, the military even ordered men to kill and they did so without a second thought.

He liked Black Rock Falls. It would seem that rather than keep people away, the notoriety of the place was making it the place to be, or visit. The town teemed with visitors but the rodeo crowd kept well away from the college and life here seemed to continue in a bubble of normality.

It was as if no one really seemed surprised that members of the football team had suddenly perished. He'd seen no outpouring of grief, no girls crying on each other's shoulders, no midnight vigils for the dear departed. He sighed. Perhaps they needed graphic slayings to stir their emotions. He grinned into the sunshine. Perhaps he should have skinned them alive and then pegged them over an ants' nest. Now that would've gotten their attention.

# CHAPTER FORTY-ONE

Jenna didn't figure her day could get any worse until she slipped out of Kane's truck and a harassed Rowley greeted her on his way to his SUV. "What happened?"

"Just had a call from one of the Blackwater deputies you sent out to keep an eye on the crowd at the showgrounds." Rowley gave a disgusted grunt. "Seems things have gotten way out of hand, fights have broken out; they're not sure but some are saying the ticket office was held up at gunpoint. People are chasing down the culprits and now the bulls have gotten loose and stamped all over vehicles in the parking lot. I was heading out to lend a hand. Walters is in the office."

"Okay, head on out there, I'll follow in my cruiser." She waved Kane inside. "Get the Dylan Court casebook written up and send Walters out to notify his next of kin. The moment Wolfe calls, I want you to head down to the ME's office and attend the autopsy. I'll be there as soon as I've dealt with this."

"You sure, Jenna?" Kane looked apprehensive. "Those boys can get rowdy, especially if they've been drinking, and Wolfe has Webber on hand, he doesn't need me there."

Jenna tapped the handle of her Glock. "Maybe, but I always have a friend ready to deal with these situations, and in addition to the deputies on scene, I'll have Rowley as backup. We can't let crimes in town slide because of our caseload. The townsfolk deserve our protection—*my* protection as their sheriff. This is a minor distraction from the case. Get at it, Kane. We have to solve these murders and I'll be back before you notice I'm gone."

"Yes, ma'am." He opened the back door to his truck to allow Duke to jump onto the sidewalk. "Call me if you need me."

She gave him a wave and headed for her cruiser, searching her pocket for the key fob. In truth, she preferred Kane to drive her in his truck. Apart from the company, it gave her time to think or work on cases to and from the office. Her cruiser looked surprisingly clean and then she remembered a group of local kids had been holding a car wash to collect donations for band equipment and she'd let them use the parking lot outside the sheriff's department. Maggie had collected a generous donation from her deputies and all their vehicles had received special treatment. She climbed inside and opened the window then headed slowly through town and out on the highway to the showgrounds. She turned on her radio, and moments later it crackled into life. It was Rowley. "Copy that. Go ahead, Rowley. Break."

*"Copy that. Ma'am, I'm in pursuit of a red GMC Canyon, heading north on the highway, containing the suspect of a hold-up at the showgrounds. The Blackwater deputies have things under control there. The paramedics are on-site treating the people injured from the bull stampede. Break."*

Jenna slammed her foot down on the gas and hit lights and siren as she flashed past the showgrounds off-ramp. Way in the distance, she could make out Rowley's wigwag lights. "Copy that. I'm right behind you. What details do you have for me? Go ahead."

*"Copy. Two suspects involved, both went to the showgrounds loaded for bear. They had a beef against the organizer about some money owed. The one I'm chasing got clean away. The other suspect disappeared into the crowd at the showgrounds but the deputies have a description of him. They're conducting a search now. Break."*

Jenna forced her concentration on the road ahead. Overtaking the slower cars, she experienced an unfamiliar rush of adrenalin. Now she understood why Kane enjoyed driving at speed. It was almost addictive. She lifted her radio and called in the pursuit to Maggie.

*"Copy that, Sheriff, and Deputy Kane is aware of your situation."*

"Thanks, Maggie. Over." Jenna gripped the wheel and squeezed the gas down a little more. She glanced at the speedometer as it reached eighty. She hadn't taken her cruiser over eighty before but pushed down the gas pedal a little more.

In the distance, Rowley seemed to be getting further away. She glanced in her mirror and thought for one moment Kane was behind her. A black truck with tinted windows similar to his was coming up fast. Even driving the beast, Kane couldn't have caught up to her in that amount of time. She reached for the radio but never made it; the black truck slammed into the back of her cruiser, shunting her forward at an incredible speed before dropping back.

Gripped with fear, Jenna let out a gasp. With "Sheriff" written all over her cruiser, whoever was trying to kill her was serious. She accelerated, taking the risk of overtaking an eighteen-wheeler to get space between her and the lunatic on her tail. She glanced in the mirror and slowed some to leave a smaller gap between her and the truck. Taking the opportunity, she reached for her radio and called in the situation. At once, Kane's calm voice came through the speaker.

*"Copy. Slow down the eighteen-wheeler. Pull him over if you can. It's unlikely whoever is in the black truck will do anything with a witness. Worst-case scenario, take the next off-ramp and head into the nearest town. Break."*

Before she could reply, she heard the air horns of the eighteen-wheeler and the black truck was almost beside her on the opposite side of the road. Heart pounding, she kept both hands on the wheel, drew a deep breath, and looked into the distance. She'd traveled this road a thousand times before, and ahead she could make out the signpost for Louan.

The black truck's engine roared as if the driver was trying to intimidate her. She forced herself to remain calm and not panic. The off-ramp was looming like an oasis in the desert. She gripped the steering wheel and hit the gas to the floor. The cruiser accelerated away and she shot down the off-ramp doing ninety, but to her horror, the black truck stuck to her like glue. A tight bend ahead forced her to brake sharply, but the other driver knew the road as well and the truck slowed but moments later was running alongside her again.

Panic had her by the throat and sweat coated her palms as she gripped the steering wheel. Ahead the road was clear with a straight run into Louan. She could hit the brakes and make him pass, but the dirt on the side of the road alongside the ditch wasn't wide enough to risk pulling over at speed. If she could make it to the gas station about two miles ahead, she'd be safer than alone on the highway.

She accelerated but the next moment the black truck tapped the rear side of her cruiser. The jolt sent her vehicle spinning out of control, and the world flashed by in a nauseating sea of green and blue then slowed. She wrestled to gain control, screaming in frustration as her cruiser slid across the highway.

# CHAPTER FORTY-TWO

"Jenna, come back." Kane stared at Maggie's big, round, worried eyes.

Nothing.

"Jenna, come back."

Nothing.

"Rowley, come back." Worry cramped Kane's stomach.

*"Copy."* Rowley's voice came through the radio loud and clear.
*"I'm north of Louan. The local deputies have apprehended the occupant
of the red truck at a roadblock. I'll take him into custody and head on
back. No sign of the sheriff. Her description of the vehicle pursuing her
fits the one owned by the other suspect. I'm not sure why the driver would
target the sheriff. Makes no sense. Break."*

Kane swallowed hard. What could have happened? "Copy. She
was looking for an off-ramp. Maybe she made it into the gas station
out of Louan? Go ahead."

*"You'd get to her before me. Break."*

"Copy. I'm gone. Over." Kane tossed the mic to Maggie and
pulled out his phone to call Jenna. When she didn't pick up, he
ran out the sheriff's department, leaving a confused Duke barking
behind the glass doors.

Moments later, he was hotfooting it out of town, sirens blazing
and lights flashing. The houses lining the streets became a brown
and red blur as he negotiated the traffic at breakneck speed. Out of
town, he soon hit the edge of the forest; here, shadows fell across
the highway in zebra stripes, flashing as he passed like "don't walk"

signs. He took the on-ramp to the highway, impressed by how his truck took the tight, sweeping bend with ease. A quick glance told him the highway was clear behind. He floored the gas pedal. "Come on, girl, show me what you've got."

The beast's engine roared its reply as he pushed it to its limit, pistons pumped and the front of his truck lifted to meet the challenge. Under him, raw power vibrated as the truck ate up the blacktop at maximum speed. All he could see was a black, winding snake before him, split down the center with a broken yellow line.

His mind focused on one thing: finding Jenna. As he sped by one eighteen-wheeler then skirted around another, he didn't slow to take the sweeping bend. As the highway straightened out, he had a clear view ahead. In the distance, he made out a nasty dark cloud billowing high in the sky. He gritted his teeth, recognizing the twisting black smoke as a vehicle on fire. The face of Annie, his wife, flashed in his mind, a memory of the day his vehicle had exploded and killed her. The thought of finding Jenna dead in the twisted metal churned his guts. "God have mercy."

He took the Louan off-ramp and headed along the road into town. Unease crept over him as he slowed to gape at the twisted black wreck wrapped around a pole in the distance. Flames licked the charred metal, leaping high into the air, and the next moment a blast rocked the silence, sending metal shards flying in all directions. He reached for his radio and called Maggie to get the fire department on scene. He swallowed hard. "I'll go take a look around but it doesn't look like anyone got out of there alive. Break."

"*Copy. Oh, sweet Jesus.*" Maggie let out a sob of distress. "*I'll contact Wolfe. Over.*" Then she was gone.

A terrible aloneness crawled over Kane as he maneuvered the truck along the deserted highway, heading slowly through the thick, black smoke. No other wrecks came into view. Only a few people used the backroad into Louan; most carried on along the highway and took the new exit to save time. He scanned the road, weaving around the wreckage from the explosion, sick to his stomach at the thought of finding Jenna, or parts of her, scattered on the blacktop. He slammed on the brakes at a glimpse of the trunk of Jenna's cruiser in the long grass. The vehicle appeared to be nose down in the ditch at the side of the road. Unable to maneuver his truck any further through the twisted, charred metal, he jumped out the door and ran through the grass beside the ditch, leaping over parts of the damaged vehicle to get to her.

Relief at finding Jenna alive stung the backs of his eyes. He stood for a beat, watching her attacking the airbags in her cruiser with a knife and cursing loud enough to make a preacher blush. Emotion washed over him with such intensity his knees weakened. He wanted to whoop with happiness but put on his game face. From her expression, she was in no mood for an outburst of joy. He slid down the ditch, splashed through the muddy water, and went to the open window. "May I be of assistance, ma'am?"

"Dave. Thank God it's you. Some crazy son of a bitch ran me off the road." Jenna turned to look at him and anger flashed in her eyes. "The stupid doors have locked on impact and I'm stuck fast in the airbags."

Biting back a smile, Kane looked her over. Her flushed face was angry and her hair all mussed up, but the way her mouth turned down with indignation told him she was okay. "You hurting anywhere?"

"Only my pride." She took a long, deep breath then let it out slowly as if to steady her nerves. "I gather the explosion was the truck that ran me off the road? He tapped the rear side of my cruiser and then shot past me at speed. Next moment, I heard an almighty crash. I figured his truck had caught fire—I could smell smoke." She winced. "Then an explosion shook the ground and I figured being inside the cruiser in a ditch wasn't so bad after all." She looked at him. "I hope he didn't hit anyone else. Can you tell if it's the black truck I had on my tail?"

Surprised by her calmness, Kane shrugged. "Hard to tell the make or model, it's in pieces. The driver wrapped it around a pole and it burst into flames. I haven't checked the occupants but it would be a miracle for anyone to survive a wreck like that." He tried the door to Jenna's cruiser but it was locked tight. "I'll get you free and then take a closer look. Where are your keys? Can you reach them?" As all the Black Rock Falls vehicles had keyless entry and ignition to allow for a fast getaway, the key fob would likely work. "I'll be able to open the doors from out here."

"Yeah, I think so. If I can reach into my pocket." Jenna wiggled around then passed him the key fob.

He aimed the smart key at the cruiser and it responded with a blink of lights. "There, the fob overrides the automatic locking system." He pulled open the door, unlatched Jenna's seatbelt, and helped her out.

"I thought I was a goner for sure." She looked up at him. "I'm sure glad I was driving the new cruiser. The airbags worked real good." She scanned the scene, on the job as usual. "I guess we'd better go and see if the driver survived, but from that awful smell, I figure he's a crispy critter by now."

"Wolfe is on his way and Maggie called the fire department." He followed her as she moved away. His natural calm had resumed and life had returned to a comforting normality. In the distance, he could hear a police siren. "That'll be Rowley. He apprehended the suspect in the red truck and he's on his way." He took her hand. "I'll help you out of the ditch."

To his surprise, she didn't argue and he climbed up the side of the ditch, pulling her behind him. He turned and looked at her. "You sure you don't want to sit and rest a while? You could be in shock."

"I've been resting for about twenty minutes. I'm not hurt." Jenna stamped the mud off her boots and looked up at him. "Mad as hell at myself for not handling the situation better, but after what I've been through of late, this was a walk in the park." She pulled out her cellphone and checked it. "My phone is fine too." She started to pick her way through the twisted metal on the blacktop. "Oh, can you smell that stink? I'm right. There's a body in the wreck for sure."

Kane hustled after her. The bitter smell of burned rubber and flesh was one he'd been familiar with in his lifetime. He reached her side and they moved closer to the wreck. From ten yards away, they could clearly see the blackened body of the driver, hunched over the wheel. He reached for her arm. "I figure we check out the surrounding area in case he wasn't alone then leave the rest to Wolfe."

"You do that and I'll see if we can get the Louan deputies to assist and block off access to this area until we clear the scene." Jenna seemed transfixed on the smoldering ruins of the vehicle. "Why did he run me off the road? I wasn't chasing him down. It doesn't make sense."

Kane peered into the ditch beside the road then shrugged. "I figure he's the second suspect in the showgrounds robbery, and when he left the showgrounds, he thought you were in pursuit of his accomplice. He wouldn't have known Rowley was ahead of you. I'd say the driver of the black truck decided to run you off the road to allow the other man to get away. He probably thought they'd both be home free once he'd disposed of you."

"Hmm, maybe, but he did the classic PIT maneuver—the one we use to stop a speeding vehicle." She looked up at him. "It takes practice to use the Pursuit Intervention Technique. I think he's a cop."

Kane frowned. "Nah, he may have tried it, but not many cops end up barbecued on a pole after completing that maneuver."

"If he isn't a cop—" Jenna stared at the blackened wreck "—I figure, there's more to this guy than we realized."

# CHAPTER FORTY-THREE

Jenna wondered if she'd ever get the stink of the rancid air out of her clothes and hair. The oily smoke had coated everything around her, giving the browning grass a weird sooty covering as if all the tops had gone through a fire. When Rowley arrived with his prisoner, she escaped into Kane's truck and listened to Rowley's update of the arrest. "So, you have the suspect in custody and recovered the money from the hold-up. Was he carrying the weapon he used?"

"Yeah, once he hit the roadblock and found himself staring down the barrels of four rifles, he threw his weapon out the window and couldn't surrender quick enough. He started talking so fast I had to shut him up to read him his rights. His name is Joey Turner." Rowley indicated with his chin to the car wreck. "I have the name of the man who ran you off the road as well. It's his big brother, Jimmy. The suspect in custody gave me a blow-by-blow. Seems his brother was talking to him on his cellphone during the chase. Said he'd slow you down so they could both get clean away. He had priors and wasn't an ex-cop."

"Kane figured it was something like that." Jenna looked behind him as Wolfe started heading in her direction. "Great work, Rowley. Take the prisoner in and book him. Contact the DA and he'll have him hauled off to the county jail to await a hearing. We'll be back as soon as we're finished here." She glanced up at Wolfe. "What do you have for me?"

"It plays out like you said." Wolfe removed his soot-covered surgical gloves and rolled them into a ball. "Speeding and he was using his phone. He lost control and slammed into the road sign." He frowned. "How many more people am I going to find dead behind the wheel of a vehicle with a phone clutched in their hands? People don't seem to realize that texting or taking calls when driving is worse than playing Russian roulette. They take their eyes off the road for a few seconds and end up wrapped around a pole or, worse, kill an innocent driver in a head-on." He leaned against Kane's truck. "I've taken what blood samples I could but we've already had witnesses from the showgrounds come forward to say he was drinking bourbon at the bar. I'm sending his body straight to the mortician. I don't need to do an autopsy."

Jenna sighed. "I'll get Walters to notify his next of kin." She looked at Wolfe's unusually strained expression. "This accident has taken up too much of your time. The clean-up crew is here; why don't you head on back to town? I know you're itching to get to the Court autopsy."

"That's done." Wolfe stared straight ahead as if thinking about something more important. "Right now, it looks like a possible homicide, if I can prove he has gun muzzle bruises on his face and temple, and match the glove marks on his thumb. He wasn't a user. I found no indication of drug use. No needle marks or the associated damage I would normally see from an addict or even a recreational user. I also contacted the college and spoke to them about the testing they do on their players: they take random urine samples and the laboratory confirmed Court's tests all gave a negative result. The last test was only a week ago. I do know he made an appointment with the counselor and was distressed by the deaths of his friends."

Nothing seemed to add up. Jenna chewed on her bottom lip. "So what killed him?"

"I've tested his blood for the usual speedball type of drugs. I'll get it confirmed but I had a positive result for morphine." Wolfe leaned one palm against the door and bent to speak to her. "The drug's readings appear to be too pure for a street mix. I figure there's more to this than meets the eye."

Jenna frowned. "What do you mean?"

"I'll know more very soon. I sent the blood samples to a special lab. If I'm right, someone used a massive dose of morphine to kill Court." Wolfe gave her a long look. "How could a college kid obtain morphine in Black Rock Falls?"

"Hmm, that is unusual." Jenna thought for a moment. "Unless his father is a doctor or works in the pharmacy?"

"Maybe but doctors and pharmacists don't just leave medications lying around, and they keep a record of their supply; they'd know if some went missing." Wolfe glanced at his watch and then ran an agitated hand through his hair. "I'll keep you up to date with the findings."

She'd known Wolfe long enough to know when something was eating at him. He was always on the job but something was wrong. "Forget the caseload for a moment and tell me what's wrong."

"Nothing." Wolfe straightened. "I'm fine."

"Oh, it's not about the pony Kane planned to buy for Anna's birthday, is it?" Jenna pushed open the door and slipped out of the truck. "We kind of forced your hand, I guess."

"No, it's not that at all, Jenna." Wolfe looked down at her and smiled. "Having you guys involved with my girls is like having a real family. Julie and Anna are always chatting about Uncle Dave or Jake and Auntie Jenna." He squeezed her arm. "It means a lot to me to see my girls smiling again, and Emily looks up to you like a big sister."

Tears pricked the backs of Jenna's eyes. To her, Wolfe and his girls, Kane, and Rowley had become the family she'd lost too. She patted his hand. "We feel the same, Shane. We've all been through so much horror since we arrived in Black Rock Falls, it's nice to have some normality in our lives."

"Which is why I don't want you to put Emily in danger. Sure, there's a slim chance the killer will grab the opportunity to take out Lyons and she won't be involved, but what we do know for sure is that if Emily runs up the mountain this afternoon, Lyons will try to seduce her in some way or another. We don't know if he plans to rape her. We can't rule out he might be the killer who murdered three of his friends and possibly Chrissie. It's pretty secluded up there, especially late in the afternoon, and you know the odds of something like this going wrong, Jenna." Wolfe dropped his hand from her arm. "It's past one and you're in no shape to go running. I'll call Emily and tell her to forget it and go straight home after class. I can't believe she agreed to become involved in your plan. It goes way past crazy. I must have been off my head to allow her to consider it in the first place."

Now Jenna understood Wolfe's agitation. She looked up at him. "I'm fine. You've checked me over and know I didn't receive a scratch. If you're worried about me, don't be. I'm functioning just fine." She rested one hand on her weapon and took a relaxed pose. "Do you honestly believe I'd put Emily at risk?"

"Well, no, but the girls are all I have, Jenna." Wolfe's eyes narrowed. "If she was your daughter, would you allow her to do this?"

Jenna met his gaze. "She could run into Lyons any afternoon when she runs; in fact, she could encounter him any time at college or in Aunt Betty's Café. This afternoon will be a controlled environment: I'll be close by and so will Kane. Heck, why don't you come along as well?"

"Having you and Kane will be enough to scare most people away. If I join in as well, the killer and Lyons will know something's up." Wolfe rubbed his chin. "I could wait in my van in the parking lot at the foot of the mountain. If I remove the ME signage magnet from the sides, no one will notice me."

"That sounds like a plan." Jenna climbed back into Kane's truck. "If you're done with the wreck, I'll ask the Louan deputies to handle the clean-up. I'll call a tow truck to collect my cruiser and we'll be back in town by two at the latest. It will give us plenty of time to get cleaned up and changed."

"Okay but if this is going to work, we'll have to plan it down to the second. You'll need to be close enough to protect her." Wolfe gave her a long look. "I'll hold off calling Emily for now but let me know the moment you hit town so we can get the timing right."

"I'll plan for a number of possible outcomes, don't worry." Jenna looked up at him. "I'll put Rowley with you, and with Webber shadowing Lyons, we'll have all the angles covered."

"Promise me you'll look after her, Jenna." A worried expression moved over Wolfe's face.

Jenna smiled. "You have my word."

# CHAPTER FORTY-FOUR

A strong wind tossed the first fall leaves into the air and then danced them in spirals along the sidewalk as Kane and Jenna walked the few hundred yards to the sheriff's office. He'd grabbed his duffel out the back of the truck along with his forensics kit when they'd dropped the truck at the carwash. He glanced at Jenna, walking beside him carrying the medical field kit. "I'm glad there's a strong wind blowing. People are already looking at us and covering their noses. I hope the carwash will get the smell out of my truck."

"It's just as well we have a change of clothes at the office and a place to take a shower, but I don't know why we couldn't have gone straight home." She gave him a sideways look as they split apart to let a mother and three young kids walk by. "We'll have to go home and change into running gear anyhow and then be at the trail way before Emily is due to arrive."

As Kane walked around a woman, her nose wrinkled with disgust and he increased his pace. "Trust me, if we'd got cleaned up then climbed back in my truck, we'd have gotten the stink all over us again. The seats need cleaning and the outside looks like it's been sitting next to a barbecue."

"Oh, Kane, that's a terrible thing to say." Jenna sidestepped a couple of kids with cotton candy blowing dangerously back and forth in the wind. "Even if the man tried to kill me, he didn't have to die that way. Can you imagine being burned to death?"

"No, I can't, but he didn't need to hold up the ticket office at the showgrounds or run you off the road either." Unable to understand her concern for the man who'd thought nothing about potentially killing her, Kane stared at her. "Or drive while talking on a cellphone."

"I guess." She glanced at him. "I wonder how many car wrecks are caused by sending messages."

Kane huffed out a sigh, wishing he hadn't looked up the numbers recently. "Last time I looked at the stats, 1.6 million car wrecks—or one in four—are caused by texting. Obviously sending or reading a message is more important than life."

"Enough about that, Emily's safety is my main concern right now." Jenna appeared to shake herself mentally. "I need to work out a plan B for this afternoon, maybe a plan C as well. I'll think on it in the shower."

He led the way up the steps and into the office with Jenna close behind. As they walked past the people waiting at the counter, Deputy Walters waved to get their attention, but Jenna had already headed for the shower. He walked toward him. "Yeah?"

"I have Chrissie Lowe's shoes." Walters held up a plastic evidence bag. "A man walking his dog found them spread out alongside the road in the grass up near the college." He gave Kane a knowing nod. "I went straight out. Nobody touched them and I put them straight in this here bag. All the details are in the report."

Kane placed his bags on the floor and examined the shoes. Someone had likely tossed them out the car after dropping Chrissie back at her dorm. "Can you send them over to Wolfe? With luck, he might be able to lift some prints off them." He looked at Walters. "Still no word on her phone?"

"Nope, it went offline around two forty-five the same morning the roommate found her dead." Walters shrugged. "Maybe someone flushed it?"

"Yeah, you never know." Kane shrugged. "I gotta go wash this stink off. Catch you later." He picked up his bags and headed for the locker room.

When Kane came out the locker room, he found Duke curled up asleep under his desk, and on top, he found takeout bags from Aunt Betty's Café. From the wonderful aroma of fresh coffee, Maggie had ordered lunch, knowing they'd both been on the go since breakfast. He sat down and waited for Jenna with one eye firmly on the clock; he'd finished eating by the time she emerged from the shower, hair glossy and smelling of honeysuckle. "Maggie ordered you some lunch."

"Great, I'll eat it on the way home." She snatched up the bags and headed for the door then paused and looked at him over one shoulder. "Coming?"

He grabbed his go-cup of coffee and followed her to pick up his truck with Duke on his heels. He strolled along beside her. "I don't think we've ever had a case with three viable murder suspects and not a shred of evidence on any of them—suspicions, maybe, but not being able to prove beyond a reasonable doubt any of them were at the crime scenes makes life difficult."

"Maybe we haven't yet but something will have to give." Jenna took a sip of her coffee. "No one is that lucky. They were all near the murder scenes. I know Emily has been asking everyone if they saw them around the time of the murders, and Webber as well. It's not as if we can put it out in a press release. I figure we'd get sued." She threw one arm up in the air. "Unless the killer makes a move this afternoon, we'll still be scratching around for evidence and suspects, but Lyons is sure shaping up as the ringleader in the Chrissie Lowe rape case. Right now, I'd be happy to solve at least one case this week."

Kane led the way into the carwash. "Rowley has the theft collar, so it's not as if we haven't solved anything, but if nothing happens this afternoon, we'll be back to square one on the other cases. I guess we can only keep throwing out the net and seeing who else we can catch because as sure as my truck is black, if this is murder, he hasn't stopped killing yet."

After changing clothes, Kane pushed a few useful items into the pockets of his jacket and waited in his truck for Jenna to come running down the porch steps of her ranch house. He'd chosen a mixture of dark greens to blend in with the forest then added a black ball cap and shades. Jenna had disguised herself quite well with casual clothes, a baseball cap, and sunglasses. She'd merge in with the other runners without much notice. For him it was slightly more of a problem: no matter what he wore, he stood out like a sore thumb. Being a head taller than most was an advantage he'd never trade, but blending into a crowd had never been something he'd been able to achieve. He pulled his ball cap down over his eyes and looked at Jenna as she slid into the passenger seat. "I figure we'll need to split up. If anyone sees us together, they'll make us for sure." He started the engine and headed down the leaf-strewn driveway and out onto the highway.

"Yeah, I already decided that, and I've worked out three possible scenarios but I'm in two minds about leaving Duke behind." Jenna chewed on her bottom lip. "He'd be able to warn you if someone was lurking in the forest."

Kane shrugged. "Maybe but everyone knows he's always with me. If they don't make me first up, the moment they see Duke, they'll recognize me for sure."

He turned the truck onto the main highway into Black Rock Falls. Once out of town, he'd decided to take the backroads to Stanton Road to avoid the traffic, getting them to the parking lot at the beginning of the trail with a good half hour or more before Emily was due to arrive. He'd had his own ideas on how to handle Emily's surveillance but glanced at Jenna and then moved his attention back to the busy road. "How are you going to play this, Jenna?"

"We'll arrive early enough to be able to split up and be at the top of the rapids, waiting on both sides of the trail." Jenna glanced at her watch. "With Webber following Lyons behind her, and both of us ahead of her, we should be fine." She turned in her seat. "Wolfe is dropping by the office to collect Rowley and they'll be in the parking lot at the foot of the mountain as backup. We all have com packs, including Emily."

"Okay." Kane kept his eyes on the road.

"I figure if Lyons makes a move, we allow it to play out." She looked at him. "We'll be able to hear what he's saying to Emily. If he's just asking her to a party, we'll keep our distance and let plan A take its course. I've instructed Emily to accept his invitation but insist she drive herself to the party." She adjusted her ball cap and pushed a strand of hair behind one ear. "I told her if he wants to run with her, she should insist he go on ahead back down the trail because she wants some alone time."

Kane smiled. "Then if the killer is lurking, she's out of harm's way."

"Exactly, and if there is no killer waiting to pounce and Lyons tries to drug her at the party, she'll have Webber as backup, as we've discussed, and we'll have the proof we need to take him down, at least for administering an illegal drug." She sighed. "If we can get our hands on his burner phone, we might be able to charge him with Chrissie's rape as well."

"It's a possibility. I'd bet he keeps it close by." Kane accelerated along Stanton Road and the smell of pine rushed through his open window. "So, what's plan B?"

"I figure it's highly unlikely he'll try and rape her in the mountains, but if he touches her, whoever is close can take him down." Jenna opened her jacket to reveal a shoulder holster. "Not the best thing to carry running but I'll use it if I have to."

Kane grinned. "Me too."

"Oh, I know you never go anywhere without a weapon. I've often wondered if you take one into the shower." Jenna chuckled, and when he didn't reply she poked him in the arm. "Holy cow, you do, don't you?"

"Well, I leave it close by." He shrugged. "It's a habit." He turned off Stanton Road and made his way through the rows of pine trees toward the parking lot at the foot of the trail. "What's plan C?"

"If everything goes to plan A, we hold back and watch. If the killer tries to take out Lyons, it's going to be before he hits the more popular trail, so somewhere between the top of the rapids and the old bridge. We'll be on our coms and able to surround him without too much difficulty."

Kane winced. "This killer is strong and super smart; he'll spot us if we get too close and it only takes a second to kill. That close to the rapids, he could just pick Lyons up and toss him over the ravine." He glanced at her. "I figure the safest thing for Emily is rather than continue to the switchback, she should take the cut-through path or maybe go back up and wait at the top."

"Then she'd be away from Webber; he'll be on Lyons' tail." Jenna shook her head. "I don't want her exposed to danger. I told her to let Lyons go on ahead and then follow in five minutes or so. We should stick to the plan or it will get confusing. She can always hang back or shoot down the cut-through to your position if anything goes wrong."

They pulled into the parking lot and Kane stopped way down the back in an area steeped in deep shadows. His black truck was almost invisible in the dark. He glanced around. Six other vehicles surrounded him but he could not see Emily's silver Jeep Cherokee or Wolfe's white van. "It looks like we're well ahead of time." He attached his com pack to his belt and threaded the earpiece through the neck of his shirt then holstered his weapon in the small of his back. He noticed Jenna was surveying the area intently before she jumped out the door. He followed and rounded the hood. "Ready?" He handed Jenna a bottle of water. "Stay safe."

"Roger that." Jenna headed up the rapids side of the trail and in seconds was lost in the trees.

Kane scanned the area one more time and then made his way across the parking lot, taking the inland trail most people preferred. The track through the dense forest led to three options. One was to take the switchback and come down along the edge of the rapids, and the second was to cut through halfway and take the shorter way back down beside the rapids. The third was to carry on up to the head of the rapids. Most people took the inland track up the mountain to avoid the cold spray and wind in their faces, but on the way down the other track, having the cool wind on their backs as they ran into the mottled sunshine was a refreshing change. He ran at an even pace, keeping his attention on every shadow. The trail was eerily quiet and he passed no other runners. He didn't mind the solitude. The silence could be an advantage, and although the scent of pine was strong with the wind in his face, if someone was hiding close by, he'd likely smell them.

# CHAPTER FORTY-FIVE

A mixture of unease and excitement washed over Emily as she slid her Jeep into a space in the parking lot at the entrance to the running trail and got out from behind the wheel. She turned on her com and slipped the earbud into her ear then bounced her head up and down as if listening to her favorite tune. It had been her father's idea, and if Lyons approached her, she could make the excuse of turning off the music and activate the mic. She couldn't see Webber's truck coming into the parking lot but he'd followed her at a distance from the college, staying well back. The roar of Lyons' red Mustang on her tail, however, was unmistakable. She pressed her mic as she reached inside the Jeep for her water bottle. "Game on."

*"Roger that."* Jenna's voice came through loud and clear. *"Kane's positioned on the forest track—head that way. I'm up at the top near the rapids. I'll follow you down when you leave. Webber will be behind Lyons. You're good to go."*

Emily went through her usual stretching exercises then swallowed hard, glancing at the three unknown cars in the parking lot. She took a lungful of fresh, pine-scented air then headed up the trail. How strange to feel so worried when she ran the same path almost every day, but this afternoon the usual crowd was missing. She understood why: most people would have forgone their exercise to enjoy the fun at the showgrounds. The rodeo went late on Friday, with the crowning of the Fall Festival queen and other events. Most people would be taking advantage of a night out. As she moved along at her usual pace, she noticed the change in the weather; the summer had vanished and the coolness that came off the mountains in fall had arrived. A fresh breeze carrying a hint of snow whistled through the tall pines in a strange whine, and the dying leaves from the undergrowth crunched underfoot.

In her earpiece, she heard Kane's voice as he communicated with Jenna.

*"Phil Stein is on the mountain, going slow about twenty yards from the switchback. I'm in a concealed position ten yards from the switchback."*

*"I'm taking it slow. I figure I'm halfway to the switchback and will continue on up to the falls."* Jenna's voice had a calming tone. *"Anyone on your tail, Em?"*

Emily glanced over one shoulder then pressed her mic. "Not yet but Lyons followed me into the parking lot."

*"I have eyes on him."* Webber sounded excited. *"He's heading toward Emily. No sign of Jones."*

*"Copy that."* Jenna took a deep breath. *"Keep heading toward Kane, Em, and then take the trail to the top of the rapids. I'll be close by."*

Emily touched her mic again. "Copy that."

Emily's heart pounded, and a twinge of fear gripped her, knowing Lyons was coming up behind her. What would he do? Instinctively she increased her pace; getting closer to Kane would be her best option but then she'd be in the sights of Stein—a potential murderer.

She kept going, taking the winding path and jumping over the twisted tree roots along the track. She concentrated on the fact good people surrounded her. Kane was up ahead and soon the trail straightened out; if he had hidden somewhere ahead, he'd have a clear shot if anyone tried to hurt her. She'd been with him to the gun range and seen him shoot. He was remarkable. No one had a chance against him. It was clear they had her surrounded, and Webber would be coming up the rear. He would stay as close to Lyons as possible without being seen. She unconsciously touched the can of bear spray on her belt.

As she moved through the twisty path, a cloud passed over the sun, darkness surrounded her, and the cool breeze became an arctic blast, stealing her breath. The forest went from beautiful to foreboding in a split second; the dim light hid the traps underfoot and she stumbled over the uneven ground. Branches snagged at her clothes and scratched her bare legs but she pushed on and soon reached the straightaway. The track widened and ahead she could make out the switchback and the trail up to the rapids.

Breathing heavily, she reached the end of the straightaway in record time and stopped to catch her breath. The pounding of the rapids was getting louder and soon would cover her voice if she screamed for help. She took a sip of water and glanced around. If Kane was hidden somewhere, he was like a ghost. A thumping sound in the distance made her turn and she caught sight of a figure heading her way. It was Lyons. *He's coming.*

# CHAPTER FORTY-SIX

Until Jenna hit the trail, she'd thought she'd not received any injuries from wrecking her car, but her back and legs ached. Yeah, she could fight if she had to, but running up the side of the mountain with a freezing wind blasting her face wasn't making her feel any better. As she made her way along the trail at the edge of the river winding through Stanton Forest, her lungs ached with each breath of cool mountain air and she found her progress wasn't as fast as she'd anticipated.

Voices ahead caught her attention and then a young couple came running around the bend, rosy-cheeked and bright-eyed. They gave her a friendly wave and chuckled as they went by. She waved back but kept her head down. As she made the final climb to the top of the rapids, another young man ran past. Not long after, her pulse quickened at the sight of Owen Jones, suspect number two, sitting on a rock and staring into the roaring water. She hit her mic. "Kane. Jones is at the top of the rapids. He looks like he's waiting for someone."

*"Has he seen you?"*

Jenna slowed to a walk then leaned over as if trying to catch her breath. "I think so. I don't figure he's recognized me though."

She stiffened as Jones got to his feet and started down the mountain toward the switchback, passing her without a glance. As she turned to watch him, he rounded the corner and vanished. "He didn't make me. He ran straight past and went round the first bend. I can't make out his position."

*"What about Stein?"* Kane cleared his throat. *"He should be right on top of you by now."*

Jenna allowed the image of another runner to filter through her mind. Had Stein already gone by? She couldn't be 100 percent sure with the beading water obscuring her vision. The young man had a ball cap pulled down over his short hair and was wearing sunglasses. It could've been him. "I'm not sure. A man did run by a few minutes ago but my attention was on Jones."

*"Roger that. It had to be Stein. No one else has gone by. Emily is close now and Lyons is on her tail; she'll be there soon."* Kane waited a beat. *"I can see Webber. We have Emily surrounded."*

Jenna moved back down the trail, slid into the forest, and positioned herself behind a moss-covered rock. "Okay, I'm in position."

As she sipped from her water bottle and waited for Emily to run by, the murder cases came to the front of her mind. She stared down the trail and her stomach dropped. Could it be a coincidence that she'd seen two of the suspects on the mountain at the exact same time and place as Lyons? It wasn't a secret he'd announced the fact he was jogging this afternoon in the cafeteria in front of everyone present. She pressed her mic. "Kane. I sure hope Jones and Stein aren't both involved in the killings."

*"I figure we're going to find out soon enough."*

"Okay, Webber." Jenna kept her attention on the trail. "I need eyes on Jones and Stein. Leave Lyons to us. Don't come to my position. Take the cut-through and wait for them to come to you. You should have cover in the trees there. Let us know if they double back."

*"Roger that."* Webber sounded out of breath. *"I'm on my way."*

Jenna hunkered down and waited for the charade to play out. Hidden in the shadows between the tall pines and the boulder, she gathered her professional calm around her and became one with her surroundings. Under her feet, the rich, leaf-covered soil was moist and pine cones littered the undergrowth. She inhaled. The forest had a different scent each season. As the biting wind cut into her damp clothes, it sent a message that fall would be short this year and winter was close on its heels.

Against the roar of the rapids, she heard the scream of a red-tailed hawk as it soared like an arrow from a tree into the sky. She watched the majestic bird and followed its silhouette against a passing cloud until the tops of the pines blocked her view. She marveled at the majesty of the birdlife in Black Rock Falls; the forest could be both a terrifying and magical place. Her friend Atohi Blackhawk once told her that no matter what terrible things happened in Stanton Forest, the beauty would remain. Rain would cleanse the soil and wildflowers and vines would cover graves. Whatever happened on the mountain today, life would go on.

From her vantage point, Jenna had a clear view of the top of the rapids. The clearing was a favorite picnic area and where she'd witnessed the fight between Lyons, Jacobs, Devon, and Jones. She would never forget seeing Jones fall into the freezing rapids or his struggle to survive as he slid between rocks on his way down the river. The memory was still so raw it sent a shiver down her spine. At the sound of footsteps, she moved her attention to the trail and sighed with relief as Emily ran into sight. As planned, Emily walked to the flat rock and sat down. She took a long drink of water and then stared down at the rapids. A few minutes passed and Seth Lyons ran into view. Jenna looked him over. He had hardly broken a sweat.

Jenna couldn't hear the exchange of words, but as if reading her mind, Emily pressed her mic button and the conversation came through Jenna's earpiece.

*"I've seen you around."* Seth Lyons moved closer to Emily. *"You're a friend of Colt, right? Colt Webber?"*

*"No, not a friend. He interns at the same place is all."* Emily stood and Jenna could see the frown on her face. *"Why, do you want an introduction or something?"*

*"Nope. I know him."* Lyons chuckled. *"We're both on the football team. I'm the quarterback."*

*"Really?"* Emily pulled the band from her ponytail, letting her long blonde hair cascade down her back, and then scooped it up and retied it.

*"We thought—me and Colt—that you might like to come to a party tomorrow night after the game?"*

*"Sure."* Emily's smile almost convinced Jenna she was interested. *"Where and what time?"*

*"Nine at my house on Pine, number six."* Lyons gave her a broad smile. *"I'll get you a ride."*

*"No need, I'll drive myself."* Emily sipped her water again and sat back down on the flat rock. *"I come up here to meditate, so I'll see you there."*

*"Sure."* Lyons touched her cheek and then turned to go. *"I can't wait."*

When he ran past Jenna, she used her com to contact Kane. "Lyons is heading back down the mountain. Emily is safe. If the killer or killers are going to strike, they'll do it soon."

*"Don't give away your position, they could be hiding anywhere along the trail. Follow the plan. They know Emily is here and she isn't a threat. Let her follow as planned and we'll take up the rear."*

"Roger that." Jenna waited a good five minutes then pressed her mic. "Okay, Emily, you're good to go. Your dad is waiting in the parking lot. As soon as you get to the broken bridge, take the track that cuts back to the inland path and head down to the foot of the trail. Then you'll bypass anyone lying in wait for Lyons along the winding part of the track."

*"On my way."* Emily dashed down the trail.

Jenna stared after her then hit her mic. "Kane. Nothing's happened or we'd have heard from Webber by now. I'll give Emily a head start then follow her."

*"Lyons should be hitting the bend in the trail by now."* Kane heaved a deep breath. *"If they were going to strike, opposite the old suspension bridge is the most secluded area and they'll have the cut-through as an escape route. It looks like we're going with plan A but I'll head back down inland and make sure Emily makes it through, then I'll cut through and meet you on the rapids trail."*

Jenna sighed. "Dammit! I figured one of our two suspects would have made a move by now."

*"The killer will make a move sooner or later. Maybe he made us, and if so this guy is even smarter than we've given him credit for."* Kane sounded calm as usual. *"Webber, what's your position?"*

Nothing.

Jenna frowned. Even over the noise of the falls, Webber should hear the com in his ear. "Webber, this is Alton. Do you copy?"

A terrible rush of unease drifted over her. "I'll head for Emily now. Emily, do you copy? Turn around and come back. I'll meet you on the trail." Jenna dashed out of her hiding place and hurtled down the mountain.

*"I'm okay. There's nobody here and the old bridge is a few yards away. I'll be heading down the cut-through track in a few moments."*

Jenna hit her mic. "Webber's not answering, something might have happened. Wait where you are until you hear from me, Em."

# CHAPTER FORTY-SEVEN

He adjusted the earpiece and slapped the com pack taken from Webber to his belt then smiled into the shadows. He'd moved through the forest like a ghost, not making a sound. Of course, he'd made the sheriff and her deputy. It was hard to miss a man of Deputy Kane's size running up a trail. Where the sheriff was, Kane was never far behind. They'd taken different paths and he'd had a momentary pang of regret for spoiling their attempts to catch the leader of Team Rapist, but he had his own plans for the spoiled, rich quarterback. He looked down at Webber's body. The noise from the rapids had made it easy to creep up behind him and engage the chokehold. The man was stronger than he'd anticipated but not as strong as him, and soon Webber's knees had buckled and he'd succumbed.

He dragged Webber's body deeper into the forest and then kicked leaves over the double tracks his heels had dug into the forest floor. He'd had no idea he was working for the cops and grimaced. How had he allowed him to slip under his radar? As he moved to the end of the cut-through track, the sheriff's voice came in his ear, ordering Emily to turn back, but he could see her not ten yards from Lyons, who was leaning against a wooden post to the old bridge as if waiting for her. He pressed his mic and hoped he sounded like Webber. "I'm at the cut-through. I couldn't come back before; Lyons was close by."

*"Roger that."* The sheriff sounded relieved. *"I'll keep out of sight and let it play out. Emily, head to the old bridge then cut through."*

He grinned. He'd fooled her.

*"Roger that."* Emily's voice came through his earpiece. *"On my way."*

He moved through the trees, and as Emily ran by, he stepped out, snagged her by the arm, and covered her mouth in one slick move. Holding her hard against him, he pulled the com pack from her waist and tossed it into the rapids then pulled the pistol from the small of his back and pressed the muzzle to her temple. "Don't move a muscle or your brains will mess up my shirt." He could feel her heart pounding against him and her breathing was rapid. "We can do this the hard way or the easy way, Emily."

# CHAPTER FORTY-EIGHT

At first, anger at herself raged through Emily. How could she have run straight into danger? The trail ahead had appeared clear. Where had he come from? Fear followed with the terrible knowledge she couldn't fight her way out of this problem. The wide-gloved hand pressed so hard against her mouth, her teeth ached. She could smell leather and gunpowder. The way the man held her, with his solid strength behind her, told her that if she moved, he'd break her neck. Terror slammed into her as the cold muzzle of a gun pressed against her temple. She froze and listened to the instructions.

"I'm not here for you, Emily. I'm here for Seth Lyons." The man pressed the steel harder against her skin. "I'll let go but if you scream or try to run, I'll shoot you. Understand? I have a suppressor on my weapon, the sheriff won't hear a thing, and Webber is down. Now this is what I want you to do." He kept the gun against her head. "Walk down to Lyons. Keep your hands where I can see them. I'll be in the bushes with my weapon aimed at your head. I won't miss. All I want you to do is distract him for a few moments so I can get close and then I'll let you go. Act natural. Got it?"

Trembling, she nodded slightly and the hand on her mouth released a little. She'd lost her com, and with her hands pinned to her sides, she wouldn't be able to alert anyone by using her tracker ring. She had no other choice but to comply, but her mind was working overtime. Webber was down. The thought he might be lying dead close by made her stomach roil. She would do what her dad had taught her: cooperate first and then the moment he was distracted, she'd try to escape. "Yes, I understand."

Holding her arms out a little from her sides, she walked around the next bend and Lyons emerged from the bushes surrounding the old bridge. The banner hanging at the entrance with "Danger" written in red had frayed and dropped to the rotten wooden slats. Long strands of canvas flapped about in the wind, slapping the ground. Beyond, the decaying structure stretched out in ruins across the fast-flowing rapids over fifty feet below. As she moved closer to Lyons, the wind carried the spray to her face. She wanted to wipe the water from her eyes, but if she moved her hands, he might shoot her.

"Hi Emily." Lyons gave her a slow smile. "I figured I'd wait for you so we could get to know each other better."

*Get something between you and the target.* Emily heard her dad's words filtering into her mind. Heart jackhammering, she moved closer to the entrance to the old bridge and leaned against one of the many pine trees lining the edge of the surging river. Her movement turned Lyons around, placing him between her and the gunman. The bushes opposite moved slightly and a man with the brim of a ball cap pulled down to shade his face moved toward them, but she couldn't see a weapon in his hand. *Are you the killer?* She swallowed the panic in her throat and looked at Lyons' smiling face. "I said I'd see you at the party. I like my space."

"You're a tease." Lyons took a step closer. "Come here, I won't bite."

Adrenalin pumped through Emily, blind panic melted away, and her path became clear. She took a step to one side. Her only option was to run. "There's a man behind you with a gun."

"A what?" Lyons spun around and glared at the man. "What the hell do you want?" He walked toward the man and pushed him hard in the chest.

"That's the last mistake you'll ever make." The other man lashed out, hitting Lyons in the face.

Emily pressed her emergency tracker ring and then turned to leap over the danger sign. She ran onto the rickety old suspension bridge. It swayed in protest and underfoot the rotten treads creaked as the bridge shuddered. Wind lashed at her and icy spray whipped up from the rapids, drenching her in seconds. She slipped and then made the mistake of looking down to the treacherous rocks and swirling water below. Unable to move, she hunched down, clinging to the railing, and then sucked in a few deep breaths to calm her shattered nerves. The noise from the rapids thundered in her ears and she doubted her dad would be able to hear any communication from her tracker, but she'd try. "Dad, if you can hear me, I'm stuck on the old suspension bridge. I've lost my com. Lyons and another guy got into a fight. I think the guy has a gun." She gritted her teeth. "I'm scared but I'm going to try and get to the other side and away from them."

Petrified, she moved in slow motion and looked ahead to the other side of the ravine. It seemed to be so far away, and many of the slats on the bridge had fallen into the river long ago. She wrapped one arm around the blackened railing and stood. The bridge moaned in protest and swung dangerously to one side. She had to make it across and moved on, step by step, testing each slat before she went to the next. Behind her the sounds of the fight came through the rush of water, and she turned to see Lyons taking a beating from the stranger.

As she turned back, the suspension bridge swayed dangerously and her palms slipped on the soaked moss and slime-covered handrail. Her heart pounded so hard she thought it would burst through her chest but she shuffled along, picking her way over the missing slats. The closer she came to the middle, the more the wind buffeted her as if it was trying to rip her from the bridge and toss her into the river. It was so cold, she couldn't feel her fingers anymore and her knees shook with each step.

The next moment an almighty ripping sound split the air and wood splinters shot past her then rushed away in the wind. The bridge jolted her to her knees and, losing her grip, she slipped in an uncontrollable slide toward a gaping hole. She grabbed at air as the supports for the handrails rushed by and then came another ripping sound. The bridge moved again, tumbling her from one side to the other. As she slammed into a support rail, she managed to loop one arm around the icy metal and came to a shoulder-wrenching halt inches from the hole and certain death.

Sobbing in terror, she looked over one shoulder and found the cause of the problem. The man did have a weapon. A knife glinted in the sunlight as he urged Lyons onto the bridge. Blood streamed from Lyons' nose and he moved without care as if on a suicide mission. She raised her voice as loud as possible. "Stop running! The bridge will collapse."

Letting out a wail of terror, Lyons ignored her, jumped over the missing slats, and headed toward her. Emily clung tight to the shuddering bridge. The wood beneath her feet bucked and creaked. The idiot would kill them. She stared through the clouds of mist behind Lyons. The man had vanished. She raised her voice in the hope Lyons would hear her. "It's okay. No one is chasing you."

He didn't so much as acknowledge her presence and kept on coming, his expression wild. Blood dripped off his soaked face in a ghoulish crimson spray around him. Decayed wooden slats fell away, floating like confetti in the wind before tumbling into the rushing water below. She held up one hand to him. "Stop!"

The suspension bridge whined and she gaped in horror as the strands of woven, rusty metal in the cable supporting one side of the bridge appeared to stretch. Wires screeched and snapped as the cable unraveled before her eyes. She stared, frozen in terror, before her instinct to survive took over. She wrapped both legs around a wooden post and tightened her grip on the slippery railing as a loud twang like the snapping of an almighty guitar string cut through the roar of the rapids. She ducked just in time as the metal cable snapped and sliced through the air a foot above her head like a whip.

An almighty moan like the felling of a great tree shuddered through the bridge and then one side of it fell away. A cry came through the wind and, trembling, she looked down. Seth Lyons was hanging by one arm to the broken side of the bridge and trying desperately to pull himself to safety. Arms and legs aching, Emily pressed her head close to her tracker ring. "Help!"

# CHAPTER FORTY-NINE

When Wolfe's voice came through Jenna's earpiece, she glanced all around, worried someone might be close by. "Copy. Wolfe, what's happened?"

*"Emily's in trouble. She's on the old suspension bridge and the last communication I received from her was, 'Help.' She's lost her com pack, and with the noise of the rapids, it's difficult to hear her. I'm heading up the mountain and bringing a rope. Rowley is still in position."*

Jenna slid from her hiding place and ran down the mountain. "I'm on my way."

*"Me too."* She could hear Kane's heavy breathing as he ran. *"I'm almost at the cut-through."*

Jenna pressed her mic. "Roger that. Webber, head to Emily's position."

No response. What the hell had happened to him now? She ran down the straightaway, leaping over gnarled tree roots and avoiding the rocks. As she rounded the bend, she caught sight of a man standing at the entrance to the old bridge. She slowed, placed one hand on the weapon in her shoulder holster, and walked toward him. He was in his mid to late twenties with short, fair hair and could be a college student, but not one who'd come under her scrutiny. "What are you doing here?"

"Trying to figure out how to save them." He pointed to Emily and Lyons dangling on the broken bridge. "I'd have called 911 but my phone is in my truck."

"Stand back, I'm the sheriff." Jenna moved closer to the edge and took in the situation. "Help is on its way."

"That guy dropped these." He offered Jenna a pile of flash drives.

Jenna pushed them into her jacket pocket. "Thanks, now stand to one side."

"Sure." The man turned away and headed down the trail.

The next moment, Kane came thundering through the cut-through track and skidded to a halt. "I found Webber crawling out the forest. Someone knocked him out, but he'll be okay. I told him to rest awhile and then head this way. Where's Emily?" He moved to the edge of the ravine and peered at the bridge. "Jesus."

Jenna turned to him. "We'll have to talk Em into making her way back, but I'm not sure how we can assist Lyons until Wolfe gets here with a rope." She frowned. "I'll call the fire department." She made the call then walked to the edge of the ravine and cupped her hands. "We're coming, hold on."

There was no time to waste, and without hesitation, Jenna stripped off her jacket and then removed her shoulder holster and handed it to Kane. "Give me your belt. I'm going to bring her in." She looped Kane's belt through her own. "I'll attach Em to me and then she won't be so scared."

"Have you lost your mind?" Kane's mouth turned down as he handed her his belt. He pulled out a small pair of binoculars and scanned the area. "Give it a few more minutes. She has herself in a good position and Wolfe will be here soon." He turned his attention to Lyons. "It will be impossible to save them both at the same time."

The loud creaking from the bridge was all Jenna needed to make up her mind. She looked up at Kane. "I made Wolfe a promise to watch out for her and I never break my word." She took a deep breath and stepped out over the abyss.

"Then promise me you'll take it slow and easy. Get Emily then we'll try for Lyons. Don't risk all your lives by trying to save them alone." Kane's face filled with anguish. "Promise me, Jenna."

"Okay, okay, you have my word." Clinging to the slippery handrail, she shuffled her feet along the metal bar attached to the dangling slats of the bridge. The rusty, wet, blackened bar did nothing to relieve her fear of heights, but she'd trained in worse conditions. She smothered her worry and moved on, taking precise, even steps. The wind pulled at her clothes as if trying to make her fall, and blasts of freezing, wet wind cut through her clothes. She kept her gaze fixed on Emily but the girl hadn't moved and was staring at the rushing water as if paralyzed with fear. "Emily, I'm coming."

She shouted to Emily to stand up and start moving toward her but the wind carried her words away. The bridge groaned and shuddered with each perilous step and Jenna had to fight against waves of rising panic. The memory of seeing Owen Jones's recent fall into the rapids rushed over her without warning. The gut-clenching horror of seeing him falling into the icy water, colliding with boulders, and fighting to survive was so real. She gasped for air, her brain insisting she was going to die. Her knees wobbled and her grip lessened on the railing. In her earpiece, Kane's voice broke through the hallucination.

*"Jenna. Jenna, listen to my voice. Just hold on. Open your eyes. You're almost there. Look, Emily has spotted you. Don't reply, just keep going one step at a time. Come on, Jenna, you can do it."*

She turned her head to look at him, gathered her wits, and then nodded. Hands numb from the constant freezing blasts of water, she moved on. With Kane's encouragement in her ear, she could face her fear and focus with absolute clarity. A third of the way across, she heard whimpering and looked down. Lyons dangled below her, his eyes desolate with fear. He was soaked through from the pounding rapids rushing by below, his face a bloody mess, and he was out of her reach. Right now, she had no way of saving him, and his life depended on how long he could cling to the rotting wood. All she could do was offer him encouragement. "Hang on. Help is on the way."

Jenna worked up a rhythm—step, slide, step—as she moved down the slope to the middle of the bridge. Ahead, Emily had finally heard her yelling and was watching her. She could see the girl's pale face, wide blue eyes, and soaked blonde hair. Wolfe's petrified daughter would need a lot of encouragement to stand up and move. As she reached the center of the rapids, the squall became fierce as if she'd stepped into a wind tunnel. Her heart rate picked up to a dizzying speed. The swaying of the bridge was bad enough but seeing slats of wood rip away and tumble into the fast-flowing water terrified her. She looked at Emily, and the worry on Wolfe's face flashed across her mind and bolstered her resolve. He was family and she refused to let him lose another loved one.

Ten more steps had her at Emily's side. "Slowly hook one arm over the handrail and push yourself up." She looped one arm in demonstration and then gripped Emily under one arm. "I have you."

Jenna heaved a sigh of relief when Emily obeyed without a word. "Okay, now I'm going to loop Kane's belt through yours, so we're joined together." The idea was more a comfort move because the belts wouldn't take the weight if one of them fell. "Okay, we're going to head back now. Your dad is waiting for you. Keep your hands and feet in contact all the time. Move one hand, then slide one foot along, then move the other hand, and so on."

"It's been moving." Emily's lips had turned blue with the cold. "Like jolting every few minutes. It did that just before it broke."

Anxiety gripped Jenna's stomach but she tried to make light of the dangerous situation. "I figure it's the rotten wood breaking away but this side of the bridge is okay." She took the first few steps, glad when Emily moved with her. "We'll be off here in no time."

*"Wolfe is here, and so is Webber. The fire department ETA is still about ten minutes. It looks good from this end, keep moving slow and easy."* Kane cleared his throat. *"Don't risk letting go to press your mic to communicate. Wolfe has Emily's tracker on his cellphone."*

Jenna turned her head to look at Emily. "Kane is talking to me through my com and your dad can hear you through your tracker. Kane told me it all looks good ahead, no more damage. Can you move a little faster?"

"I'll try." Emily had a determined expression on her face.

The bridge shuddered and whined with every step and the howling wind tugged at their clothes. Aware the next step could have them tumbling to their deaths, Jenna kept up a conversation with Emily, and having her there bolstered her courage. They passed by Lyons. He'd stopped whimpering and had climbed up to hook one arm over a metal strut. Above him was an empty gap and twisted metal; he had no place to go and remained suspended in midair. She glanced to the entrance to the bridge and a chill ran through her. Wolfe was there with a rope in hand but he obviously thought the bridge would not support another person's weight.

Twenty yards to go, she could clearly make out everyone's faces. Kane and Wolfe stood at the edge of the bridge, feet spread and ready to grasp them the moment they arrived. Jenna sighed with relief. "Not much further, Em, keep going."

The next moment a ripping scream cut through the thunder of the falls, the bridge shuddered, and a noise like the devil himself had leapt out of hell echoed through the mountains. "Hang on, Em." Jenna wrapped her arms around the handrail and her legs around the metal support bar. She turned to see Emily copy her.

In an almighty roar of tearing metal, the second cable broke, slingshotting them at an incredible speed toward the side of the ravine. Behind her, Jenna could hear Emily screaming as they flew through the air. She clung on tight as they shot toward the edge of the rapids. Sheer force plucked them from the bridge and they fell, crashing into the thick undergrowth lining the ravine. Pain shot through Jenna's arm as they tumbled together, bouncing over rocks toward the fast-flowing rapids. The ground and sky became a blur of colors. Air rushed from her lungs and then the world went black.

# CHAPTER FIFTY

Kane watched in horror as the bridge swung back in a scream of twisted metal. Jenna and Emily were nowhere in sight, but Lyons had been flung up and onto the bank. He was within reach. When Wolfe ran up beside him, Kane grimaced. "I can reach Lyons. I'll go down; toss me down the rope and haul him up."

"And leave Emily and Jenna? No damn way." Wolfe stared down the rapids.

"We can't leave him there, and I figure they've been thrown onto the side of the ravine downstream a ways." Kane slapped Wolfe on the back. "I didn't see them fall into the water and Emily was strapped to Jenna; they'll be together."

"Jenna, do you copy?" Wolfe sounded desperate.

Nothing.

"You'd better hurry." Wolfe glared at Kane. "That son of a bitch isn't worth saving."

Kane wanted to agree but had a duty of care to Lyons. He turned away and dropped over the rock face. Moments later, he found Lyons battered and bruised but trying desperately to climb up. He got behind Lyons and pushed him up ahead of him. At the top, he forced him down on a boulder. He had to keep Webber's involvement a secret and stared at Lyons. "Rest a while and then follow us with Webber. Take off and I'll arrest both of you. Understand?"

He took Lyons' nods as affirmative and turned to Wolfe. "Bring the rope. Webber, call 911 and get the paramedics here pronto, and then wait where we descend and direct the firefighters to our position when they arrive." He gave Webber and Lyons a long look. "I'm trusting you to do the right thing. Lives are at risk—can I count on you?"

"Yes, sir." Webber pulled out his phone. "We'll do as you ask."

"I'm not going anywhere." Lyons held his head.

Kane picked up Jenna's jacket and weapon and then took off at a run with Wolfe close behind him. They charged down the trail, crashing through the bushes lining the edge of the ravine. The wall of the gorge fell away in layers, some with pines and juniper bushes growing among the boulders. The moss-covered rocks and damp vegetation made it slippery underfoot. He slowed, searching in all directions for Jenna and Emily.

"There." Wolfe pointed to a huge boulder resting precariously on the edge of the rapids. "See them?"

Kane could just make out the arm hanging limply over a juniper bush. He pressed his mic. "Jenna. Jenna, do you copy?"

Nothing.

"Emily, Jenna!" Wolfe cupped his hands around his mouth. "Call out!"

Only the sound of rushing water came from below. Kane dropped Jenna's things and then looked around wildly for a suitable tree. He grabbed Wolfe's rope, tied it securely, and then tossed it down the ravine. "I'll go first. Do you want me to carry the medical supplies?"

"No way." Wolfe gave him a stare to freeze the rapids. "You're wasting time."

"Okay." Kane dragged gloves from his jacket pocket and pulled them on. "I hope you have gloves." He grabbed the rope and started backward down the ravine.

"I never leave home without them." Wolfe stared after him. "I'll be right behind you."

As he made his way down, a feeling of dread fell over Kane. No cries of pain or pleas for help drifted up to him, only the roar of the falls. No sound came through his earpiece. Yeah, Jenna could've lost her com in the fall, but heck, she was tough and she'd call out if she'd seen them. Jenna had been close to death too many times this week and determined not to allow her to die, he dropped onto a ledge and crawled to the edge to peer over. "Oh, shit."

Kane's gut tightened in anguish at the sight of Jenna and Emily wedged between the rock face and a massive boulder hanging precariously above the fast-flowing water. On each side, the soil had eroded, leaving little support. He assessed the situation and turned as Wolfe moved to his side. "I know you want to go rushing down there but we can't risk dislodging the rock; it's hanging by a thread. We'll have to split up and move in slow." He scanned the area, taking into consideration each foothold. "We'll head for the flat rock. That area appears stable, and if I can reach them, I should be able to pull them clear before the boulder falls into the rapids. If you take the right and use the saplings as handholds, I'll go down the rocks to the left, it's faster."

"It's almost a sheer drop." Wolfe stared at him and then nodded. "Okay, I figure if anyone can climb down there and survive, you can." He hoisted up his backpack and moved off at once.

Kane dropped over the edge of the ravine and, finding footholds in the rock face, moved down at a steady pace. He'd reach the women first and swallowed hard at the thought of finding them both dead. His heart raced and sweat beaded on his brow but fear had no place in a rescue mission. He dragged in a deep breath and dropped into the zone, pushing his emotions into the far reaches of his mind and only concentrating on the task ahead. To his right he could hear Wolfe calling out to Jenna and Emily every few minutes. From above he heard voices; the firefighters had arrived and one glance skyward confirmed they were getting organized to drop down stretchers.

Relieved help was at hand, he kept moving, ignoring the constant cold spray lashing him. The handholds moved unnervingly under his fingers and his boots slipped on the moss-covered rocks. He glanced down and, gripping the base of a juniper bush, slid down the last few feet to land on the flattened plateau five yards away from Jenna and Emily. Remaining cool and professional now could mean the difference between life and death for his friends. He examined the immediate area then moved forward, taking careful steps. The loose rocks beneath his boots shifted with each step and rushed down like birdshot to pelt Jenna's back. Her arm moved and then her head. "Jenna, can you hear me? Don't move."

"Oh, shit." Jenna turned her head toward him. "I think my arm's broken. What happened?"

"You're suffocating me." Emily's muffled voice came from behind her.

Gut tightening with relief at hearing their voices, Kane shuffled closer and raised his voice. "Don't move! You're hanging just above the rapids. Wait for me and I'll pull you clear."

"Wait!" Wolfe came in from his right, crawling on all fours. "Don't move them, they might have spinal injuries."

"I'm sore all over but my back and neck seem okay." Jenna turned her head to look at Emily. "You okay, Em?" Jenna looked back at Kane, her face filled with concern. "She has a head injury. She's bleeding real bad."

"I can move my fingers and toes. My ankle is hurting and I've got blood in my eyes." Emily's voice sounded surprisingly calm. "Sore lower back but everything seems okay, Dad."

Kane edged closer and glanced over at Wolfe. His next move could send the women falling to their deaths. Directly in front of him, the rock face dipped slightly but had a ridge wide enough for him to stand. To get both women to safety, he'd have to drag them out at the same time and then roll back onto the flat rock, bringing them with him. He didn't have time to explain, and the expression on Wolfe's face told him he was fully aware of the danger. "Jenna, are you still tied together with the belts?"

"I can't tell." Jenna frowned. "I'm stuck tight against Em."

"Okay." Kane watched in horror as small rocks rained down on each side of Jenna as the underpinning of the boulder slipped away. "Emily, can you move real slow and wrap both arms around Jenna's waist and hold on tight? Jenna, hang on to Emily. I'm going to have to pull you out. It's going to be rough."

Heart thundering, he waited for Jenna's signal. "Okay, here we go. Hang on."

Wind and icy spray pelted Kane as he stepped onto the narrow rock, spread his feet, and bent his knees. He took hold of Jenna's belt with one hand and slid the other around her thigh. The boulder moved, slipping another inch toward the swirling rapids. It was now or never. He sucked in a deep breath and, using every ounce of strength, lifted the women out of the crevice. One step, two, and then three backward had them falling back onto the plateau in a tangle of bodies. He rolled Jenna toward him and grabbed Emily's arm to prevent her slipping away. He winced at her blood-soaked young face blinking up at him. Wolfe dove in to help and they all sat on the plateau, breathing heavily. A grinding noise tore through the air like a chainsaw and the massive boulder shifted then rolled like an out-of-control bowling ball into the ravine. The almighty crash vibrated through the mountain, sending a shower of dust and pebbles over them. Kane looked down at Jenna and shook the dust from his head. "That was too close."

"Are you guys alright down there?" A voice came from above Kane. "We're on our way down."

Kane looked up at the faces of the firefighters and gave them a wave. He looked down at Jenna. "Help is on its way."

As Wolfe tended to his daughter, Kane eased Jenna into a sitting position and unbelted her from Emily. Jenna shivered and he shrugged out of his jacket and wrapped it gently around her. She had scratches and bruises and bits of grass and twigs sticking in her hair, but somehow she'd survived. "I'm starting to wonder how many lives you have. This is your second dice with death this week."

"Says the man who just climbed down a sheer rock face without a rope." Wolfe grinned at him as he removed his jacket and covered Emily. "How many for you, Dave? You must be into three figures by now."

Kane shrugged. "I don't think about it."

"Me either." Jenna frowned. "I wouldn't make a very good sheriff if I worried about getting hurt. It's the nature of the game." She sucked in a deep breath and looked at Wolfe. "I'm not going to make it back up top without pain meds. I'm okay, no headache or dizziness."

"That bad, huh?" Wolfe wrapped a bandage around Emily's head. "Dave, there's morphine in my field kit. Check her eyes; if she looks okay, you can give her a shot." He slid the kit toward him.

Kane made Jenna look into the sun then back a few times. She was freezing cold but lucid, and her pupils reacted normally. "She looks fine." He pulled out the plastic container labeled "Morphine" and took out a prepared syringe. The sight brought back memories. He'd carried the same pack during his tour of duty. Without any preamble, he pulled up the leg of Jenna's shorts and plunged the needle into her thigh. When she let out a howl of protest, he caught the flash of anger in her eyes. "Okay, which arm hurts?"

"The left." Jenna trembled against him. "I must have put it out to break our fall." She supported the wrist with her other hand and grimaced. "It feels broken."

"Hmm, looks painful. I'll wrap it but the paramedics are on their way. They'll be here by the time the firefighters have you up top." Kane narrowed his eyes on her. "You're going to the hospital, so no complaints, okay?" Small rocks pelted them and he glanced up. "The fire department are on their way down. You'll get to ride up in a stretcher."

"I hate those things." She indicated toward the twisted metal dangling over the ravine. "Did Lyons make it?"

Kane looked up from bandaging her wrist and nodded. "Yeah, he's waiting up top with Webber."

"Some guy gave me a bunch of flash drives and said Lyons had dropped them." Jenna looked up at him. "They might be the evidence we need to arrest him. He might have been the killer after all."

It was dark by the time Kane made his way back down the mountain with Rowley and Wolfe. He'd insisted Webber go to the hospital after noticing the bruising on his neck. After Emily had insisted she was fine and didn't need to have her dad along, Wolfe had reluctantly remained behind. Although a small group of people had gathered to watch the firefighters in action, they'd soon dispersed once the paramedics had taken everyone down the mountain. He'd asked the bystanders if any of them had handed Jenna the flash drives but no one had come forward.

"Why is this guy so important?" Rowley glanced at him.

Kane pulled the flash drives from his pocket. "He's a witness. When Lyons ran onto the bridge after Emily, he dropped these drives. Lyons is insisting someone was up there threatening him and they got into a fight. I was on scene seconds later and I didn't see anyone."

"Did Jenna recognize him?" Wolfe fell into step beside Kane.

"Nope." Kane pocketed the flash drives again. "She didn't see where he went because she was watching what was happening on the bridge."

"Emily would've seen the fight, but after sustaining a head injury, there's no way I'm going to allow questioning until I'm sure she's okay." Wolfe raised one eyebrow. "Are we clear on that, Kane?"

"Sure." Kane shrugged. "I guess the doctors won't allow us near Lyons either. I'd sure like to know if he accidentally dropped the flash drives or if it was an attempt to dispose of them in the ravine."

"If they're the missing ones from the safe at the frat house." Wolfe frowned. "How did they get into Lyons' possession? Unless he took them."

Kane looked at Rowley. "Did you watch everyone coming down the trail?"

"Yeah, and I've taken photos of everyone." Rowley slid his phone out of his pocket and opened the file. "Recognize any of them?"

Kane stopped walking and scanned each image. "Nope. Jenna said the guy she spoke to was tall and muscular with a buzz cut. He had a blue cap hanging out the back pocket of his jeans and wore a black T-shirt." He paused at the images of Jones and Stein. "Where did our suspects go?"

"They went to their vehicles and drove away." Rowley took back his phone. "They came off the trail about five minutes apart. They never returned. I figure they went back to their dorms."

Kane rubbed his chin. "I'm heading home to get out of these wet clothes. I'll feed Duke and settle the horses and then take some clothes to the hospital for Jenna." He looked at Rowley as they walked into the parking lot. "There's nothing more we can do today. I'll leave you to lock up. We'll talk to Lyons in the morning. I figure he'll be kept in hospital overnight."

"Roger that." Rowley smiled at him. "Can you give me a ride to the office?"

Kane nodded. "Yeah." He turned to Wolfe and frowned. His friend's expression had turned to granite. "What's up?"

"What's up, he says as if he didn't risk Emily's and Jenna's lives up there. It's just another day's work for you, isn't it, Kane?" Wolfe's eyes bored into him. "Just so we're on the same page, this is the last time you're involving any of my daughters in one of your crazy schemes. Emily could've died today. It ends here, Kane, or I'm walking. Have I made myself clear?"

"Perfectly." Kane met his stare. "We had her covered, but I didn't account for the bridge collapsing. You were listening on the com, Jenna ordered her to run to me." He sighed. "I'm sorry, man. You should know I'd never intentionally place any of your kids in danger. You're like family, and Jenna would rip me a new one if you left Black Rock Falls. She loves those girls like sisters."

Not sure, for once in his life, how to handle the situation, he waited for ages as Wolfe stared into space, his anger palpable. Beside him, Rowley had an expression of disbelief on his face. Kane cleared his throat. He had to say something to encourage Wolfe to stay. "You have my word, Shane. That used to mean something."

"Okay." Wolfe gave him a curt nod. "There's something you need to do for me before you hightail it up to the hospital to see Jenna."

Kane opened his hands. "Just say the word."

"Take a look at the flash drives and call me. I'm not sure I can wait until tomorrow to know if they're the evidence we need in the Chrissie Lowe case." Wolfe's mouth turned down. "If they're the missing drives, Lyons sure had us fooled."

*

The nursing staff at the hospital had been amazing. Once Jenna had the results of her X-ray, they'd helped her out of her wet clothes and she'd showered and washed the filth from her hair. The crack in her wrist was painful but she would get away with only wearing a brace; the bruise on one hip and the other scrapes just added to the assortment of bruises she'd gathered during the week. She had to admire the nurses for asking discreet questions and giving sideways glances at Kane when he finally arrived with her clothes. If she'd been a battered woman, Black Rock Falls General wouldn't have let her down.

She glanced inside the bag he handed her to find toiletries, a nightgown, slippers, and a robe. "I'm not staying. I'm good to go as soon as I'm dressed." She waved a packet at him. "They even gave me pain meds."

"Yeah, I know, but they told me you need bedrest, so this way there's no arguing when we get home." Kane sat on the edge of the bed. "I know you won't have eaten so I've ordered Chinese takeout and I'll drop by and collect it on the way home." He gave her a long look. "I'm staying overnight in case you need anything."

Jenna smiled at him. "I'm sure I'll be fine but I'll probably hurt all over in the morning."

"I'd say so." Kane pushed the hair away from a bruise on her forehead. "I'll be checking on you every couple of hours during the night. Concussion has a habit of creeping up on people." He sighed. "I can't believe you and Em survived the fall. I was expecting the worse."

"I'm not surprised. I didn't think we'd survive either. We landed in the bushes and they slowed us down, but I couldn't stop us rolling back toward the water." Jenna leaned back and studied him. "You had your battle face in place when you came down the ravine. It's kind of intimidating, you know. I figured you were going to raise hell and then you calmly dragged us to safety."

"Is Emily okay?" Kane frowned. "I know Wolfe came by to collect her."

"She's fine. She went home hours ago but Wolfe insisted we drop questioning her until the morning. She has a sprained ankle and they put three stitches in her head. She has bruises all over but hasn't complained and figures her moon boot is a new fashion accessory." Jenna smiled. "Webber dropped by as well, he's fine. He'll have a sore neck and a husky voice for a while though."

"That's good. I'm relieved they're both okay." He shook his head. "Though Wolfe is not too happy with me for including Emily this afternoon."

"She'd planned to run there anyway; she does most afternoons. It was only a matter of time before Lyons made a move on her. When Wolfe calms down he'll realize she could've been up there all alone." Jenna studied his face. Something else was bothering him. "It's not just Wolfe, is it? Are you mad at me?"

"No, we're fine. It's the flash drives that guy gave you, the ones Lyons dropped." Kane looked away, swallowed hard, and then stared at his hands. "They're the uncut versions of the videos of the young women Lyons and his teammates drugged and raped. Not a few—twenty, maybe more—and now we have absolute proof who was involved apart from Lyons. The three murder victims and Josh Stevens."

"So we'll be making the arrests tonight?" Jenna frowned. "Have you seen Lyons since he arrived here?"

"Nope. I couldn't get near Lyons. They're keeping him overnight for observation. Apparently, he was raving when he arrived." Kane grimaced. "Maybe it's for the best. I'm not sure I'm the best person to question him right now."

Jenna gaped at him. He wouldn't look at her and his back was rigid as if he was on the edge of losing his temper. She touched his arm and taut muscles met her palm. "You look as if you're going to explode. What the hell is on those files?"

"I've only skimmed through a few and they're very disturbing." He scrubbed his hands down his face. "They made me ashamed to be a man."

When he wouldn't meet her eyes, she squeezed his arm. "You're the most respectful, kindest man I've ever met, and you make me feel safe. Heck, you make the whole town feel safe."

"Do I?" Kane lifted his gaze to hers but only deep sorrow filled his eyes. "Thanks, but right now, I wish I wasn't a deputy."

Jenna sighed. "How so?"

"I keep thinking Lyons will get some high-profile lawyer and he'll walk." Kane cleared his throat. "We can't allow that to happen."

"We have to enforce the law." Jenna bent to look at him. "Once he goes to trial—and he will—it's out of our hands."

"Yeah but I'm not thinking like a cop right now, Jenna." Kane flicked her a lethal glance. "I'm fighting a primal instinct to go drag that smart-mouthed animal outside and teach him how to respect women—Kane style."

# CHAPTER FIFTY-ONE

## Saturday

After Jenna considered everything that had happened on the mountain, she couldn't discount Lyons as the person responsible for causing at least one of the accidents that had killed his friends. She ignored the ER doctor's orders to rest and decided to go into the office. Although in considerable discomfort, and bone-weary from Kane waking her every two hours to make sure she hadn't fallen into a coma, or whatever, she'd already organized two arrest warrants. As usual, Kane had left at daybreak to tend the horses and completed his exercise routine before making breakfast at seven. Not that she complained; in fact, she kind of liked the attention.

She'd remained in her office, updating case files and leaving Kane and Rowley to hunt down Josh Stevens and Seth Lyons. As the case involved serial rapists, she'd made a call to the local FBI office. Cases involving serial rapists went way above her pay grade, and they had people to deal sensitively with victims. She glanced up as Kane walked into her office, showing no hint of weariness. "What do you have for me, Kane?"

"I have Stevens and Lyons in custody." Kane flipped open the file to display an image of a young man with dark curly hair. "Stevens is in interview room one for questioning and hasn't asked for a lawyer; I figure he wants to cut a deal." He sighed. "We picked up Lyons from his house and he's not saying much. He's in room two but I figure he'll lawyer up as soon as we show him the evidence."

"I'll talk to Stevens first." Jenna leaned on her desk. "I spoke to the DA and he'll drop by later. He wants copies of the flash drives and then his office will hand the evidence over to the FBI. He's confident enough of the women will come forward. Apart from getting justice, they have another reason: Lyons and his accomplices had considerable estates. There'll likely be a number of lawsuits for damages against them."

Jenna pushed the hair from her eyes and looked up at him. "I went over the evidence to consider if Lyons is implicated in Jacobs' death, but the DA considers it to be circumstantial at best and we don't have enough to charge him."

"We have the rapes and blackmail." Kane frowned. "If Josh Stevens confirms our suspicions, they'll both be spending a long time in jail."

Jenna pushed to her feet and bit back a moan of discomfort. "Okay, let's see what he has to say."

She followed Kane down to the interview room, waited for him to swipe his card, and then followed him inside. After taking a seat, she switched on the recording device and stated her name, and Kane did the same. "Mr. Stevens, you've been read your rights and agree to questioning, is that correct? Please state your name before replying."

"Josh Stevens and, yeah, I've waved my right to have an attorney present at this time but I reserve my right should it become necessary."

Jenna flicked Kane a glance then moved her attention back to Stevens. "Are you studying law?"

"No, but I watch TV." Stevens leaned back in his chair. "Okay, ask away."

Jenna took the digital notepad from the file. "We've seen the rape files, the uncut versions Lyons kept in the safe at his house. This is why you're under arrest. We've identified you as one of a number of men involved." She regarded him closely. "We know drugs were involved to an extent where the women involved were in no condition to give their consent."

"How can you prove we drugged them?" Stevens' mouth twitched up in almost a smug smile. "You don't have any proof."

"We have Chrissie Lowe's autopsy report." Jenna stared at him without blinking. "By the end of the day, we'll have testimonies from other women on the tapes. You see, now that we have you and Seth Lyons in custody, and the other men involved are dead, the women feel safe enough to come forward. The court will protect their identity. This part of the interview process isn't why I'm here. I want to know if Seth Lyons was involved in blackmailing the victims to keep them quiet."

"Do I get a deal if I throw him under the bus? I don't want my name all over the media." Stevens leaned forward and clasped his hands on the table. "If his dad finds out, my life is over."

"Your life is already over, Josh." Kane glared at him. "You think the DA will give you a get-out-of-jail-free card for talking? You'll be charged as a serial rapist, we have all the proof we need." He leaned forward. "But as Lyons was the ringleader, any information you supply now may go in your favor. You might get lucky and receive a lighter sentence."

Jenna collected her thoughts. "Was Lyons involved in blackmail?"

"Yeah, he used the images and video files to keep the girls from crying rape, but he used them to keep us in line too." Stevens pushed a hand through his hair. "This is why I didn't participate after the first six or so. I told Seth I had contracted an STD. He used the tapes to prevent any of us shooting off our mouths about the parties, and he used Alex and Dylan as his muscle if one of the girls threatened to expose us."

A cold chill ran down Jenna's back. "And what did he threaten to do? Surely he couldn't use the images or he'd incriminate himself."

"He said he'd kill us." Stevens gave her a long look. "The girls were easy to convince. He threatened to post their videos all over the media, but he'd make sure none of our faces were visible. Seth was good at manipulating images and video files."

"Okay." Jenna made a few notes. "Did you ever see him threaten any of the men who died recently?"

"Sure, all the time." Stevens frowned. "That doesn't mean he killed them."

Jenna moved in harder. "Where did he get the drugs?"

"I'm not sure." Stevens shrugged. "He always had something to slip into a girl's drink. Some girls he'd shoot up halfway through, depending on how long we needed them." He chuckled. "We had one freshman in his room for three days."

"You think this is funny?" Kane's fist smashed down on the desk. "What if Chrissie Lowe took her own life rather than face living with the shame of what you did to her?"

"Not me." Stevens held up both hands. "I didn't touch her."

Jenna lowered her voice. Beside her, Kane had regained his composure in seconds but his deadly expression remained. She leaned forward and took an almost conspiratorial pose. "How did that evening play out?"

"Alex Jacobs and Pete Devon drove out to the college and took the janitor's car. They went to meet Chrissie." Stevens shrugged. "Seth never gave the girls a ride; he always sent one of the guys. When she arrived, he gave her a few drinks and then took her to his room. I didn't do anything. He gave her a few pills and then Jacobs held her down. I just filmed it."

Biting back the urge to slap his arrogant face, Jenna kept writing. Although she had no need to write notes with the entire interview on tape, the process focused her. "And afterward?"

"From what they said, they drove her back to her dorm around two, dumped her on the grass, and then took the car back to the parking lot and returned the janitor's keys to his office. The girl had left her shoes in the car, and on the way back Alex chucked them out the window." Stevens leaned back in his chair.

"Did they threaten her or strike her?" Kane glared at him.

"Jacobs gave her a slap to wake her and then Seth gave her a warning before she left. He told her if she opened her mouth, he'd have her sister the following weekend."

"Her sister?" Jenna raised her gaze. "The one in high school?"

"I guess." Stevens smiled at her. "Seth was careful who he chose; he always said he picked someone who had something or someone to lose. They were the easiest to control."

"Did they mention her phone?" Kane drummed his fingers on the desk.

"Nope, just her shoes."

"Okay. I'll have a statement typed up for you to sign and then I'll call the DA." Jenna stood. "You'll need a lawyer. Do you want me to call someone?"

"Okay, call me a lawyer but I don't want Sam Cross." Stevens didn't appear the least bit concerned about facing possible jail time. "Call my family lawyer. I'll give you his number."

Jenna gave him a nod, closed the interview, and turned off the tape. She followed Kane out into the hall and leaned against the wall. "How did Lyons react when you hauled him in?"

"He went ballistic." Kane's mouth twitched into a smile. "It took two of us to take him down and cuff him. Rowley wanted to Taser him and I admit the thought had crossed my mind, but I didn't want his lawyer crying foul."

"Maybe you should sit out of the next interview and cool down." Jenna cleared her throat. "I know you're angry but this isn't the Kane I know. Can you reboot? I really need your professional side in these interviews."

"Sure." Kane let out a long sigh. "I'm glad we have Lyons in custody. I won't jeopardize the case, Jenna. You have my word."

"Okay." Jenna lifted her chin. "Do you figure he's capable of murder?"

"Yeah, anyone who can inflict that kind of violence is capable of murder." Kane shrugged. "Maybe Jacobs wanted to stop after Chrissie died. Hell, maybe they all did, and it made him angry. He likes to be in charge; controlling people and dominating women is his thing. He figures his friends owe him loyalty. Yeah, he could've snapped and killed Jacobs. I figure Lyons is the only person he would trust to spot him."

"True." Jenna frowned. "And Lyons having the flash drives doesn't mean a thing. In hindsight, Lyons could've taken them out of the safe before Court overdosed. He'd never admit it, would he? We'll never find out if he was at any of the murder scenes, his friends will cover for him. The only thing worrying me about Jacobs' death is motive. Lyons needed him on the team to make the NFL. That was something his daddy couldn't buy him."

"Maybe not—there are lots of great players on the bench. As long as he shone out as a star player, the others were disposable. It had to be something else." Kane shrugged. "Right now, all we have on him is blackmail and serial rape."

"I need to know who he fought with at the old bridge." Jenna pushed her hair behind one ear. "Who could it have been?"

"We'll get Emily to take a look at the images Rowley took on the day." Kane shrugged. "She might be able to make an ID."

Jenna turned to walk to the next interview room. "Wolfe will be here soon with the final results from the autopsies." She looked over her shoulder at Kane. "I hope he's found evidence against Seth Lyons or Steve Lowe. I can't ignore my gut feeling that one of them is a very smart killer."

# CHAPTER FIFTY-TWO

If Jenna had to describe the difficulty of walking into a room to interview a man she despised and act in a professional way, she wouldn't be able to. Facing a person who'd ruined so many lives made her skin crawl. Seth Lyons was a monster but she put her sheriff's mask firmly in place to deal with him and hoped like hell she'd be able to keep Kane from leaping across the table and beating him to death. She nodded at Rowley, who was standing outside the room, and stared through the one-way mirror to the man inside interview room two. With his wrists cuffed to a ring on the table, Lyons' head hung down and he was panting like a cornered animal.

Holding her head high, Jenna walked inside with Kane at her heels. Without preamble, she turned on the recording device and camera. "Mr. Lyons, you've been read your rights and understand them?"

"Yeah, Sheriff." Lyons' eyes shifted to Kane. "Your deputy explained and I agreed to speak to you, okay? I don't need a lawyer. I didn't do anything wrong. I'm the victim." He moved his head slowly to her, and the look he gave her was contemptuous. "You're wasting my time. Get on with it."

Before she could start the interview, her cellphone chimed. "Excuse me." Jenna paused the tape at the sight of the DA's phone number. "Sheriff Alton."

*"An agent from the FBI called. The first four women they've contacted agreed to come forward and testify against Lyons and his friends. I'll give*

*you their names. This is only the start, Sheriff; by the end of the day I figure we'll have many more."*

*We have him.* Jenna tried unsuccessfully to suppress the bolt of excitement rushing through her. She glanced at Kane and allowed her mouth to twitch into a small smile. "Thank you." She made notes and then went through her folder and selected a number of photographs. She placed them face down on the table and restarted the interview.

After giving the time and people present, and again making sure Lyons was aware of his rights, she met the man's sullen gaze. "I'd like some more information about the fight you were involved in on the trail up by the old bridge."

"It was nothing." Lyons looked at his hands.

"That's not the impression Emily Wolfe had; she said you were in fear of your life." Jenna leaned forward in her chair. "Do you know this man and did he threaten you with a weapon?"

"Just drop it, okay?" Lyons moved around in his chair. "Nothing happened. I went on the bridge to help Emily, is all."

Jenna glanced down at her notes. She needed a description or a name. "Come on, now, you must know this guy. Why did he attack you? Who is he? We'll haul him in for assault."

"I attacked him." Lyons smirked at her. "He wanted to act the hero and chase after Emily. He wouldn't back off, so I hit him. End of story. Can I go now?"

"The interview isn't over yet, Mr. Lyons." Jenna stared at him. "It's come to my attention that you're in the habit of inviting young women to your off-campus house with the intention of raping them."

"Me?" Lyons' eyes never left her face. "You have the wrong man."

"Do I?" Jenna placed the compromising images taken from the uncut media files on the table before him. "This is you and your friends, raping women, I believe?"

"You can make what you like of those photographs but I know the truth." Lyons' mouth curled into a sadistic grin. "They all came willingly and never made a complaint. Some women like group sex, or are you too frigid to understand a good time, Sheriff?"

Beside her, Jenna heard a low growl come from Kane and she exchanged a meaningful glance with him before turning her attention back to Lyons. "I understand these four women are speaking to the FBI as we speak." She saw the raw rage in his eyes. "In fact, all these witnesses will testify that you and your friends drugged and raped them at a party at your house and then blackmailed them to keep quiet." She shrugged. "Your friend Josh rolled over on you in the Chrissie Lowe case too. We have all the details about the night she died and evidence to back up his statement. In fact, we have all the flash drives and enough witnesses to keep you in jail for the rest of your life and then some."

"Do you want to give us your side of the story?" Kane leaned forward. "This is your chance."

"I don't have a story." Lyons glared at him. "I don't need to rape women—they come to me willingly. I'm the quarterback; they all love me."

"Uh-huh." Kane folded his arms across his chest. "That's why Chrissie Lowe killed herself after your date."

"Can we move on to the night Alex Jacobs died?" Jenna needed so much more from Lyons. "Did you spot him on the weights?"

"Nope." Lyons pulled at the cuffs, making them jangle against the hook in the table. "If you're going to accuse me of killing him as well, I want a lawyer."

Jenna shrugged. "Very well." She took down details and closed the interview. As she stood, she looked at him and smiled. "How's it feel to be on the losing team?"

# CHAPTER FIFTY-THREE

Wolfe scratched the two-day-old stubble on his chin and stared at the results of the blood tests taken from Chrissie Lowe and Dylan Court. Nothing was adding up; in fact, all his findings seemed contradictory. He'd made his final determinations and didn't believe Jenna would approve. He'd checked his findings a number of times and they'd all come out the same. Unconvinced, he'd visited the college to speak to the coach and members of the faculty who'd accompanied the players on their trip. All had said the same thing and confirmed that Pete Devon had taken a number of big hits over the days before his death. They'd also mentioned that Dylan Court had taken the deaths of his friends hard, to the point of seeking professional help. He signed the death certificates and let out a long sigh then turned his attention to Lyons' test results from the hospital.

Although Lyons had been out of control on arrival at the hospital, the tests had detected no alcohol or drugs in his system. What had made him charge onto an unsafe bridge like a lunatic remained a mystery, and so far, he wasn't talking. The arrogant young man didn't seem the type to run from a fight, and from Josh Stevens' statement, which Jenna had emailed to him earlier, Lyons had controlled everything and everyone in his house.

After collecting his results and shoving them into a folder, Wolfe headed for the door. At the reception, Emily sat chatting with Webber. He hadn't questioned her about her ordeal, preferring she had a good night's sleep, and figured going over a near-death experience once with everyone present would suffice. "Ready to go?"

"Do you want me to take care of reception?" Webber stood and helped Emily to her feet.

Wolfe shook his head. "Nope, I'll lock up. You come too; you'll be needed to help sort out this mess."

"Dad." Emily gave him a worried look. "You mad at me?"

Wolfe locked the door and turned to her. "You're a grown woman and I respect your decisions, but risking your life after all we've been through is upsetting." He let out a long breath. Being a single father was becoming harder each year. Once, his glare had them all scampering to their rooms, but as they grew into young women, Emily and Julie in particular needed more tact than an angry growl. "Kane shouldn't have involved you. It was unprofessional and I told him so."

"You know Dave would willingly take a bullet for any of us." Emily's face drained of color. "You heard his orders over the com. Jenna sent him down the back trail and then he took the cut-through track to meet me. He was following orders and he figured I was safe with Colt covering me. I can't believe you blamed him, Dad. He's like your brother. Heck, he's one of the family." She chewed on her bottom lip. "Jenna risked her life to save me. She could've waited for the fire department, but no, she came onto the bridge to help me, same with Dave. He didn't hesitate to climb down the rock face to save us. That's what family does, Dad." Her eyes filled with tears. "You used to be like that too."

Wolfe looked down at her and cupped her chin. "I know I don't take so many risks now because I'm all you have. I made a promise to your mom to always be here for you." He dropped his hand. "Wipe your eyes or we'll be late for the meeting. And in case you're worried, I sorted everything with Kane. We're good." He headed for his truck. *Oh boy, my girls sure have a way of twisting my heart.*

*

The aroma of coffee and cinnamon buns greeted them as they entered Jenna's office. With everyone squashed around her desk and talking at once, it was like walking into a cage filled with turkeys. Wolfe dropped his files on the table amid the cups, coffee pots, and plates of buns and then helped Emily into a chair. He looked at Jenna. "Morning, ma'am. How's the arm?"

"I'll do." Jenna was looking pale and drawn. She stood and went to the whiteboard. "Okay, so many things happened yesterday, we'll need to correlate everyone's stories into a timeline." She glanced back at Wolfe. "Are there any findings we need to consider before we go on?"

Wolfe tapped the folder on the desk. "I have made a determination in the cases. They're not what I expected, and the reasoning behind each one is complicated. I suggest we deal with each case separately, and I'll give you my cause of death as we go. It will make more sense if we deal with Chrissie Lowe's rape first. I have ruled her COD as suicide, I'll elaborate later."

"Okay." Jenna moved down to the end of the board. "This morning we interviewed Josh Stevens and Seth Lyons; you have all received a copy of their statements. Stevens verified Chrissie's movements on the night she died. As you can see from the timeline, she left the student hall at nine. We now know she got a ride to the party with Jacobs and Devon, was drugged and raped, and then around two was returned to her dorm. It was then she wrote a text message to a number we can't trace." She looked back at Wolfe. "Any luck finding out who she messaged?"

Wolfe shook his head. "It could've been an attempt to contact her brother but there was no reply. From what I could ascertain by pulling every string I have, her brother's team went down in enemy

territory. If any of them survived the wreck, they won't for long."
He stared at Webber and Rowley. "That information is classified and
does not leave this room."

"I trust my deputies." Jenna added notes to the whiteboard.
"Okay, let's move on. Lyons is talking to his lawyer but he won't be
getting away with anything. We have video proof he was involved
in Chrissie's rape and many others. I've turned a copy of everything
over to the DA's office. The FBI has spoken to a number of victims
from the video files and found some who are willing to testify. The
DA refused to cut a deal with Josh Stevens and he is currently on
his way to the county jail to await a hearing. I believe due to the
evidence against him he's opted to plead guilty to rape but will
be testifying against Lyons in an effort for leniency." She looked
back at Wolfe. "Do we have solid evidence to corroborate Stevens'
statement?"

Wolfe opened his file and searched through the documents. He
was old-school when it came to reports and he liked having the
paperwork in his hands. "Yeah, I found prints on Chrissie Lowe's
shoes that match Alex Jacobs. The hairs found in the vehicle match
Jacobs and Devon. The shoes were found where Stevens mentioned
in his statement." He glanced back through his notes. "The date-rape
drug, jet, which Webber reported Lyons mentioned, was the one
used on Chrissie Lowe—it all ties in. There's no doubt Lyons used
the same method with each of their victims. I'm sure now that the
threat is over, the FBI will encourage more women to come forward
to testify and make claims for damages."

"Okay, so we can inform Chrissie's parents that apart from Lyons
and Stevens, the men involved are deceased. I'll go and speak with
them as soon as we have charged Lyons." Jenna looked at Wolfe.
"Okay, moving on to the other cases. Up to now, we've had three
possible suspects, but I believe Lyons may have been involved as well."

"I figure we'll need to compile all the evidence we have from yesterday." Kane's gaze moved around the group. "Although Lyons made light of the fight with the guy on the trail, we need to know who he is and what scared Lyons enough to jump onto an unsafe bridge."

"I know why." Emily sucked in a deep breath.

# CHAPTER FIFTY-FOUR

Worried when the color drained from Emily's face, Jenna took her seat at the desk and looked at her. "In your own time, Em. What happened when you headed toward the old bridge?"

"A man grabbed me from behind and pressed a gun to my head. He said he would shoot me." Emily swallowed hard. "But would let me go if I did what he said, and he only wanted me to distract Seth for him."

"Oh, Emily, why the hell didn't you tell me this last night?" Wolfe looked grief-stricken. "Are you sure you want to do this now?"

"Yeah, Dad." Emily squeezed his arm. "I'll be fine."

"Did you recognize him?" Kane leaned forward when Emily shook her head. "What did he look like?"

"I didn't see him, he grabbed me from behind." Emily glanced at Wolfe. "I couldn't do a thing, Dad, he was strong and had my arms pinned to my sides."

"I understand." Wolfe took her hand. "You survived, that's all that matters now."

Jenna nodded at Emily. "Just take it slow, Em. No one is in trouble. We just want to figure out what happened."

"I walked up to Seth. He was waiting for me by the bridge. I turned him around so I could see the other guy but I didn't see a gun." She looked at Kane. "He was tall and muscular and wearing a blue ball cap, black T-shirt, and jeans. He had the cap pulled down over his eyes and his face was in shadow. I couldn't make it out." She sighed. "Before you ask, he could have been Stein or Jones—they're the same build and he was some ways away."

"What about this man?" Kane held out a photograph of Steve Lowe. "Was it him?"

"Maybe." Emily looked at Jenna. "They're all much the same."

"Okay." Jenna smiled. "Go on, what happened next?"

"All I could think about was what Dad had taught me: distract and then run. So I told Seth there was a man with a gun behind him and then I ran onto the bridge. I figured he wouldn't risk following me." She let out a long sigh. "I heard Seth yelling at the guy but I didn't look back. Next thing, the bridge started swaying and shuddering. I turned around and Seth was coming after me, and his face was bloody. The man wasn't there and I told him so but he kept on coming, fast. Next moment the bridge broke and he was just hanging there. Then I saw Jenna and Dave. You know what happened next."

"Do you figure the guy who gave you the flash drives at the bridge could've been him?" Kane looked at Jenna.

Jenna sighed. "Maybe but he didn't look like he'd been in a fight, and from the state of Lyons, he'd have gotten in a few punches. I didn't see a weapon either." She looked at Webber. "Did you see who grabbed you?"

"Nope." Webber rubbed his bruised neck. "He had me out in seconds. I didn't so much as hear a twig crack."

"The man who gave me the flash drive could've witnessed the fight. It shouldn't be too difficult to track him down if he's studying at the college." Jenna sighed. "Big guy with a buzz cut. Could he be on the football team?"

"There are four or five big guys with buzz cuts on the team." Webber narrowed his eyes. "Come to think of it, the guy Court took down to the cellar was big. I didn't see his face but he was wearing a blue ball cap under his hoodie. I recall seeing it sticking out, light blue."

"Maybe he removed his cap and acted nonchalant to fool you." Kane rubbed his chin and looked at her. "He didn't want to be seen running away, so he hung around for a few moments to give you the flash drives." He shook his head. "Rowley took photos of everyone who came down the trail and you said he wasn't one of them."

The hairs on the back of Jenna's neck rose. "So where did he go?"

"Maybe he found himself a vantage point and watched the rescue. Not many people hang around to assist the cops." Wolfe let out a long sigh. "Jenna, did you see a weapon?"

"No." Jenna shrugged. "I was a little preoccupied at the time to notice where he went."

"He didn't pass me." Webber filled a cup with coffee. "If he didn't go down the trail, he must have gone up. Maybe he watched from where they launch the kayaks and then came down later?"

"In the dark?" Jenna shook her head. "By the time everyone left the mountain, it would've been pitch-black. Only a lunatic comes down the falls trail in the dark, and it was cold last night. He must have slipped by us."

"He didn't come down either trail." Rowley looked offended. "I had them both covered until Kane and Wolfe arrived."

"Okay, but there's a million ways out of Stanton Forest. Just to cover every angle. Rowley, get a list and images of all the male students around twenty to, say, twenty-eight, and we'll take a look." Jenna sighed, pushed to her feet, and indicated to the whiteboard. "We've no hard evidence to prove Stein or Jones were involved in any of the possible homicides. Sure, they had reasons to pick a fight with Lyons on the mountain, but from the images Rowley took on the day, neither of them wore jeans, so that rules them out, and none of us saw Lowe on the mountain." She looked around the faces before her. "Can anyone give me a solid reason why any of these men could be responsible? Everything we have is circumstantial at best."

"Suspicions aren't enough for an arrest warrant." Kane sighed. "Which brings us back to Lyons."

"He wasn't so brave without his friends around him." Emily rubbed her hip and grimaced. "I saw his face. Whoever that man was, he scared the hell out of him." She shuddered. "Seth was running for his life."

Jenna's phone rang and she returned to her desk to take the call. "Yes? Okay, I'll be right out." She held up a hand to halt the buzz of conversation. "Livi Johnson, Chrissie's roommate, is outside. I'll go and talk to her."

In the reception area, Jenna smiled at the young woman. "Yes, what can I do for you, Livi?"

"It's just I found this when we were cleaning the noticeboard in my dorm." Livi handed her a newspaper cutting containing an image of the football team. "See, some of the faces of the players have circles around them? I figured it was a bit spooky as three of them are dead now." She handed the paper to Jenna. "See here at the bottom of the page? Chrissie wrote that—she always added an emoji and her initials to messages. I figure those were the animals who raped her."

Jenna swallowed hard at the emoji of a sad face and the initials "CL." Chrissie Lowe had reached out from the grave to tell the world who'd raped her. How had her team missed this vital piece of evidence? "It was on the noticeboard?" She frowned. "Where is that in relation to your room?"

"She would've had to walk right by it on her way. It's in the hallway." Livi shook her head. "It was covered with a sign-up list. It went up the day I found her. Someone must have posted it real early. This was underneath it."

Jenna squeezed Livi's shoulder. "It must have been a shock for you to find this."

"Strange that three of them died in accidents, isn't it?" Livi's eyes searched her face. "It's as if she had an avenging angel."

Jenna stared at her for a beat. Of course, Wolfe hadn't released the causes of death to the press but rumors and gossip spread like wildfire across a college campus. He wouldn't issue a statement until he'd made a determination in each individual case. She nodded. "It is strange, isn't it?" She led Livi to the door. "Thank you for bringing this in."

Saddened by the simple emoji, Jenna stared at the newspaper cutting and then pushed a hand through her hair. She gathered her composure, walked back into her office, and handed the clipping to Kane. "A voice from the dead. This was pinned to the noticeboard in Chrissie Lowe's dorm. How did you miss it?"

"I searched for notes." Wolfe frowned. "I gave the noticeboard a cursory scan but it was packed with information. I honestly didn't see a newspaper cutting. It must have been covered by something else." He pulled out his phone and scanned the files. "Here's an image of the board I took that morning. See, no newspaper cutting."

"I looked at the noticeboard as well." Rowley frowned. "I took a copy of the college newspaper she had in her room with an article about Seth Lyons in it. It's in a bag in the evidence room but she hadn't written on it."

Jenna took Wolfe's phone and zoomed in all over the board. She found the sign-up sheet, and peeking from behind it was the edge of the newspaper. "Livi said she found it under a sign-up sheet and here it is."

She dropped into her seat, suddenly aware of every bruise on her battered body. "Right now, we have no other alternative but to hunt down the mystery man on the mountain. I want to know why he picked a fight with Lyons and why Lyons was so afraid of him." She sighed. "Get me a name, Rowley."

Her phone rang again. She answered. "Okay, Maggie, send in the DA."

The door opened and the DA walked in and looked around the crowded room. Jenna smiled at him. "We're going over the evidence."

"I've spoken to the lawyer representing Seth Lyons and he is aware of the evidence we have against his client." The DA looked pleased with himself. "With the account from Josh Stevens and the witnesses piling up against him, the lawyer's going to encourage Lyons to plead guilty."

Jenna smiled. "That is good news."

"Do you have anything to tie him in with the deaths?" The DA looked hopeful.

"So far all we have is circumstantial evidence on all our possible suspects." Jenna sighed. "Everything points to Lyons being involved but we have no proof."

"I asked his lawyer if Lyons would disclose the name of the mystery man and he refused, saying the fight was personal and had nothing to do with anything else." The DA smiled. "If Lyons is responsible for the deaths in some way, proving it will be impossible. He had the motive and the smarts to kill without leaving evidence. He also would've been able to get close to his victims without causing suspicion." He shrugged. "We may never prove he killed them, but with twenty-five rape charges against him, and blackmail, during sentencing I'll be stating a precedent in a recent case in Billings of twenty consecutive life sentences given to a serial rapist. I doubt either of them will ever be released from jail."

Jenna stood and shook his hand. "That's great news! Kane and I will go and speak to Chrissie's parents this afternoon. I'm sure it will give them a small amount of closure. Thanks for coming by."

"My pleasure. Have a good day, Sheriff, Deputies." The DA headed for the door.

Jenna glanced around at the faces staring back at her. "I wish we had more proof."

"I know you want to find the answers, Jenna, but sometimes there's not enough evidence to support homicide." Wolfe looked at her and shrugged.

"Yes, I know." Jenna sighed. "We've solved the rape of Chrissie Lowe and charged two suspects with serial rape and blackmail. We've caught the man responsible for the armed hold-up at the showgrounds and returned the money. It's a good week's work but we still have four unsolved deaths."

"Make that one death by unknown causes, one accident, and two suicides." Wolfe narrowed his gaze. "As I mentioned before, I've made a determination on each case based on the evidence." He looked at his notes. "As I mentioned before, Chrissie Lowe committed suicide. I wasn't convinced until I examined the cuts to her wrists under a microscope, and the angle suggests she cut herself."

Jenna heaved a sigh. "That was expected. Go on."

"I have reason to believe that Devon could have sustained the marks on his ankles from other means; they'd had group sex previously, and after looking at the tapes, I can't rule out the possibility he received the marks at that time. Also, by speaking to witnesses, his head injury could have been caused during football practice. He could have sustained a concussion before entering the pool, slipped, and fallen." He looked at his notes. "The only death I'm leaving with an open verdict is Jacobs'. I can't prove he dropped a barbell on his neck or that his spotter accidentally dropped it on him, but as I don't have a shred of evidence either way, I have to leave his finding open."

Jenna could not believe her ears. "And Court?"

"I have no proof Court didn't sustain the facial injuries during the fight on the mountain or on the football field. I do have evidence to support his state of mind the night he died. Two of his friends had just died and he'd been seeking professional help. He was alone with a needle still in his arm and the evidence points to suicide. The man he took to the cellar could've been a dealer. I have no hard evidence anything else happened."

Suddenly lost for words, Jenna stared at him. "What? You mean after all this time you've changed your mind on all the cases?"

"No, before this, I've only made assumptions—we all did. It's my job to prove cause of death, and I'd never make a determination until I'd considered all the evidence. I require absolute proof of homicide before I stand up in court and testify to convict a man for murder." Wolfe lifted his grim expression to her. "It's only been a week and I came today to give you my final determination. If you find new evidence, I'll reopen the cases." Wolfe collected his documents and lifted one eyebrow. "Sometimes the dead don't talk."

# CHAPTER FIFTY-FIVE

Wolfe's conclusions percolated through Jenna's mind on the drive to the Lowes'. She glanced at Kane. "He's right."

"Huh?" Kane flicked her a bemused look then returned his attention back to the road. "About what?"

Jenna sighed. "What Wolfe said about not convicting a man without proof. I was just so sure we were looking at homicides."

"Me too, but in the end there just wasn't enough evidence to charge any of our suspects." A nerve in Kane's cheek twitched. "I'm sure we didn't miss anything."

Jenna chewed on her bottom lip. "Shane looked worn out today. I know he's been working late to search for any shred of evidence to bring about a conviction."

"He's been pulling triple shifts in the ME's office and assisting us on stakeouts; I'm not surprised he's exhausted." He pulled into a parking space outside the Lowes' house and turned to look at her. "He's on the edge of leaving town too, Jenna. We can't involve his girls in cases again."

Jenna turned to look at him. "I know." She adjusted the sling holding her injured arm. "I guess as we've all gotten so close, Emily became a natural part of the team."

"Put that to one side while we speak to the Lowes." Kane examined her face. "You look annoyed, and right now they need compassion. Losing one child is bad enough but not knowing what their son could be going through right now, or if he's alive or dead, must be horrendous."

Jenna nodded. Kane would be aware of the horrors of a military chopper going down behind enemy lines. "Have you been in similar situations?"

"Yeah." Kane's eyes had a faraway look. "If they've been captured, they'll be tortured. Wolfe told me in confidence, the government is hoping for a negotiation but the chances are slim. There's not much communication between the radical groups, so if they capture one of our guys, for them it means the end of a very nasty road."

Jenna fumbled with the seatbelt and groaned. "Okay, let's go and speak to the Lowes. I hope knowing the men who hurt their daughter are dead or heading for jail will give them closure."

"I don't think anyone ever gets closure, Jenna. The anger takes a long time to go away." Kane leaned across her and pushed open the door. "Will you be okay? You're sheet-white."

"I'll be fine." She forced her mouth into a smile. "I'll take some pain meds when we're through talking to them."

The walk to the Lowes' front door gave Jenna a minute to collect her thoughts. There could be nothing worse than facing a family who'd lost a child. She'd have to break the sad news of Chrissie's death being ruled a suicide. She would give them a concise and clear statement offering them a brief outline of what they assumed happened. Wolfe had sent all the information to the state coroner's office and they would decide if an inquest was necessary. If so, the coroner would reveal the horrific details of their daughter's suffering. Right now, she hoped to soften the blow. She'd noticed two vehicles parked in the driveway and hoped she'd find both of Chrissie's parents at home. Not notifying them beforehand wasn't an oversight. She preferred to deliver this kind of information in person, and phone calls usually led to disclosure of information.

She glanced up at Kane as he pressed the doorbell to an older-style red-brick home. From inside she could hear the chimes. The door opened and a tall, gaunt man in casual jeans and sweater opened the door. "Mr. Lowe?"

"I am." Mr. Lowe gave her then Kane a look of deep concern. "Is there news of my son?"

"No, sir." Kane shook his head. "A member of his team would come by to speak with you if there was any news."

Jenna cleared her throat. "Is your wife here? We have some information to share with you both."

"Yes, come in." Mr. Lowe held the door open and stepped to one side. When a teenage girl walked into the hallway wide-eyed, he turned to her. "Go get your mom and then go to your room. We have something to discuss with the sheriff."

The girl turned and hurried away, and Jenna followed Mr. Lowe into the family room with Kane close behind. She stood waiting for Mrs. Lowe, and when a rake-thin woman with a pale complexion arrived, they all sat on sofas facing each other. Jenna wanted to be as compassionate as possible. "We've come to inform you that we've made an arrest in Chrissie's case."

"Only one? The medical examiner informed me she was raped by more than one man." Mr. Lowe's face filled with anger. "What's his name?"

"We've reason to believe four men were responsible; one will be pleading guilty and the other three are dead." Jenna kept her voice low in an attempt to calm the man before her. "Another man we have in custody admitted to taking photographs. The images he took implicated the other men. He is currently in the county jail awaiting a hearing. He'll plead guilty and spend a long time behind bars."

"Dear Lord. My sweet innocent girl." Mrs. Lowe lifted her sorrow-filled eyes. "Was Seth Lyons involved? Chrissie's roommate Livi came by and told us she went on a date with him the night she died."

Jenna nodded. "Yes, he was. He slipped through our net for a while." She sighed. "But Seth Lyons will spend the rest of his life in jail. The other men involved died in various accidents and one from a suspected overdose."

"I'd have spoken to the son of a bitch myself but I don't venture out much these days." Mr. Lowe wheezed, coughed, then touched his chest. "Emphysema."

"I'm so sorry." Suddenly lost for words, Jenna swallowed hard. "I'm sorry to inform you, the ME has ruled Chrissie's death a suicide."

"We gathered as much after we spoke to Livi." Mrs. Lowe shook her head. "I wish she'd told us."

"Is that your son?" Kane stood and walked to the mantel. "A Navy Seal, you must be very proud, sir."

"Yes, that's Jack." Mr. Lowe pushed to his feet and sucked in a breath. "That photo was taken the week he left. He'd been home on leave for a few days and then the call came and he was off again." He shook his head. "He loves the life and lives for his team. I hope he makes it home." He turned to Jenna. "I'll never give up hope."

"That's a fine attitude." Kane nodded. "When he comes home, we'll come by and thank him for his service."

Glad of the respite, Jenna stood and peered at the photograph. She did a double take and then swallowed hard. The smiling face slammed into her memory and her mind whirled with the implications. Heart pounding, she fought for words, unable to drag her eyes away. "He's… ah… a fine-looking young man." She handed Mr. Lowe the photograph. The need to leave had become urgent. "We should be heading back to the office now. If there's anything you need, please don't hesitate to call." She handed Mr. Lowe her card.

"Thank you." Mrs. Lowe gripped her arm. "For finding justice for Chrissie."

Unable to reply, Jenna nodded and headed out the door. She walked swiftly back to the road without saying a word. She climbed into Kane's truck, anxious for him to get behind the wheel. "I recognize the man in the picture."

"Oh yeah?" Kane leaned back in his seat and his eyebrows knitted into a frown. "I didn't know you knew any Navy Seals."

Heart thumping, she stared at him. "He's the mystery man or I've seen a ghost."

"He's MIA, Jenna." Kane sighed. "You must be mistaken."

A rush of euphoria hit Jenna like a tidal wave. It all made perfect sense. "Think about it, Dave. What if Jack Lowe is alive? After suffering a horrendous rape, Chrissie sent him a text naming the men who hurt her and telling him her intentions. She destroyed her cellphone. She could have flushed it down the toilet for all we know, and if he *had* gotten the message, he couldn't have contacted her. Last she'd heard, he was MIA, and after almost a week, she'd lost hope and reached out to him beyond the grave. Maybe she believed he'd be on the other side waiting for her. She couldn't face Lyons blackmailing her and took her own life." She stared into space for a beat. "I figure Jack came back and murdered most of the men involved. He delivered the evidence of their guilt right into our hands. How else could he have gotten hold of the flash drives if he wasn't Court's killer? I don't believe for one minute Lyons would risk taking such damning evidence with him out running." She stared at him. "Jack risked being recognized to give me the evidence against Lyons."

"You can't prove Jack Lowe is alive, and if he is, you've no evidence he killed anyone, Jenna. I trust Wolfe's findings. He didn't find enough evidence to prove the men were murdered." Kane gave her an incredulous look. "No one tried to kill Lyons either, or he'd have been telling anyone who'd listen. In any case, frightening a guy isn't the same as killing him; and trust me, for a man with Jack Lowe's abilities, killing Lyons would've been a walk in the park. If he'd seen the footage on those flash drives, he'd have a good reason."

Jenna kept her voice low and in control. "He found a way to avenge his sister. I can feel it in my gut."

"If you figure you saw Jack Lowe, I believe you, but we have no evidence, Jenna. Zip, nada, and the ME ruled out homicide. If he was on the mountain, there's no case for him to answer." Kane frowned. "If Wolfe says Jack Lowe's on the other side of the world risking his life for our country, he wouldn't lie. Right now, MIA means he's either dead or being tortured in some godforsaken prison." Kane started the engine. "Military guys all look much the same in uniform, but we'll drop by to see Wolfe. He'll find you a better photo of him from his files."

# CHAPTER FIFTY-SIX

After Kane and Jenna arrived at Wolfe's house, and informed the girls they'd be holding a birthday party for Anna at Jenna's ranch, Kane gave Wolfe a brief explanation for disturbing his evening with his family. He followed Jenna into Wolfe's secure office. More like a safe room, the six-inch steel door protected the secrets inside. It was Kane's first invitation into Wolfe's inner sanctum and he took in the various computers and military phones and a wall lined with top-secret codebooks. He whistled. "Wow, no wonder you requested such a large house with separate accommodation for a housekeeper. When did you manage to get all this built?"

"When Jenna put in the requisition, a team moved in and it was all done by the time I arrived. They even moved in my electronics and the books from my other house. They sure wanted to keep you guys safe, and they still do. I send in weekly reports." Wolfe tapped a white telephone. "That's a direct line to the Pentagon." He sat in a chair behind the desk and looked at them with one raised eyebrow. "So, what's so top-secret you need to use my cone of silence?"

Kane explained, and moments later Wolfe went to work. He had an image of Jack Lowe on the screen in seconds.

"That sure looks like him." Jenna leaned forward and stared at the screen. "He could be the man on the mountain. He matches the description of the person Emily saw and the one Webber saw go into the cellar with Court. If I did see Jack Lowe, he has a clear-cut motive." She leaned back in her chair and folded her arms over her chest. "You wanted new evidence—well, here it is. This is reasonable doubt, surely?"

"It's hearsay at best. No one else identified him." Wolfe looked at her. "Now you've seen a better photo of him, are you 100 percent sure?"

"My focus was on Emily and I only had a brief glance of him, but from what I recall, he resembled Jack Lowe." She stared at the image. "Isn't that enough to reopen the case?"

"No, I'd need more evidence, and so would the DA. I'll stand by my findings, Jenna. Even if you did see him on the mountain, it proves nothing. You couldn't stand up in court and testify he was a threat to anyone, and from Lyons' statement, he'd testify the same. You told me the man you saw wasn't carrying a weapon and showed no evidence of being in a fight. I've ruled the deaths as accidental or suicide, which means there's no case to answer." Wolfe tapped away at his laptop and then turned it for her to view the screen. "See for yourself: Jack Lowe is still reported as MIA, and I can't find any trace of him being in the country since he left on his tour of duty. As far as I'm aware, none of his team have reported in since the chopper went down. By now, we have to assume they're all dead."

"So you're saying I saw a ghost?" Jenna lifted her chin and stared at Kane.

Kane shrugged. "I don't believe in ghosts but I do believe you met someone on the trail that resembled Jack Lowe." He narrowed his gaze. "The press release you asked Rowley to issue mentioned a reward for the guy who gave you the flash drives. Maybe he'll show and put your mind at rest."

"I hope so." Jenna shook her head. "But if I'm right, he'll never come forward."

# CHAPTER FIFTY-SEVEN

Lightning cracked and thunder rolled around the chopper. Jack Lowe gazed into the black clouds. It was as if the sky cried out with anger against the cruelty his sister had endured. As the high winds tossed the chopper around, he ignored the elements and stared again at the message on his phone. It would haunt him for the rest of his life.

*Jack, I know you'll never read this but I have to tell someone. Earlier tonight four members of the Black Rock Falls football team drugged and raped me. You know them, Jack. Lyons, Court, Devon, and Jacobs. Seth Lyons threatened to do the same to our little sister if I went to the sheriff. They have pictures and a video of me, Jack. Mom and Dad would be so ashamed if this was spread all over social media. They're like terrorists to women on campus and Lyons told me I'm not the only girl they've done this to. My roommate tried to warn me about them. I've been such a fool, Jack, and it's best if I end this now. Like you, I'm not afraid of dying. See you on the other side, big brother. xxx ☺*

Heart aching, Jack gripped the cellphone so hard it cut into his palm. Her message had remained unanswered for ten minutes before he'd returned to base after one hell of a mission. His chopper had gone down but most of the team had walked away without a scratch. He'd been out of contact with base for a few days, but after completing the mission with a depleted team, he'd returned to base. At the debriefing, Jack had discovered his status was MIA and would remain so until his unit had completed the retrieval of all the members of his team.

He'd turned on his phone and sent her a message but his reply to Chrissie had remained unanswered. Devastated, his gut told him he'd missed the window of opportunity to save her by less than fifteen minutes. How many more young women's lives would these men destroy? The creed he lived by had played in his mind: *I humbly serve as a guardian to my fellow Americans, always ready to defend those who are unable to defend themselves.*

He'd pulled in a few favors and within the hour was on his way home on a fake passport. After arriving, he'd gone straight to Chrissie's residence hall and the scuttlebutt surrounding her suicide had near shattered him. He'd dropped into a different zone, engaged a protective shield to ease the pain, and then gone about gathering intel on the run, with the help of his drone. People had little idea how easy it was to spy on them and discover their innermost secrets. Infiltrating the influx of new students for the fall semester had been easy, after making friends with the football team the previous semester. It had been by pure chance that during his downtime, a friend had asked him to replace him as the medic for the college football team for a couple of weeks and this semester he'd slipped into the college without question. Having field medic training had paid off in spades. He'd also used his expertise to disable the college CCTV cameras, hack the mainframe, and, like a ghost, hunt down the targets. It had only taken a few days to take out the trash.

He'd not gained any satisfaction by killing Jacobs, Devon, or Court, and their faces would never haunt him, but he would remember Seth Lyons. The disgusting animal had wet himself when he'd told him he was Chrissie's brother and given him the reason he was in Black Rock Falls. He'd dangled the flash drives in front of his face and grinned. After messing up his pretty-boy face, he'd threatened to disembowel him and hang him from the nearest tree by his entrails if he gave the cops his name. Hoping Lyons would leap to his death into the ravine, the man had decided his own punishment by taking the coward's way out and opting for the bridge.

Yeah, he'd taken a risk by sticking around to make sure the sheriff had all the evidence she needed to ensure Lyons would rot in jail for the rest of his miserable life, but it was worth it. Moments later, he'd vanished like smoke and then called the team to evacuate him. Later, when the news had come through about a reward for the man who'd given the sheriff the flash drives, he'd arranged for one of his buddies to drop by the sheriff's office. With a similar build and features, they were often mistaken for each other on base. His friend had donated the reward to a charity for battered women. As his friend had an iron-clad alibi, having arrived in Black Rock Falls on the morning of the bridge collapse, his ruse had worked.

Jack allowed his humanity to slip through one more time to read Chrissie's message again. He brushed away the sting of tears in his eyes and then, with his mask firmly back in place, he hit delete. His mission was over and it was time to return to base. *Rest easy, little sister. I'm done here.*

# EPILOGUE

## One week later

A shimmer of excitement ran through Jenna as she stepped onto her porch and surveyed her ranch. It was an incredibly beautiful day. The sun shone and not a cloud marred the blue sky. The scents of fall came to her on a surprisingly warm breeze as if nature had made this day special to mark one little girl's birthday. Wolfe's youngest, Anna, had stolen a place in her heart, but she enjoyed spending time with all his girls. Emily and Julie had become close friends, and it was great to have someone to go on shopping trips with and not be the sheriff for one day. Best of all, this year she'd persuaded Wolfe to allow her and Kane to arrange Anna's birthday party. Surprisingly, Anna had only invited three friends from school but insisted that Rowley, Webber, and Atohi be there as well. The little girl had asked her shyly if she could have a big person's barbecue and horse rides. How could she refuse?

It had been a busy week, tying up loose ends and writing reports. The FBI had moved swiftly and contacted more of the young women raped by Lyons and his friends. Fifteen had come forward, and as the proof of the crimes was unchallengeable, Samuel Cross, the lawyer, had found himself inundated with queries about compensation. As the majority of the offenders were loaded, he'd agreed to represent them all in a number of class actions for damages. Lyons had pleaded guilty at his hearing and was awaiting sentencing, but like Stevens, he would spend the rest of his life in jail.

The day a man with a buzz cut had walked into the sheriff's office to claim the reward had been the cherry on the cake. At last, she'd been able to tie up all the loose ends and close the case. He'd claimed he'd come home on leave and taken a walk when he ran into Lyons and Jenna but hadn't witnessed a fight. He'd gotten there after Lyons had run onto the bridge and found the flash drives on the edge of the ravine. After Kane had shaken his hand and thanked him for his service, Jenna had stared at the man for a long moment before checking out his story. A Navy Seal like Jack Lowe, the resemblance between the two men was uncanny. When he'd left, she'd looked at Kane. "I'm sure glad he came by. You have to agree he looks like Jack Lowe."

"I never doubted you, Jenna." Kane had smiled at her. "I'd have figured the same thing."

The rodeo crowd had left, and after the usual Saturday night dance, the town had thankfully returned to normal. Soon the chill of winter would arrive and Kane had offered to take her for a weekend at the new Black Rock Falls ski resort—just as friends, of course. It would be a luxury. Hot chocolate, skiing, and nights in front of a log fire… Bliss.

The warm comfort of friends surrounded her as Kane strolled back to the porch. He'd spent a great deal of time attaching balloons to the driveway and now walked back, chatting with Atohi, Rowley, and his girlfriend Sandy. She smiled at them. "You've all done a great job."

"The ponies are very gentle." Kane slapped both men on the back. "Thank you for bringing them; it will mean all the kids can ride and Anna is going to love her gift."

Jenna opened the front door and went inside. "Her pony is so pretty. Thank you so much, Atohi."

"The mare is gentle and I've worked with her this week to make sure she has no vices." Atohi looked at her. "She'll be perfect. Her name is Raweno and she'll take care of the young one."

Jenna looked over the gifts piled high on the coffee table then led the way into the kitchen. She'd made the birthday cake, and although it tilted slightly to one side, and Kane had helped her with the frosting, she considered it quite an achievement as she had only one good arm. As Kane moved around the kitchen, filling bowls with various snacks and candy, Jenna handed Rowley, Sandy, and Atohi drinks from the refrigerator. "So, who plans to do the cooking?"

They looked at each other and a smile spread over Rowley's face. "Shane."

"He's the master of the grill." Kane chuckled. "Wolfe has many talents." He cocked his head as if listening. "I hear vehicles."

Emily and Wolfe were bringing all their guests, and after taking a quick look around the rooms, Jenna headed for the front door. As the children spilled out of the trucks, she moved down the steps to greet them. "Happy birthday, Anna." She bent to hug the little girl.

"I can't wait to ride the horses. I saw the ponies in the corral. Are they for us to ride?" Anna looked at Kane and beamed when he nodded. "Can we do that straight away, Uncle Dave? Daddy can help with the barbecue."

"Don't you want to open your presents first?" Kane crouched down to look at her. "And Jenna made you a cake."

"I'm not sure they'll sit still long enough." Wolfe chuckled. "All they've been chatting about is the horses."

"Yeah, they've been driving me nuts." Julie pulled a face. "Horses, horses, horses."

Jenna laughed. "The cake can wait. They'll need a boost once they've run out of energy." She gave Atohi a wink and he slipped off toward the stables.

"Great!" Emily grinned. "I'll help Jenna. Julie will help with the girls."

"Oh, all right." Julie waved Anna's friends toward the corral.

As Jenna followed, holding Anna's hand, the little girl lifted her big blue eyes to her. "Can I ride with Uncle Dave? My friends can all ride and they'll be fine on the ponies."

"Not this time; you'll be staying inside the corral with your friends." Kane took Anna's other hand. "But I'll walk beside you if you like."

"I can ride your horse on my own?" Anna's eyes rounded.

"No need, look." He pointed to the stables as Atohi led out a magnificent paint pony. "Happy birthday, Anna."

The little girl's face lit up with so much joy, tears pricked the backs of Jenna's eyes. Wolfe moved beside her and she turned to look at his reaction. "I think she likes her present."

"It's been a long time since I've seen her that happy. Thank you. I appreciate it more than you know." Wolfe rubbed his hands together. "I'll get the fire going for the barbecue."

Under the guidance of Julie, Atohi, Rowley, and Sandy, the procession moved off around the corral. Jenna went to stand beside Kane and smiled at the way Duke leaned against his leg, his eyes closed. The kids had worn out the dog already. She mimicked Kane's pose of one foot on the bottom rung as they watched the little girls. "I knew when I woke up this morning it would be a special day. This is like having a real family."

"Yeah, it is." Kane slipped his arm around her waist. "People say you can't pick your family but I figure ours turned out just fine."

# A LETTER FROM D.K. HOOD

Thank you so much for choosing my novel and coming with me on another thrilling adventure with Kane and Alton in *Break the Silence*. If you'd like to keep up to date with all my latest releases, just sign up at the website link below. Your email address will never be shared and you can unsubscribe at any time.

*www.bookouture.com/dk-hood*

If you enjoyed my story, I would be very grateful if you could leave a review and recommend my book to your friends and family. I really enjoy hearing from readers so feel free to ask me questions at any time. You can get in touch on my Facebook page or Twitter or through my blog.

Thank you so much for your support.
D.K. Hood

@DKHood_Author

dkhoodauthor

www.dkhood.com

dkhood-author.blogspot.com.au

# ACKNOWLEDGEMENTS

Many thanks to all the wonderful readers who took the time to post great reviews of my books and to those amazing people who hosted me on their blogs.

Made in the USA
Coppell, TX
10 May 2021